ALEXEY KOVTUNOV

GHOST
IN THE SYSTEM

BOOK FOUR

MAGIC DOME BOOKS

Ghost in the System
Book # 4
Copyright © Alexey Kovtunov 2025
Cover Art © Ivan Khivrenko 2025
Cover designer: Vladimir Manyukhin
English translation copyright © Benjamin Patrick Miller 2025
Published by Magic Dome Books, 2025
ISBN: 978-80-7702-516-4
All Rights Reserved

THIS BOOK IS ENTIRELY A WORK OF FICTION.
ANY CORRELATION WITH REAL PEOPLE OR
EVENTS IS COINCIDENTAL.

OTHER BOOKS BY ALEXEY KOVTUNOV:

THE HEALER'S WAY

A Portal Progression Fantasy Series
by Oleg Sapphire & Alexey Kovtunov
Books 1-18

ME AND MY DEMONS

A Portal Progression Adventure Fantasy Series
by Oleg Sapphire & Alexey Kovtunov
Books 1-4

THE VILLAGE

A Litrpg Progression Fantasy Series
by Dmitry Dornichev & Alexey Kovtunov
Books 1-5

Table of Contents:

CHAPTER 1

*YEGOR MIKHAILICH: Kasp! ***! We're being attacked!*

"What's with you?" Eva was looking at me in surprise.

I had just jumped a little bit, and my face visibly changed when I read the next message:

*Yegor Mikhailich: They've taken half our shield! One more minute and we're f*cked!!!*

"So…" I shook my head. "You got one minute to figure that junk out. Then open a portal to Petergrad. That's all I got."

Allow Eva access to Kaspiana Arch of Unlimited Portal? Yes/No

Yeah, for sure. Why would I have even asked otherwise? I mean, I did have to move the girl from the last column to the second one, otherwise the System wouldn't allow it. Now she was a second-class citizen. But that was still better than a fourth-class one. For now that was where abso-lutely everyone was, besides Brownie, and we would have to deal with putting them all in their places later. Separate the useful people from the rest. But that was for later...

Choose the location of the exit.
Amazonia — 2 un./sec.
Gorodovtsevgrad — 1 un./sec.
District 09 — 189 un./sec.
Petergrad — 2 un./sec.

Well, we had enough seconds. Turned out this piece of crap, by which I mean the gold arch, also eats up our shield's energy. And with a hefty ap-petite, for every second you use it.

Even if it was totally possible for me to teleport, taking a whole army with me would be a problem.

There was a whole ton of functions in the in-terface, but I just didn't even get around to check-ing them out. Yeah, for sure, it would be super in-teresting to dig around in every section, but as the minutes passed my vassal got closer and closer to becoming nothing more than some less-than-pleasant memories... So we had to hurry up.

"But I didn't..." That was the last thing I heard from Eva.

The next moment the space within the arch first went all wavy, and then started swirling into a funnel.

Was it frightening to go in a place like that? Well, yeah! But it was necessary.

So I immediately took a step forward.

Safe to say that the feeling was strange. It was

like I should have felt something, but for some reason I couldn't feel anything at all. I just popped out near the gray stele in the store with no problem. Then for a few moments I could still hear crackling behind me, and when the portal closed, the room was lit up by a bright flash.

Well, here we are.

Outside I could hear dull thuds of something wooden, shouting and moaning from monsters I didn't recognize, and a feeling of panic and weakness in the air. People were running, trying to defend themselves through the windows, but that was not going too great for them.

"Kasp!" Ah, right, I teleported in my corporeal form and I forgot to put on my hood. Okay, fine.

"Who's there?" I went up to the window, but... I didn't get it. That was definitely not a zombie. I mean, zombies aren't made of wood, right?

But in addition to the unknown creations made of wood, there were other ones too. Ugly beasts, looking as if they had been sewn and grafted together using flesh from different creatures and people. They were furiously trying to break through the shield, but the wooden ones were blocking them for some reason. It was like two armies were competing to see who could break through the defenses first.

But nobody would. Screw those guys. These people still have taxes to pay me.

"Those... Over there is someone. Or something. But they are being controlled by people, hiding there!" Yegor pointed somewhere in the distance with his hand. All I could do was nod, finally get my hood on, and dematerialize.

It was no big problem to find the two idiots. The young guys were sitting off to the side on their incomprehensible monsters, just screwing around. The one who looked older was sitting atop a pile of concrete lumped together to make a dog. I think I could confidently call that piece of shit a golem. No mistake. More than that, I felt like the chunks somehow made of wood were the same sort of Unique production. Just made of wood.

The golems were made, certainly, by the hands of their maker, but mass production had also left its mark. I mean, they were mostly made of furniture...

Anyway, a golem made of plywood sure is a wooden golem, right? Or maybe particle board, nothing else. And that's what these ones were. Thankfully, burning these things should be a piece of cake.

The second guy, clearly younger, was sitting atop a "natural" creature made of, I must say, what was once alive. Six human legs, a dark hairy body, wings torn off an overgrown rock dove, and a head that was either from a cat or one of those mop dogs. But it was pretty well messed up, to speak precisely.

In any case, all these kinds of things were looking down a swift destruction. They should not exist in my world, much less my city.

The two dummies were just carrying on a casual conversation. They were counting their chickens, discussing how much inventory space they would get from the people here and making remarks on this or that animal. That is to say, they were obviously bored, because in their mind they had already won, and it was all too easy for them.

"Well, how long do you think it will last?" asked the younger one.

No matter how much I tried to get an idea from what they were saying about why they started this attack, I couldn't do it. Every second it became more clear that they did it just because they could. Just for funsies, nothing more.

Nah, I have to read their minds. I wondered what was going on in there anyway.

Even though it wasn't as easy as it was under the shield of Kaspiana, I was still able to dig around in some of their memories. And I even implanted some of my own thoughts!

These guys turned out to be brothers. I was digging around in the younger one's head, but it didn't really matter. They were both dumbasses. A rare sort of idiot, which they had been even before the apocalypse started. It just let them fully show off their inner character without any fear of reprisal in the form of legal consequences.

But they really weren't that worried about it before either, since their dad would get them off the hook.

As soon as I figured out what kind of people they were, I wanted to slam my slungshot into both of their heads right away. Ah, but that would be too easy of a death for them.

GHOST IN THE SYSTEM

Before the apocalypse they had entertained themselves by destroying others. Whoever they could. Servants, passersby, subordinates, anybody could end up on the receiving end. Pasha personally thought that everyone owed him as his birthright, and he constantly demanded everyone around him to pay that debt. Almost to the point of making them bow before him.

Whatever, I wasn't going to dig deep into their memories anyway. No way. Spoiled brats, with all that entails. I had no interest in people like that, and now, seeing how they thought, I could even say I was disgusted.

What did they attack them for? For flesh, of course!

Yeah, that's what it was. I didn't know the older one's reasons, but the one whose head I got into was just going to dismember the bodies and take them back to their lair so he could make more chimeras there.

Honestly, I didn't see a point in his class. If you could hide golems in your inventory and put a whole army on the battlefield in just a few seconds, then what were you supposed to do with these freaks? Nothing! Yeah, they might be stronger than the wooden dummies, and some of them might even have the barest hint of intelligence, but as far as I was concerned, it would just be easier to fight one-on-one. And while I was thinking all that, I didn't forget to whisper it into their heads as well.

The wood guys are definitely going to get

through first and take whatever they can for themselves... We have to hold them back...

As expected, it worked like a charm. The thought I had implanted was hovering somewhere on the edge of this guy's conscious mind. Right away, he frowned and started ordering his monsters to get in the golems' way as much as they could.

He pulled the same thing with the older one. But it took him a bit longer with that one. He didn't really care about the attack anyway, just here now testing out his new portable army. At the same time he was hoping to increase his inventory space with the people inside the building. That way he could carry around a bunch more golems.

Eventually, somewhere in his lazy thoughts I was able to catch onto a real thread. The brothers were always competing. And that competition was not always healthy. So I could play on that...

His army is better, and it's already crowding out mine... I have to slow those beasts down a bit.

It took a bit, but he fell for it. Sure, the two armies didn't start fighting openly with each other, but they were attacking a lot less actively. First one of the fleshy monsters would accidentally crush one of the wooden golems, then the other way around, with a sharp spikey piece of wood poking through another gross monster.

The motley army, thus messed up, suddenly lost all its effectiveness, with the boys, pretending that nothing was happening, kept chatting casually with each other all the while.

"How many tons of meat do you think it'll be?" asked Pasha, as if in passing.

Even I was surprised. No, in his mind that was clear as day. He was sick in the head and he needed to be destroyed in any way possible, but even so, to speak that casually and unbothered about completely normal people as if they were just meat?

I couldn't even imagine it. Yeah, maybe I'm not the most psychologically healthy person myself. But no matter how you slice it, in that building, besides the couple dozen armed idiots, there were a bunch of kids, women, and other people who couldn't fight. And what, you're just going to put them through the grinder? To make those gross monsters he could just rats. Breed them at industrial levels and feed them with zombie corpses. They'll multiply quickly, and you got zombies coming out the ass now.

All that is to say that he could have been a decent chimerist, but instead he became a piece of shit.

"If I'm being honest, I don't know how much meat is there." I appeared behind them, already swinging my slungshot. "But there's definitely a ton of bullshit in your head…"

After saying I disappeared. Why did I appear at all and distract their focus? Because otherwise they quickly would have noticed that both of their armies were fighting in the wrong place. Absolutely wrong.

The beasts and constructs had been given

clear instructions. Mess with each other. And now, slowly but surely, they were even forgetting about the shield, becoming more and more aggressive with each other with every passing second.

I had definitely gotten their masters distracted at the right time. The guys had instantly forgotten about their minions, completed focused on the danger to them personally. They got out their weapons, sitting down and glancing around nervously.

I didn't even have to turn on my Aura of Fear, since they were already shitting themselves.

And now it's time for them to kick the bucket.

My spiked ball flew out at an inconceivable speed, slamming right into the back of the younger one's head. I materialized it just a moment before it hit him, ready to watch how far his brains flew out of his head, but...

FWOOSH!

Right before the slungshot slammed into his empty head, the place was lit up by a bright flash and the Chimerist disappeared.

Son of a bitch!

He teleported? Where to?

Trying to answer those questions stopped me from smashing the older one's head right away, although he had frozen in surprise.

No big deal, I'll just dig out all your thoughts, find out where that asshole got off to, and knock his skull open. And then I'll clean up the rest of this mess...

But as soon as I started getting close, a smiled

appeared on his face. Within a moment everything was lit up with a bright flash, and the other asshole escaped his fate too.

But that was just temporarily. If I had to, I would find them. And I did have to.

But still, it was annoying. I didn't think there were artifacts like that. And what's worse, that two freaks like that have them.

Probably it was something like a teleportation stone that took you right back to your home stele. It must be somewhere nearby. What was frustrating, though, was that they realized right away that fighting with me was pointless, so they didn't even try to get involved, deciding to just run away.

Would we have more issues with them? I was sure we would. But most likely next time their army would come without their leaders. They would be attacking Petergrad, so no need to worry about Kaspiana. I mean, even if they found it, those piles of wood couldn't even break through the shield, even if we didn't try to fight back at all.

So whatever.

M-M-MO-O-O

I didn't even have to turn around. I knew that the bull was running out of the store. And behind him came the rest of the team, so all that was left for me to do was fly up a little and watch the bits and chunks of flesh flying around the place.

There was only a meager handful of creations left of the once-mighty army by the time my comrades showed up anyway.

Both the golems and chimeras had gotten the

orders to mess each other up, and without their masters to control them, they went full out on the slaughter. Even when our hooved friend, the two elves, and a few more people showed up, it did nothing to distract them from their fight, which made them easy targets.

Somebody had even got the bull an axe. A big battle-axe, to be precise, but in his hands it still looked pretty small. I didn't have time to admire the weapon. Just ten hits and it turned to dust. Grugg, not having really cared about the weapon, just started using his horns then. And his huge paws could deal some good damage too. In any case, the wooden golems turned to wood chips just like that in his hands.

The elves were focused on the chimeras. The girl was armed with a bow, while her brother had decided to level up his hand-to-hand combat. Even starting from nothing, it was worth a try. And even without a class, he was doing great!

He removed their extra limbs with quick, nimble movements, and when a chimera finally turned its attention to its annoying opponent, he easily avoided all their attacks. And he could jump surprisingly high. I would have to weigh them, but it seemed to me like those fully-grown elves could not weigh more than 70 pounds. But that was just judging from their movements.

The girl jumped onto a gutted semi-truck lying nearby without breaking a sweat. And without even using her hands. Just a couple quick movements and she's already up there showering down a hail of arrows on the monsters. And she was shooting with care, making sure to hit the wooden ones with fire arrows and the fleshy ones with normal arrows.

I had no intention of getting involved, since everything was fine as is. Plus, if you didn't get any experience for creatures like that, there was just no reason for me to destroy them. There were specially trained people, bulls, elves, and cactuses for that.

Hey, why had Gosha not shown up? And the bear was too lazy to even come see what was going on... Soon he would settle down in Kaspiana entirely and you won't even be able to drag him away from there.

I mean, yeah, they both did have a ton of things to do, and the reserve team was doing just fine without them.

Could I take them for my own? I mean, it was better to take people to tests that wanted to go. Neither Igor nor Bale really seemed to want to. Plus Brownie wasn't raring to go either, and just said okay because there was no one else...

I'll give it some thought. Right after I finish dealing with the portal. And after I figure out what to do with my ability for concentrating energy. That one was urgent, the interrupted lesson.

But before even that I had to see what rewards I got after the attack on the village. And it couldn't hurt to scarf down a whole ton of potatoes, finally, which would buff me up significantly. And it would be nice to fly to the US. Most of my vassals had never even seen me face to face. Just the slave whose name I didn't even remember. I would have to talk to him too, since I was his master after all. I would make him fan me if it was hot over there, or whatever they had there...

Oh yeah, how could I forget about giving my new mini-army their classes? I had to deal with that as soon as possible too.

I also had to learn about spirits. Every once in a while I would catch sight of their shadows, here and there, but since our last encounter I didn't really feel like making contact with those monsters. The most decent one out of all of them seemed to be the penguin. He just stood by, watching me, not being aggressive at all, but still, even my buffed-up Aura of Fear had no effect on him.

So I had a to-do list up the ass, to say the least. Way too long, but I had to start with something. I think it makes most sense to take care of stats and potatoes. You should never put those off for later, even though that meant I was constantly dealing with them.

Then I would focus on the ability, and only after that would I start looking through the rewards dropped by the horde of deadies. I would just keep getting more of them, since new monsters were always coming to the village from the forest. It was not hard to deal with them if you just stayed inside the shield. And now we didn't even have to go outside it, since all the resources we needed could be gotten under the cupola, at least for now. Well, except iron.

And then the portal, for sure...

That's what I was thinking about while I waited for the rest of the two armies to be beaten into the ground. That took a little more time than I thought, but whatever, we managed it without any casualties among the taxpayers. Of course, now they would have to wait for their shield to recover, but that was their problem, not ours. We got through with just a little bit of mess. Or rather, the bull made a mess, while the rest did it all quite calmly.

Our hooved friend loved to shout, so God forbid anybody from the village, most likely Gosha, should teach him how to swear. That would be a serious problem. I was afraid to even imagine what kind of profane expressions the relatively small brain of our cow could think up.

So that's why I decided to leave my subordinates here for now. They could get to know some people, communicate with them, and protect my vassals from zombie attacks. The first group had already appeared, so their services would definitely come in handy, and they could work on their abilities at the same time.

Kasp: Eva, get me out of here.

I didn't have to wait long. The girl immediately got what I was asking for, and a wide crack soon opened up right next to the gray stele of Petergrad. Although it would be better to call it a funnel, since that's really what it looked like.

I stepped into the hazy, semi-transparent circle, feeling light-headed for just a moment, and then soon found myself standing right next to the arch.

"Phew…" I shook my head. It doesn't matter, I just get more and more used to these kinds of teleportations. "So, let's get some food, huh?" I suggested, and the girl immediately perked up.

"I'm not done figuring out how the arch works…" She was trying to show how responsible she was. But I could see that the girl really wanted to eat, and probably had been wanting to for a while. So I just nodded for her to follow me.

It was not hard to find a place for lunch. I just sat right on the edge of the village, turned on my Aura of Fear for a bit, which probably took Eva's appetite away completely, but left absolutely no people around us.

The girl would get used to it. Or she'd just be pissing herself all the time.

"Bon appetit!" I smiled at her when the two tables full of all kinds of delicacies appeared before us.

Her appetite came right back, but before she could reach out for the food, I grabbed a slice of pizza off her table and started nibbling on it.

"Okay, now you can dig in." I smiled even wider, since I had gotten a skill point for that slice. Which was pretty rare.

Eva dug into the delicious food, forgetting everything else on earth. I just sat and watch the joy in her eyes. The girl loves to eat, awesome. But I had to take some stuff too.

I started popping one purple potato after another into my mouth, and then came the blue ones. Where did I get so many of these? 21 purple ones and 63 blue ones! Thankfully that didn't take too much time, and soon, ignoring the girl's loud chewing, I finally closed my interface.

"Ah, not bad..."

CHAPTER 2

Name: *Kasp*

Level: *25*

Class: Ghost

Stats:

Body (42): Strength (16), Dexterity (13), Constitution (13)

Mind (51): Intelligence (18), Reaction (17), Perception (16)

Spirit (73): Repository (29), Conduits (44)

Available Stat Points: 0

Skills:

Active: Appropriation (epic) (20), Aura of Fear (rare) (1), Aura of Ice (epic) (10)

Passive: Energy Vampire (rare) (20)

Additional: Dematerialization (Class Skill)

Available Skill Points: 10

Abilities:

Martial:

Craft: Concentration of Energy (10)
Available Ability Points: 22
Auction
Inventory 1540 lbs.

SOMETHING LIKE THAT. I think I got some good buffs. My senses were exceptionally good. Hard to even put it into words. When you put that many points in at once and are using up your calories in the process, you really feel amazing.

My eyesight and hearing had gotten better. Noticeably. I could now clearly see how grossly Eva was eating. It was even a little repulsive, with her chewing so loudly and grossly.

I got about ten different points from the purple potatoes. I put the stat points into my Conduits right away. Like usual, I wasn't going to bother with opening them up, since I needed all of them right away. Even the physical ones helped a lot. Except maybe Constitution. That one I didn't need at all.

Plus my stats raised by about another twenty or so from those purple potatoes.

Then came the blue ones. I couldn't even look at them now, it would just make me throw up, the sight of them. I slammed them down, so many, I didn't even know when I would ever have that much in my mouth again. 63 potatoes, what do you know, can you believe it?

My stats got a little closer to max from them. Especially my Strength. And my mana, too, so now I could control my flight better. And my speed, if not multiple times faster, was at least significantly improved.

It made no sense to try it out under the cupola, so I wasn't even going to test it. Here I was the king, a god, capable of moving from one end to the other in a fraction of a second, a mile a minute.

Plus I got skill points and ability points, although I was much luckier with the former. As far as I could recall, I only had very few available, so I would soon get one of my skills up to a new limit. The additional effects were always interesting, especially when I could pick them. But I would just level up my vampire aura anyway. It might be just blue, which meant that the System wouldn't give me a choice, but the skill was unbelievably handy.

Without it, given how active I was, I would have to constantly stop and gather up potions. But now my health and mana just recovered on their own, drawn even out of my allies…

But they were used to it. If I put the aura at max distance it would work on them for a long time, and practically no one even noticed. Their strength just came back a little faster.

I had just given up on stealing. It was so much easier to get stuff by beating it out of enemies. Plus, honestly, I hadn't meet any people for a long time. At least not any I could steal from.

Still, I should have lightened those two brothers' pockets though. Even though they might have just been full of golems, I should have at least looked through all the trash to see if they had any artifacts that could help them run away from me.

Ah, whatever. I didn't have the time to be stealing. Next time, if there is a next time, I'll rummage through their pockets, and then kill them.

I felt like putting ten points in to improve my first rare skill. By reaching level 30 it would improve how quickly I absorbed energy and increase the maximum radius, while also lowering the minimum. Although I wasn't sure about that last one.

But if it was like that, my short-range effectiveness would be scalable, and I could confidently call my vampirism a real, actual attacking ability.

I thought that was almost my best ability. I mean, the psy-claws had never shown up. I hadn't even seen something like them at auction.

Once I deal with the portal and all that stuff, I'll take a look at the treasury. Something must be in there by now. I mean, at least 30 would be enough. And if it wasn't... Well, I would have to whip my vassals into shape.

"What's up with you?" Eva had finished both hers and my lunch and staring at me in surprise.

"You ask that question pretty often." I smiled. "I was messing with the interface. Trying to figure out what to put where... Anyway, it doesn't matter. You go take care of the portal, and come tell me, personally, everything you know. In the meantime..."

Well, she didn't need to know, so I just dematerialized and headed for the other end of the village. And I didn't forget to hit the square with an Aura of Fear either. What are they doing screwing about here, go work!

It was striking that the people almost never went past the shield. They were afraid. Even in the day, when the zombies were less active and got lost in the forest. I hoped that when it got dark they would come out and things would heat up a little here. That would be much better, because I wouldn't let them forget that the shield had weakened and so the people would get rewards and levels. Which would result in them being more useful to everyone. And get me some tribute, of course.

I was starting to understand our old government. The IV of taxes was seated deep in my veins, and I wasn't planning on taking it out any time soon. It was a great feeling to know you could reap the rewards of other people's labor and nobody could do anything to you about it.

Even if they wanted to get rid of me, I... Well, I wouldn't do anything. It was my stele, and I was going to stay here.

Now my Skill. I had been putting this moment off for a while, and now it was here. I put one point into it, and my mind suddenly was in another world...

Yetis. They were starting to rile up already. Soon they would be wearing loincloths to hide their hairy gifts and jump around the spirit of heat.

The spirit was a formless blob, but what more could you expect from a hastily constructed creature, even if it came at the cost of the life of one of the tribe? Just a blob. It was better than nothing, you had to assume.

Now I was taken again to the process of creating a spirit, but this time with a different tribe. These ones lived high in the mountains, so their conditions were definitely much worse. So they had mastered the art of making even the simplest spirits much better.

I focused entirely on the process, reading all the thoughts of the snowy man who was fastidiously gathering up all his energy and concentrating it into a single point. Eventually a little spark appeared, growing larger with every second.

Now this I understand, the fire spirit! Not at all the same bullshit my last teachers were trying to get me to do. You could warm yourself by it, you could shoot it at your enemies, and you could even burn the grass in the fields in autumn, if nothing else. I did that my whole childhood, and now I wouldn't even need matches.

Before getting kicked back to my drab reality, I managed to watch a few more tricks with my ability. But those lessons seemed completely nonsensical, although I still studied everything carefully, even the things that seemed to be the least important.

All of this would definitely come in handy. Concentrated energy could definitely do more than just heat up a place. I could see how I could use my ability to heal wounds, restore other people's mana or my own, and much more. There wasn't just enormous potential, no, it was almost endless. But it wouldn't take a year to develop it. Maybe a month. Possibly even a week or two would be enough. It would hold off until I had some free time, but now I had to get the knowledge down.

After recovering my breath and running through the memories of that icy, white world, I lowered down to the ground and shut my class skill off. I had learned how to do it while I was in my corporeal form, so I would have to try it in that same state now.

This time my memories were fresh, and a bunch of details had been filled in that I had been missing before.

So the process of creating a simple silly spirit didn't take me long. I did it step-by-step just like the mountain yetis. On top of that, I recalled that, even though he was a master of this skill, he had used a lot of energy on it, nearly on the verge of passing out, if not dying.

I didn't even feel bad. Just used a hundred points of mana, that's all. I would just suck it up from my subordinates if I needed it. Or even from this spirit itself. Nothing came here for free.

I got a small but fairly bright spark. Unlike the last one, this one seemed pretty lively. It flew around, checking out the world around it.

But in five minutes it went out.

Okay, that's annoying. But I had time. Eva was still hopping around the portal, sometimes wasting the shield's energy on trifles, but I could forgive her. Then she would be talking to me in…

Yeah, she had twenty minutes left of the time I gave her.

So I set about making a simple fire spirit again.

Or a heat spirit? Who knows?

This time I got one that was much larger and well-formed. Altogether it looked not like a microscopic spark, but rather more like a small gout of flame.

It would show up and disappear, teleporting a few feet back and forth.

And after five minutes my new friend didn't even go out, still flying around, studying its creator. But it really could hardly have any kind of brain. It was just a ball of energy, nothing more.

But really, where did these spirits come from? What was the reason for them to come to be naturally? So many questions and so few answers.

As an experiment, I dematerialized, so I found out that the spirit didn't go anywhere. It was just that I could see it when it was radiating heat, and when it ran out of energy it was just left in its normal state. Which was incorporeal.

In my ghost form I could see it in a completely different light. I wondered if the yetis knew that their spirits didn't look anything like flames or sparks. I would say they were more like little worms. Maybe with wings. But it was so small that I couldn't really see it that well.

Whatever, it was cool! Live, my little friend! I won't hold you back. And I expect great things!

Like Eva telling me soon how the portal should be used. After that I should probably be able to go to America. It was only after the apocalypse that I could travel abroad, but hey, good enough for me.

"Fifteen minutes!" The girl raised her hands as

soon as I appeared. "And then you can do whatever you want with me?"

"Really whatever I want?" My eyebrow raised all on its own. Eva smiled coyly in response, then kept messing around with the golden arch.

Actually, I had meant to send her to go get clay. The settlement needed new houses, and it would be a lot easier to move that valuable stuff around with a portal. If we used it to get the big guys out, then we could get ten tons of it in mere minutes.

But fine. 15 minutes is 15 minutes. In that time I could see where the resources go when they're sent to the warehouse...

Turned out they just disappeared. The big guys threw the contents of their bags past the door and that was it. No special effects...

Some idiot had built this shed, calling it a warehouse for the System, but put it right next to the forest. The clay, though, was like 200 yards away, so getting it was much slower than it had to be. Could I tear it down or something like that and put it closer? Most likely the System wouldn't let me, but I still had to try.

Of course, I could wait. But I hate dicking around. So I had good reason to stop by the town hall.

No, I definitely didn't want to deal with the stele, especially since Brownie was on that day and night. As far as I knew, there really weren't that many functions yet, and half of them were still blocked.

Well, it was certainly worth it to check the rewards. At least the ones that hadn't managed to get to the suffering inhabitants of the village.

Eventually it became clear that the majority of the abilities that I had recently bought at auction were just lying on the table. And that was pretty annoying.

"Oleg, what the hell?" I pointed at the pile of rewards by the stele. "What did I get all this stuff for?"

"Uh... well... Let me say that we're holding off with classes for now. So we're not handing out the abilities that nobody's picked something for yet." He put his hands up. "You're not getting it...?"

"Okay, so..." I picked up a gray scroll that said Carpenter on it. "Do we have anyone who works with wood around here?"

"A couple of them, but they're not doing anything with the System..." Brownie just shook his head.

"Then give it to them! At least one of them. He can get a Carpenter class, why not? He'll enjoy his work and get experience for it!"

We had to fight it out a little bit. We even opened up the list of people, handing out responsibilities to most of the population within just a few minutes.

And we even have green craftsmen! What are they doing now?

"Oleg. You're a pretty cool dude. But you are doing some dumb shit..." I shook my head, having learned that our green Chef was chopping wood at the moment.

"Ah, what do you expect? The only person with access to the list is you! I asked who wanted to do what and they just went wherever! We have to build things, give people places to work, and only then can we start doling out jobs!" Brownie was started to get riled up now too, and honestly, there was some truth in what he was saying. We did need buildings, not just places to live, but ones that were designed for specific purposes.

"Fine. But find some builders, they'll at least help you some. And the resources will store up fast, don't worry..."

How awesome would it be to trade resources? System! Get an auction together for settlements next phase, please!

I was asking from the bottom of my heart. It wasn't going to do it now, for sure, even if it meant to. Still, it would make sense to be able to trade resources with your vassals, at least. I mean, it wasn't hard to get concrete in the city. Literally everything was made of it over there, and getting here would be pretty hard. So what difference did it make which storehouse it went in? The System was teleporting the materials wherever it wanted anyway.

I had gone through most of the stuff already, and what was most important was that it was all opened already. There were all kinds of weapons, shields, and armor. The only things left were the stuff that only had a small chance of being good for me.

*Helmet of Discharge (rare) (Static Shock)
1000/1000*

Description: Mana 100/100. Static Shock is a support skill. Costs 1 mana/second. Upon activation it starts sending weak discharges into everyone within a radius of 5 feet.

Warning! Your allies will also be affected by the charges if they come within 5 feet!

Awesome. It was made of metal with a sharpened tip. Right at the end there was a point sticking out, about an inch and a half long, with a little ball on the end. That was probably where the lightning came from.

"Ah! Kasp!" Brownie put his hand on my shoulder. "You thought we wouldn't check them?"

All I could do was shrug. Sure, the discharge was pretty weak, but it did make even Oleg drop the notebook in his hands. And that meant that weaker enemies would have a hard time attacking because of the charges.

Did I need the helmet? Not really, except maybe as a joke, to fly around my enemies and make of them with it. But my hood didn't fit over it. So it would be better to just hang it on one of the bull's horns, let him play with it.

All the epic stuff was all gone already. Plus the guys who took part in the test had already opened up their unique rewards. Brownie said there weren't as many of them as you would like. But still, there had been some good stuff. For instance, our Saboteur had gotten a sapper kit. That was amazing, because you could make land mines with it!

Oleg didn't go into details, but he did tell me that the landmines were normal, explosive ones. They were easy to make, and hiding them was no problem either, especially for a Saboteur. Well, at least since he had gotten that kit.

Plus the artifact let you deactivate enemy mines when you found them. And also take them for yourself.

If you asked me, that was pretty cool.

Somewhere in that epic trash heap I found a massive hammer. Its main advantage was its durability. It had something like 10 thousand or more, and when it was used passively it constantly refilled on its own.

It also buffed Strength and Constitution pretty well, but not shit for the rest.

"And?" I asked, staring at Oleg in confusion. "What they hell are they still doing here?"

"Yeah, I wanted to ask you if we should give them to the bull," Brownie said, not looking up from his writing. "He'll break that hammer too. We've given him so many items already, but we thought it would be a shame to waste the epic one on him."

True. It didn't matter what you gave our horned friend, he would break it. They had tried to dress him up, making him a fair-sized loin-clothed just for that purpose. Not for his physical health, but for their mental health.

But he had still terrified half the village with his equipment.

But our ungulate companion had even broken that at the first opportunity, although entirely by chance. Same with System items. A weapon? Two hits and it was done. Armor? Even if he put on, let's say, gloves, they would still only last a few hours. He had a talent, to say the least.

But the hammer should be able to hold out. If need be, we would set someone up who would get Grugg repair kits. In bulk.

I took all the single-use items for myself. There was a couple of interesting land mines and some grenades, including one large frag grenade. It was a massive ostrich egg, covered with shrapnel. According to the System, it should blow up real good, covering an area of hundreds of feet with shrapnel.

It would definitely come in handy.

I tossed a couple other uncommon grenades into the depths of my inventory. I had wanted to leave some for Glash, but Oleg had already done that for me. He had given the flying girl everything she needed, which had made her indescribably happy. And given the shit-eating grin on the guy's face, it was even possible that she had rewarded him for it somehow.

Otherwise I would have to wonder why he was so... much calmer than usual, let's say.

But I wouldn't read his mind to check, at least not this time. Sure, I could take a peek in the Berserker, he was always going nuts in a fun way, but Brownie was just boring in that regard. He didn't have any acting talent at all.

When all was said and done I ended up with

frag grenades, fire grenades, air grenades, and holy grenades. As usual. But in addition to that standard set, I also got a new one.

Vacuum Grenade (uncom.)

Description: Upon activation, creates a vacuum point which will pull in anything within a radius of 30 feet. Lasts for 10 seconds.

A kind of black hole, most likely. Would it swallow up the material, or just attract it inward? Well, there was only one way to find out.

"Anton took a couple too, for his experiments," Brownie said, looking up from his writing. From what I could gather, he was keeping a sort of log. Would I have to remember that later?

"What kind of experiments, exactly?" I decided to make sure before I dematerialized. By now Eva would have finished studying the portal and was now flopped over the grass she had trampled all over.

"Ah, you know..." Oleg shrugged. "Scientific ones, I guess."

Good answer. I wasn't expecting anything else. Especially from the bear. I decided to get out of there then. This silence was starting to drag on.

"You done?" I appeared by Eva, and she immediately started.

"Yeah! Check it out! So damn much! But it's working... Now! Where you wanna go?

She didn't let me get a word in edgewise. She talked and talked for almost two minutes, but that whole time she didn't give me even a scrap of useful information.

"Alright, good. You better just show me, because talking is clearly not your strong suit..." I said, stopping the flow of useless words.

"Yeah, no problem!" Eva shouted and then stared into space for a few seconds.

Within a couple of moments the undulations that I was already used to had appeared in the arch, and the girl's face had lit up in a smile.

"Well, are we going?" She pointed at the portal with joy written all over her face.

All I could do was shrug. She would definitely refuse to tell me where the funnel was taking us. It was like she wanted it to be a surprise.

"Ladies first." I stood by the arch and pointed my hand at it. Eva didn't take a second, jumping right into the blurry whirlpool of the portal, disappearing in a flash. "Here goes nothing," I murmured and followed after.

CHAPTER 3

"THIS IS A JOKE, right?" I stared into the girl's eyes, but she met my gaze with guilt in them. "You're pulling my leg, huh?"

Eva said nothing, simply letting her gaze sink to the ground. But what was there to say? We were in Japan!

It was the middle of the night here now. You could see the horizon getting brighter, little by little, but there was still a long way to go until dawn. We had ended up right in the middle of a forest, quite a picturesque place, no doubt about it. If you were a tourist, you'd be thrilled, but...

"I, uh..." Eva perked up after a couple of minutes. "Thought it would last longer..."

In fact, everything should have gone fine. The girl's plan was to maintain the portal on this side, we end up in Japan, look around, see how things were, what the weather was like, enjoy the romantic atmosphere, and then head back. Nice and easy, right?

Eva had held onto this unfulfilled dream for a long time, that she would come here, so she had entirely forgotten about her responsibilities, to assess her own abilities, and about the untested capabilities of the portal.

Was she an idiot? Yeah, definitely an idiot. But it really was pretty here. I wouldn't say where we were from was so bad, of course, but there really was something about this mountain.

"What's this place called, then?" I asked the girl, pointing to the mountain.

"Fujiyama!" She was annoyed, even looking offended. Hmm... She had sent me god knows where, to the other end of the Earth, and now SHE was offended?

Well, fine. Anyway, it was totally possible for us to think of something in this situation. Especially since it looked like portals could be opened up in other places than vassal villages.

"Okay. You opened a portal here, so that means you can get Brownie to do the same? Have I got that right?" I started thinking out loud once Eva stopped pouting. "Or not?"

"No..." She shook her head. "You would need my class for that. At least a gray one, anyway. But something definitely connected to portals or teleportation. We just feel all that differently, so there's no way I could ever explain it to the bear."

So he wouldn't be able to, then. Anybody could use the portal, but for us, regular people, we only got limited functionality from it. The girl, though, could do whatever she wanted with it. It increased her abilities and powers, completely trivializing the process of finding the place she needed, really just letting her do a whole bunch else too.

Plus it was a lot less expensive for her to teleport.

But really, I was an idiot too, kind of. I should have checked what the conditions were for us to return, and basically just watched the girl carefully. If I had just jumped back into the hole before it closed...

No, then she would have been left here completely alone, and surviving in post-apocalyptic Japan? Pretty unlikely. At least with me she would have a chance.

I chewed Eva out a little bit, so she would feel suitably bad for what she had done, then dematerialized, flew up in the air, and took a look around. There was no point in standing around yelling at each other. It wouldn't get us closer to any sort of goal, anyway. But what even were our goals right now, then?

To go back? Yeah, that'd be nice. I still had a full treasury over there, all of Anton's creations, and a bunch of other stuff. Like those two assholes, just asking to get their asses kicked.

Damn, that spirit had flown behind me, but hadn't gone through the portal. I wondered if it would burn the shed down in annoyance...

In fact, getting back would be that hard. For me. I would just have to wait for the next test, beat everyone there, and set my return point as my home region. Piece of cake. But then I would have to leave this dummy for the slant-eyes. And from what I had heard, those midgets didn't take kindly to our kind.

On the other hand, there was one other perfectly valid option. Getting myself a vassal. Someone would agree to it, anyway. It didn't have to be willingly, either. You know, the power of persuasion is a many-sided thing. You can use it in a lot of ways.

"Okay, tell me what you can do, in detail." I sat down on the ground, leaning my back against a tree.

She had decided to open the portal in a fairly picturesque place. Which was good, because if it had been in the city, we would have been fighting beasts right away. Or zombies, however it shook out.

Even though I had already tried to get a handle on her abilities, it was still interesting to listen again. I did have to take out a couple of packs of deadies that were wandering in the woods, but that was no big problem. The animals here had clearly had a bad time of it, since there had definitely been more people here at first. So the deadies had cleared out the local fauna well and fully. Or maybe not, who knows? It was also totally possible that the animals had quickly adapted and just hidden themselves real well. The main thing was that they weren't bothering us.

During our conversation, Eva had no desire to

face any deadies whatsoever, but I was somehow able to get her to show some guts. And also how she survived and fought with the zombies before.

It turned out to be simple. Her portal would suck in the victim and then put it out some feet above the ground. The girl's main weapon was gravity. And a couple of weak skills that her admirers had given her once upon a time. I always say that chicks have it just a bit easier, no matter the situation. Nobody gave me nothing, which was pretty insulting.

The first skill was a jump. At first glance, it should have been really good for her, except it attracted too much attention. It was like teleporting a short distance, something like 30 feet. But that teleportation came with a loud crack and a flash of light. Obviously you weren't escaping unnoticed. It was an uncommon skill, which meant it might surprise you with some nice additional effects later. But that wasn't guaranteed.

The second one was passive. Aura of Improving Physical Stats. The girl had hardly put any points into it, so there was almost no use to get from it. All of her allies within a 30-foot radius would get a buff to all their physical stats totaling one-fifth of their value. If she leveled it up, and used it on a whole crowd of people, that would be amazing, no doubt.

You could take a hundred people and sell all of them a book of that. And then you would get 100 Hercules out of them.

"Don't level up the aura. Right now you have a

different job to do," I advised Eva. "And that active one could save your life, you never know…"

"It has saved me, more than once. It just uses a lot of mana." The girl smiled.

I was just about to send her on her way, but at the last moment I noticed what she was wearing. Regular clothes? Just one System ring? She didn't have a weapon either, from what I could gather.

All I could do was shake my head sadly. How confident could you be in the durability of the shield? We had a ton of common weapons and armor. Not to mention that I had 1,223 spheres in my inventory! And that was taking into account that I had spread a significant amount of them through the village, and from now on I was trying not to pick up the gray trash.

So what could I do? Keep the inhabitants outside the shield so they didn't put their guard down?

"Here, open this." I tossed a blue sphere into Eva's hands. I had a whole eight of them, and 35 green ones on top of that. Almost certainly we could get a decent set from that which would raise my personal Portalist's chances of survival tenfold.

"Hey!" She blinked in surprised, staring first at the sphere, then at me. "This is rare! I've never even seen one yet!"

She'd never seen one, right. Because if you drop a rare monster from a height of 30 feet… It just gets angry, nothing more. That's why she'd never seen one.

"Open it up already. I wanna know what's in it." What I was really itching to do was test out my theory about luck. I usually just got all kinds of trash. Even the rare ones dropped loot that did me no good at all.

"Check it out!" Eva held out a scroll. Her hands were visibly shaking from nervousness, but still, she had gotten a pretty interesting item.

Wand of Space (rare) (Repository +10, Sense of Space)

Set: Space Wizard Clothing 1/8

Description: Sense of Space is a passive ability. It allows the wearer to better sense the surrounding area. It assists them in using space spells.

Set Skill: Return. Allows you to teleport to a point chosen in advance. Costs 90% of your mana.

"Son of a bitch! You son of a bitch!" I shouted, as soon as I had read the description.

"Me?" squeaked the girl in fright, but I just waved my hand at her.

"It's got nothing to do with you..."

Oh, what? I was pissed! The System is so good to some people, but it just screws me over, over and over.

Okay, Eva was not a Space Wizard, just a Portalist. Yeah, an uncommon one, but still. Her specialization was in opening and closing portals. Ideally closing them after everybody who needed to had gone through them and come back... But fine. She would be smarter next time.

But this wand was definitely in her field and would certainly help her use her class ability. And it was an uncommon drop, too. I mean, instantaneous teleportation happens in space. Which means it's still space magic.

I shook my head and gave Eva another sphere. Then another, and another, until she was fully decked out.

Now she had a pretty good set of System armor, even if it was a little ragtag, along with a weapon. It was a decent outfit, especially since I hadn't even offered any gray spheres.

Some of the items did us no good, so I put them up for auction right away, at half market price. A Shield of Justice, an Ice Axe, Iron Boots of Might... These were all definitely unnecessary, even for me. Only the axe might have been kept, but the description wasn't very impressive. I had a slungshot and a bow, and for extreme situations, the hammer. And that was more than enough for now.

From a blue sphere we got our weapon, which was a small, fairly comfortable crossbow. It didn't seem to have any special effects, except for one, which was to make bolts, since it didn't take normal ones. If you thought it up, then you could pretty easily spend a little more mana and add specific effects to the bolts. Something like fire bolts, ice bolts, poison ones, that sort of thing. Say you used all your mana on the weapon, then it would take ten hours to refill, but that was still pretty cool.

Plus it had a place for four arrows, and one could be loaded in advance. So I had to use up my mana a few times on the weapon so I could make all sorts of arrows four times in a row.

I even got a bunch of treasures for myself, like a rare blinding grenade and another magic wand. This one let you lift up a clump of earth about 5 feet in diameter into the air with a wave of your hand. It was kind of like a localized earthquake. Somewhat silly, but you could still use it. Maybe to knock down a bunch of zombies, or to knock over a wall.

Basically, we were all decked out. And while we were doing that, I became fully convinced that the System was definitely playing favorites. Like that Tamer, for one. I would have to see how she was doing when we got back. Because somehow I just always forget about all the inhabitants of the village, paying just the slightest mind to their activities, or in those short times when I appear in the village at all. I just save them and save them all the time, and then never get repaid for it later. It's not right.

"Well, try it out!" We had gotten out of the forest pretty fast and run into a small horde of deadies.

I had nothing to fear, so now Eva would have to get used to either fighting, or hiding herself well. Otherwise we weren't going to get anywhere far.

I mean, at least now, while we were in the outskirts. It would be a whole different thing when we got to the dense parts of the city. There Eva could fairly easily teleport between buildings without having to worry about running into a whole horde of powerful monsters on the street.

A fireball broke through the pre-dawn twilight, and right as the arrow hit one of the big guys' bellies, there was a sudden large fire. The bastard burned quite well, much better than with the green arrow for my bow.

However, it didn't seem to do any damage to the big guy at all. And he and the zombies around him pinpointed exactly where the shot came from, immediately rushing towards us in a big group.

The Japanese suburb was so nice. Little cookie-cutter houses, narrow streets, and not a single place to hide from these pissed-off deadies. At least not for a normal person.

Suddenly I found myself wondering what Eva would do. So I waved at her, and instantly disappeared into thin air.

"Oh you... Did you ditch me?" The girl didn't know what to yell at me at first. Probably she wanted to curse me out, but she didn't haven't the same upbringing as Gosha, obviously. But we would fix that, no worries.

I had no intention of answering her at all and just set about watching after gaining some height. From here I had an amazing view of the whole mountain, the city in the distance on the ocean shore, and whole host of tall buildings, half-destroyed.

Hmm, strange. I had been expecting at least a few million-strong hordes of zombies covering the entirety of this little island. But there were only a few here. The group that was now chasing after the panicking girl was just about 30 individuals, and only at most five of them were mutated. And one sentient one, although I wasn't sure about that. It was light work, my slungshot wouldn't even get tired out. But I was just here to watch.

Eva started running back through the narrow street, heading for the forest. But two leapers had appeared behind her, and they could easily catch her in just a few seconds.

But the girl had no plans to run away forever, dodging the first hit by instantly teleporting some feet away… There was a clap, a flash, and she was already back, standing on the roof of a fragile two-story building. Yeah, maybe houses like that were great for places where you had earthquakes every day, but I still cringed at the sight of their paper-thin walls.

Even a deadie who wasn't a big guy could easily break them, so how the people here even manage to hide from the deadies at all? Thoughts like that bummed me out, since I didn't just need a few people, but whole camps of survivors so they would at least have a stele.

Ugh, what a mess. But somebody had to be left in this city, almost certainly.

In the meanwhile, Eva was really going off. She unloaded her whole armory, then threw the grenade I had given, then…

And that's all. From then on she started teleporting from roof to roof, confusing her enemies, gradually putting distance between them.

I should have at least given her the Ice Axe,

because without arrows she wasn't going to be able to do anything... Unless she could hit them with the wand? Ehh, maybe...

"Okay, bunny, that's enough hopping." I appeared on the roof next to her. "You only beat five of them, that's pretty weak..."

A little chastising and then I quickly took out the rest of the zombies, grabbing all their goodies. The crystals would certainly not go amiss, and it would be a shame to throw away the rewards. I would really enjoy using those grenades, for sure.

"Let's hop off to town." I nodded at the girl, ready to get moving. I knew she would be able to travel much easier herself. But I didn't need portals, since now my Conduits were so high level that I could fly around 300 miles per hour. "You know some places there? We need to find people."

"We could go to Fuji... It's about 20, 25 miles, straight shot." She shrugged. "But my mana's about out, so we gotta wait."

With a face expressing as much pain as possible, I passed her a flask of blue liquid. Eva's face suddenly lit up, she smiled brightly and threw her arms out to hug me, taking a step closer...

I had to disappear into thin air, and so she nearly tumbled off the roof. Was she planning to kiss me right here? We were in the middle of nowhere! A real shithole, and we had to get home, not all this stuff!

What a dumbass.

"You idiot..." mumbled Eva, pulling herself together and getting ready to open a portal.

I flew behind her, seeing bright flashes off in the distance where she was teleporting.

I don't know how Portalists pick their end points, but she was doing it pretty well. Maybe the wand was helping, or maybe she was just lucky. In any case, by the time dawn was breaking we were near a much bigger city.

The skyscrapers towering over the sea could be seen already from far off, and even thought we might get there pretty soon. And we hadn't even seen a single zombie the whole way...

"So where do you think they all are?" asked the girl, as soon as I appeared next to her. "At first I saw a couple more packs of zombies, but the closer we got to the water, the fewer there were. The last five miles or so was just nothing..."

The Japanese guy had told me already. Or rather, I read his memories about this place during a test. Here he had personally witnessed a ton of terrifying things, how all sorts of monsters crawled out the water, eating everything in their path, zombies and other living things alike. All so they could get levels and mutations.

The sound of metal scraping down below came to my ears as if in response to my thoughts.

And here are the people...

I ordered the girl to stay there and wait, then dematerialized and flew after five Systemniks.

One of them was pretty strong, but only by the standards of the Japanese. About six foot tall, broad-shouldered, dressed in plate armor. It was creaking up a storm, for sure, but it was only thanks to that that I was even able to the notice the group.

One tank with a shield and a club, two swordsmen, an archer, and a mage. That last one had activated some skill which made the group very hard to pick out with the naked eye. All of them were semi-transparent and blended into the scenery.

By my eyes were not naked, and my ears were sharp as Cyrush. So I easily followed their tracks.

They were heading towards the water, which bugged me a little. They most likely weren't going home, but on the attack. Which meant I would have to wait until that was over.

I could have just pulled the coordinates out of any one of their heads, but that wouldn't be fun. Especially since they seemed to be head for a specific destination, and it would be worth seeing what it could be.

In half an hour we had reached the shore! It was relatively quiet here, which was enough to put you on edge. The Japanese were also obviously tense, but still kept their outward composure, starting right away to get ready for...

An ambush? Did they come here to hunt? That would be fun.

The fighters scattered some mines and System traps right on the beach. Then they found cover and took harpoons out of their inventory. They were fairly massive instruments, definitely weighing above ten pounds. Which meant that each of them had certainly killed at least one person.

But I wasn't there to judge. No, just to watch

and see how and who they were hunting here. The water seemed calm for now, nothing was climbing out of the depths, and it would be pretty annoying if they just set up crab traps, waited, and then went home to roll up some sushi.

But no. Eventually the mage got close up to the water and, without turning off his stealth effect, took a zombie out of his inventory. A dead one, sure, but the corpse stank bad.

He sent the rotten body straight into the water, then the wizard immediately ran back to his fighters without looking back.

Okay? Are we waiting for them to bite? I can wait…

Thankfully, I didn't have to float in the air for long. Within just a few seconds the water by the shore started churning. At first I could see a few toothy fish mouths through it. They started tearing the dead flesh to pieces, ripping each other's gains away and fighting vigorously.

Gradually the number of fish got bigger and bigger, and for a while it would have been possible to throw harpoons into the water. There would have been loot no matter what, enough for dinner. But the people just kept sitting, patiently waiting for something else.

Hey! The body is almost all eaten! Where you gonna get another one?

But it turned out they were waiting for a reason… Soon the water started churning even more, and the deeps of the sea gaped open, releasing a new, much more terrifying monster…

CHAPTER 4

"WAIT, YOU SERIOUSLY THOUGHT you could handle..." I was walking back and forth, staring at the massive, overturned body. "Is that some kind of valor for you? Or are you just that stupid?"

The Japanese just lay on the ground nearby, blinking their eyes, dumbfounded.

And for real and true, the language barrier was in full force. They simply did not understand me. Plus, they were pretty cold. Those guys were clearly not used to cool frost in the middle of summer. Especially since they didn't have anything like that in winter here. They were lying on the ground, shivering, their teeth clattering. This was especially noticeable from under the dull helmet of the armored fighter. His shaking came with a whistling noise that was unavoidably annoying.

"Ehhh..." I shook my head again, realizing that now I would either have to get inside of one of their heads or use the chat. The first option was questionable, since I knew what kind of perverts the Japanese are. I would be getting all sorts of garbage...

Kasp: Hey, you speak the local language, if we need it, right?

The message went to Eva and I was left to wait. The loot from the monster was already settled warmly in my inventory, and its crystal could wait for the moment. I didn't want a corpse like this to just disappear. There was still something I could get from it.

Eva: Kasp! Was it you making that loud sound? What happened?

Well, okay... She didn't even answer my question, just tossing out her own. What's going on their heads, I wonder?

Kasp: Not important. Teleport somewhere higher up and look at the sea. Once you see the crab on the beach, hop over to it. That's where I am.

Once again we had minutes of waiting ahead. Somewhere off in the distance I heard a dull tap, letting me know that the girl had teleported successfully. Another ten seconds or so to spy the crab and then...

Eva: WHAT?! THAT'S A CRAB?!

I didn't see any reason to answer a question like that. Yes, it is a crab. A big one, sure, but it didn't stop being a crab for all that.

Soon the space next to me broke out into cracks and my friend dropped out with a bright flash. Her eyes told me that the monster I had felled had left an indelible impression upon her. It would be too boring to wait for her to pull herself together, so I just got right down to business.

"Tell them to show us where their camp is. Because the devils are just silent, not evening opening their mouths." I waved over at the samurai in their dogpile. "You want me to give you the whip? But that didn't help me too much..."

"You asked them about their camp using a whip?" shouted Eva. "And now you're surprised that they won't tell you anything?!"

"What, you think I'm a complete idiot?" I was surprised and offended. "I asked them using the chat and spoken words... I used the whip to hit them."

It turned out that Eva did not speak Japanese, so typing in chat was way easier and faster than the spoken word. I hadn't gotten used to it yet, but then again, I didn't have to talk to people that much anyway. Luckily for me.

While they were getting to know each other, I decided to check the fallen monster for useful items once again. I suddenly recalled how I had killed the monster.

The Japanese had been expecting a smaller fish. Clearly they had gone fishing like this many times before, but they were just unlucky today. But unbelievably lucky that I had been around.

As soon as the crab broke onto dry land, those idiots decided to commit their beloved seppuku, rather than running away and not looking back. Or maybe it was hara-kiri, I don't know exactly what they call this outright suicide, especially when it's a group all at once.

The crab climbed onto the shore, grabbed what was left of the corpse, and was about to return to his own element, when one of those idiots threw a harpoon at the monster.

The toothed pole somehow pierced through the thick chitinous armor, and the rope pulled taut like a guitar string, stuck fast in the ground. Then the rest of them followed the idiot's lead, throwing their own harpoons, pinning the unlucky crab to the beach, leaving him no choice but to go on the offensive.

The fight didn't last long, since the powerful claws easily tore through first the chains and then almost finished off the guy decked in plate armor. The only thing I did like was the mage's attack. He gathered a cloud sparking with a number of charges around himself, then concentrated it in front of himself, letting out a bright ray that hit the monster right in the belly.

The sturdy tank got some cracks from that hit, but it still seemed to be too little to finish him off. But quite enough to piss him off. So the furious crab began tearing up the littoral landscape in his attempts to snatch up the fleeing people.

To be honest, I didn't decide to get involved in the fight for a while, since I was wondering how long the Japanese could hold out. And to my surprise, they did a good job of fulfilling their main task for about 10 minutes. Running away. And right towards the city. They hid skillfully, avoiding all attacks, but eventually they did get stuck in a dead end.

Actually, the crab made the dead end by vomiting up a green liquid up to a hundred feet away. The pool immediately started hissing and flowing in all directions, cutting the poor suckers off from all avenues of retreat.

Why didn't the crab just start vomiting right on the people? Probably because it was hungry and it didn't want to ruin the meat, since that sort of spit up would make any food turn into foul-smelling goop. Obviously Monsieur Crab was a real gourmand.

And it was that that let the people survive. Remembering that I still didn't know where their camp was located, I decided right then and there to join the battle.

It didn't last too long, given that the creature was cold-blooded and reacted badly to low temperatures.

And while the crab was pretty dumb, it still had enough sentience in it for that to be a terrible trick. I turned all my auras on at once, focusing on sucking out its energy, then started flying after the monster, which was running away in a panic. He wanted to get back underwater, but by the halfway point he had already started slowing down. And with every foot his steps got slower and slower.

I had already hit him a couple of times. Right where the mage's ray had hit him earlier. Even though his regeneration had already started closing up the damaged area, still, I had managed to find the weak point.

The first hit made the beast shake his claws and spew acid all over. I patiently waited for the mutant to stop dancing, then I hit him again, right in the same spot.

This time I increased my slungshot's mass, so that the iron ball could cause the solid chitin to crack open again. And right in there was where I threw the mine I had readied in advance.

For that I had to materialize on the monster's pokey back and get my arm dirty all the way up to the elbow, but it was worth it.

I was afraid to even imagine what was happening under his armor, but when it exploded, everything around was splashed with a thick, iced soup from the entrails of the crab. Without taking even one more step, the mutant simply went weak, falling to the ground with a crash.

Well, just five or ten more feet and I might have had to test how I moved under water. It was an intriguing idea, I had to say. Who knew what was going on on the ocean floor right now? In the deepest abyss, and just in the watery depths themselves…

Whatever, screw that for the moment. Right now I was interested in what was inside the crab and where the tenderest meat was. Besides the aforementioned, I didn't find anything else interesting, except that I did decide to take a claw as a souvenir. I would hang it in the town hall and show off in front of everyone.

Now I could take the crystal, no worries, but

first I had to talk to the monster hunters. However, they wanted to get the crab's body from me so bad that I had to get my whip out of my inventory and turn my Aura of Cold on. Now they were just sitting, depressed and upset.

Of course I had taken their weapons away, and also didn't slack on cleaning out their inventories. Nothing much worthwhile to speak of, but better to avoid any possible surprises in advance.

"Well? What are they saying?" I went up to Eva. "If it's nothing, there's always the whip."

"We don't need the whip... They wanted to get the crab meat and you took it from them!" She was angry and stared at me reproachfully.

Well shit. Pale and fuzzy little narrow-eyed kids. Evil uncle Kasp came and took the poor boys' food. Well, huh.

"Are they sure?" My hammer appeared in my hands. The slungshot would not have had the desired effect, since it was practically invisible. Plus it used up mana in its corporeal form, no need to waste.

The Japanese immediately changed their tune, so soon Eva was staring daggers at them too.

What reason was there to lie? Clearly they would believe me. Even if I said that the Japanese were really trying to fornicate with this crab. That sounds a lot more believable anyway.

"Fine, let them take what they need from this crab and then show us their camp." I waved my hands, understanding that we wouldn't have any more problems with them. Although I might have to hit people with the Aura of Fear once a while, they eventually did become meek and obedient.

Eva used the chat to convey my words and the fighters, not believing their eyes, hopped up from where they were sitting. For a while they chattered in confusion, making a show of bowing, but after I shouted at them they scurried off.

I had to give them their weapons back so they could take it apart. Not like that group could do much to me anyway, even if they wanted to and mustered all their force. Nobody was going to heal them up in any case, so their wouldn't be any problems. However, judging from the way they were looking at the girl, I would have to keep an eye on them. Eventually they would get over their fear, might even go hit on her, but she was a big girl, she could teleport them a few feet underground if need be. Or I could help, no skin off my back.

In any case, the Japanese guys threw themselves on the fallen monster like a pack of dogs on a thrown sausage treat. Soon enough the chitin cracked open from sword and club hits, then came chomping sounds, with the people talking quietly amongst themselves the whole time.

Finally, after half an hour, they had taken the crab apart. An impressive amount of it went into the fighters' inventories, but they still had to carry some of it by hand. Like its legs. They each weighed about 70 pounds, so they wrapped them up in ropes and made the armored one drag it behind him.

"They're not worried that we're tagging along? I mean, we could attack their camp and stuff like that..." I asked Eva, but she just shrugged.

Most likely they had called reinforcements against us a long time ago. If not, that meant they just didn't have any more fighters. But I felt like we were in for a surprise no matter what, since they were whispering suspiciously amongst themselves.

I informed the girl of my worries so she would follow the group at a safe distance. In fact, jumping from roof to roof was a great way for her to travel when you considered that there weren't any flying monsters there at all.

And that wasn't even to mention that the seaside was super boring. We had been on the beach for two hours now, and nothing had come out besides the crab. It was strange. I would have to dig around in the heads of the Japanese to see the latest news from this place. But first I would need to get a stele.

The people hoisted their loads onto their backs and wandered off somewhere into the city. They called me insistently to them, showing me what they wanted with gestures and even trying to communicate with the chat.

But I had it on silent so I pretended that I couldn't understand anything. I had something like 200 unread messages which would take me at least half an hour to get through, and that was definitely too much for right now.

And what's more, my new friends were really

nervous. I was floating about 15 feet over their heads, and now and again they would look around, trying to figure out where I was.

Well, no need for that. The mage was just thinking about me. He sent a message to his people and a few dozen fighters had moved on us, and a couple brigades of "fishermen" should be coming from the water any minute now.

How naïve, for them to talk in an open group chat without worrying at all.

Okay, so what would I need to take the settlement? It didn't make any sense for me to wipe them out completely, since then I would just get a stele, not a vassal. Then I would have to find some dumbass to agree to set it up and become my subordinate, and that would just be a whole bunch of wasted time.

Should I kill the leader? That was definitely possible, but then what if his people turned out to be faithful minions. Then I would once again just have to wipe them all out. It was a problem.

I was sure there would be some way to take it more peacefully, at least a little, but until I got right to their center of the city, I wouldn't know it. So, for the moment, my goal would just be to touch the settlement's stele.

Soon the first fishers showed up. For a while they tried to follow their companions surreptitiously, making their way right next to the group. Or rather, they were following me, but they couldn't actually find me at all, so they were in no hurry to join the rest of the crowd.

What kind of person was I to make these decent fellows hide in the shadows?

"Guys, come out, nobody's going to hurt you here." I waved my hand, turning to face a heap of busted technology. That was where five fresh fighters were hiding. "And help carry those crab legs, just look how your friend is sweating over there." I pointed at the tin can, clanking and wheezing as he was.

My appearance was a signal for them to attack. The furious Japanese guys showed up out of their hiding spaces, throwing themselves into their attacks with shouts. A few flashes from offensive abilities could be seen, but they whistled off multiple feet away from me. I could fly much faster now anyway.

The funniest thing was that they had about no weapons. None at all. They were carrying them in their inventories, fully trusting the System to keep their stuff, so now they were empty-handed. Come on, like I wasn't going to clear out their storehouse in advance, along the way. Without appearing at all.

And I had also managed to absorb most of their mana, so those were the only attacks they got. They simply didn't have enough to even make it worth trying.

Since everything was going so well, why not get the kinks out a little? My stats had increased significantly in the last few days, and I somehow hadn't gotten around to testing them out in battle. In the real fight I had only used my Conduits. So now I could have a little fun.

BWACK!

I appeared right in from of the group commander, giving him a good smack right on the jaw. My glove, fully covered in a whole host of protective plating, cracked into my opponent's face, and he went limp, falling to the ground like a brittle fall leaf.

And so much the better! Especially if you consider that the man was a little shorter than me, but weighed at least twice as much.

The fisher groups hardly were any different from each other. A mage commander as support, a tank, and three attacking classes, capable of doing maximum damage both at a distance and in close combat. A perfectly fine choice, most likely draw from video games.

But I was surprised to find that the most powerful member of the group was just a Healer, or something like that. This guy would definitely need his skills, since his jaw was definitely broken.

Next up was an armored fighter. He was significantly smaller and lighter than his commander, the massive plate metal notwithstanding. In the end, the only difference in the fight was the sound of the hit. First there was the sound of hitting a bucket, then the clattering of armor to the ground.

The rest didn't take much effort or time either. Except that one did manage to hit me in the face, which garnered him a nice kick in the gut. The Japanese guy, doubled over, flew a few feet backwards and landed with his ass knocked right through the back windshield of a sedan.

Hm...

Yeah, I had gotten more Strength, quite a bit. I was throwing the close-combat fighters around, and they should be leveling up their physical stats for a bit. But clearly they had some serious problems with potatoes around here, just like with their other food. Plus their levels left something to be desired, since the strongest one was level 22, and the poor archer was just level 11. I wasn't about to hit him too hard, since I wasn't planning to kill anyone.

"Now get up and help your friends carry their stuff." I got my whip out as a warning, giving a few light warning shots to the legs of some unlucky guys.

They got their shit together pretty fast. The first one to come to was the sumo commander. He groaned and moaned for a while, then a bright flash of white light crossed his face and his jaw cracked back into place.

After that he almost passed out again, but his friends, panting and aching in their backs, were able to keep him from falling down.

Soon enough my first captives had explained to their friends that it was stupid to attack me, and they shouldn't do it again. Actually, I don't know what they were saying, constantly staring at, but I sincerely hoped I was right.

But who was I kidding? Now they were all waiting for an army from the city to come reinforce them. They had sent everyone against me, so a bloody and difficult battle was ahead. Or at least that's what they thought.

Soon we started moving on again. Another group of "fishermen" got close, but I paid them no mind. Was just all of Japan intending to attack me or what? I had limbered up, checked my physical stats, so there was no need to show off any more. I had one goal, and I needed to achieve as soon as possible.

About ten minutes later the main army appeared on the horizon. The soldiers had taken up position in two buildings on either side of the street and were fully prepared to attack me as soon as I showed up.

They sure had done a good job of camouflaging themselves. A lot of them were wearing invisibility cloaks, seeming to be made of jellyfish hides, if those even exist.

A few dozen archers and a heap of mages were sitting around behind intact windows, patiently waiting until they could unleash their entire military arsenal. The rest of them, close-combat fighters, had taken positions on the first floor. Why they had even brought them here, I don't know. But whatever, they can be there.

The fishers that I had taken captive stopped sharply, standing and looking around, waiting for me to appear in my corporeal form. They were certain that I would want to know why they had stopped and I would just have to ask them personally, but...

Eva: I think I found it. It's right by the tallest building here. Will you fly over, or should I show you?

I'll fly there myself, Eva. All on my own.

62

CHAPTER 5

"HERE'S WHERE THEY live?" I stared down in surprise, having landed next to Eva. "It's pretty nice, I have to admit..."

"Yeah, I liked it too. Built real nice..." I had to agree with Eva. True fact. "But there's just too many left there."

Actually, even though the main army had been sent after me, there was still a decent force left in the settlement.

On the other hand, if they had done anything else, I would have considered them stupid. Entirely stupid. Sending off your force to fight a unknown person, one who's not even your enemy, just some strange dude, and leaving your settlement unprotected would be the very height of idiocy.

But there were only about 20 people who could be considered real defenders, the rest just being craftsmen, probably, of which there was definitely more than a hundred, all working together in harmony.

Of course, I could admire how other people work till the end of time, but that's not what I'm here for. I only had a little bit of time. It would be about forty minutes before the ambushers realized I hadn't been there for quite a while, before they got back here. Give or take, but I didn't think it'd be more than an hour.

The Japanese had hidden their settlement, although not too well. I think that rather than zombies they were more afraid of attacks from the sea, so they put their stele right on the street, directly between two fairly tall buildings. They were like two unbroken walls, and the street itself was covered by a solid-looking fence made of concrete and steel.

There was no issue with resources here, just gather up all the trash around and there you go, you got iron, concrete, asphalt, and whatever else. Well, except that wood was a no-go, but I didn't see anything too terrible about that.

I may not have had basically any time to spare, but reconnaissance was sacred. So I flew down to check out the settlement up close.

What really stood out was that their shield was large. They either had a high-level gray stele or at least a green one here. Somewhere around 300 feet in diameter, if not more. That might make them a problem, since getting through a shield wasn't that simple, and if were durable too... I might, at worst, not have enough time before the reinforcements arrived, but the fact they were in the middle of the city did make my job a lot easier.

I would just pick up a bunch of heavy items off the ground and throw them from a great height. Eventually the shield would give out. The main thing was just that other stuff not going flying through the cupola, because who knows if the System might consider, say, a piece of wall to be my opponent's weapon or one of their tricks. And I wouldn't want to destroy the city itself, because that was how they were going to have to pay me their taxes...

Plus, I had to recognize their skills. These guys really managed to do construction and crafting much better and faster than us. Everything was built under the cupola now. And right up to the limit, with the buildings higher in the center of the settlement and smaller two and three-story buildings on the edges already. And that was all so they never had to go outside of the dome, as far as I could tell.

The living space might be cramped, but there was enough for everyone. And that totaled, for now, more than 200 people in a pretty small area. And a large number of crafting places too. They had leatherworkers, builders, and even a smith. I never even noticed before how well the dome kept sounds in. But now that was strikingly clear, given that a few hundred feet in front of me a large man was beating on a piece of metal with a hammer as hard as he could, but for me it just sounded like the ticking of a clock.

The streets inside the settlement were clearly not designed for transportation. Barely two people could pass through them, just six feet across at their widest. But that was normal for them, since there really wasn't much space.

I was honestly kind of embarrassed by what I saw. They had a weak stele and significantly fewer people, but everything was built up and put together so much better. Sure, they had resources out the wazoo, although getting clay would be harder than, let's say, breaking a piece off a home and throwing it into your inventory, but still...

So yeah. Judging by the pieces of the crab that they were carrying, they all had quite massive inventories. About 200 pounds, if not more. And that immediately changed my view of those people. What were they doing before they started developing their crafting? I had a hunch that they hadn't increased their inventory space with dolphins.

Then again, who knew? I hadn't gone through the functions of their stele, and all my other vassals had also paid no attention to that super important thing. Maybe the basic class here was some kind of Storer. And he could share those abilities with all the inhabitants, you could suppose. Or just with those nearby, but even that would be pretty amazing.

Whatever the case, I would have to check it out.

Anyway, I tried breaking through the shield, but I just bump up against an invisible barrier.

Even though I knew it wouldn't work, it was still worth checking, in any case. Maybe I hadn't been able to get to the bitches because they had been sent a challenge?

Hmm...

Oh, why am I wasting time on nonsense? There definitely is a way for the System to do that, so I could just beat them on my own terms. Just ask Brownie to mess around with the stele and challenge our pals to a duel, and then we're basically done. I would take advantage of that if I couldn't manage to get in.

"Can you open up a portal for me?" I appeared behind the girl, so I had to grab her by the hand. And once again she nearly jumped off the roof in fright.

"Dammit! Why you gotta be like that?" She was upset, but calmed down immediately once she got one of my oh-so-sweet smiles. "Y-yeah... I can, but not too far..."

"What about under the shield?"

Now she couldn't answer. But that was what I wanted to know the most, if it was possible. It seemed like it shouldn't be. But who could punish us for trying? Not the Japanese, that was for sure.

To do so we went down a few stories, hid in one of the rooms, and then the girl started right off on trying to break into the settlement.

Eva frowned, closed her eyes, and even spit on the floor, just in case, while I started looking around this living space for the well-to-do Japanese person who once lived here. Most likely he had been digested in the belly of a sea monster long ago and was now lying on the sea floor in the form of natural waste.

There wasn't much left from the room itself. The inhabitants clearly got their wood from furniture, but why they took out all the appliances you could only guess. Most likely they also had a System engineer who made powerful weapons out of trash, which blew up all on their own right in the laboratory.

But if our Anton actually showed his class, theirs would have been much less likely to.

No to mention getting through the shield without a fight like ours.

"Oh!" A bright flash appeared in the room Eva was sitting in, and then came some smoke.

I found the girl lying on the ground, blinking her eyes. She was conscious, but she definitely had taken a hit, and there was no open portal to be found. I wasn't even mad, though, since this is what I expected.

"Almost!" she suddenly shouted, taking a small green mana potion out of her inventory.

"Nah, wait up. Chill." I put my hand on her should. "What do you mean, almost?"

"I would have been easy to open it through the arch!" she shouted. "For real! If I worked on it a little, I could totally open a portal under the cupola, but I just don't have the skills for it now."

Well, now that was intriguing. It would work, she just needed some practice... Portalists had just become a much more valuable class for me. I mean, really, being able to attack without breaking the shield was quite valuable.

"But I can't pick the place over there. I have no idea at all where the portal will open up..." The girl closed her eyes once more, concentrating on her task, and I had no intention of distracting her, so I headed toward the window.

The exact center of the settlement was only a few hundred feet from here. In general, not being able to pick the place where the portal would open was no problem for me personally, but if we sent Grugg to attack them later, then it would be an issue.

Let's suppose the window opened up right under the dome, way up high. Then what? He would simply fall and hit the ground, damaging only the ones who were unlucky enough to find themselves below him.

If only I found some catgirls. A whole army of them. They could land on four feet, and even if they shat in everyone's shoes and stole our rewards from under the door, still it would be better than a massive bull. He wasn't even that useful in daily life, but alas, it is what it is.

I still had to deal with the elf girl too and also find something for her brother to do.

There was so much to do, and I was just sitting around on this godforsaken island, unable to go anywhere. I couldn't even fly away, since I had this Portalist tagging along, and it's not like I could put her in my inventory. This would be so much easier with Gosha. I should have turned him into a Portalist instead of making him grow all sorts of junk. Although Cyrush did give me hope. I mean, the giant cactus had done a good job of fighting a whole horde of zombies twice already.

There was one other interesting thing. Let's say the shield won't let me or a whole zombie pass through. That would be a bummer, but not the end of the world. So what if I threw Gosha into it? Or what about Cyrush? In theory it was not a weapon, just some thingamajig made by the System. And what could just some artifact and a plant do? They should be let through, in theory, but I couldn't be sure.

"Ah!" Eva shouted once more, another failure. But this time it clearly went a lot better.

It wasn't hard to see her success, since there was now a commotion going on in the village. The fighters were rushing out of their houses, taking up positions on the wall, fully preparing for an attack. Most likely the System had informed them of the invasion attempt and now they were all waiting to see where the enemy would come from.

That was bad.

"Okay, wrap it up." I waved my hand. She wasn't going to succeed anyway, since the ones they had sent after me had been called back, probably. No, it had to be like that. I didn't think the people in this settlement were that stupid, and they could definitely put two and two together. "Get ready to run away if anything happens. I'm going in, under the shield…"

"Under the shield? It seems to be impenetrable

everywhere…" Eva was surprised, but I had stopped listening.

I dematerialized and then first flew upward, grabbing everything that wasn't nailed down along the way. Broken glass, leftover furniture, shattered doors. Everything worked. The main thing was just not to throw away the reindeer leg or the crab meat, since I still wanted to use them for food at least once.

As soon as I got high enough, I sent all that stuff down with a nice toss, at the same time flying off to refill my ammunition. I also saw how the trash was slamming into and breaking apart against the shield.

And that meant my method would work, but I just didn't know how long I would have to be throwing all of that to break through the shield.

But right after that attack the people down people started moving. Although really their efforts weren't very fruitful, given that still nobody could see the enemy.

On the next pass I took just one thing. I had noticed right away that a broken chunk of the brick wall was sitting just wrong on the street, so I put it in my inventory. The chunk wasn't too big, less than 1000 pounds, but a bigger one wouldn't fit. Somehow I had collected a significant amount of shit.

The brickwork went flying, and I hovering in the air for a bit. It was just interesting to see how the stone slammed against the invisible barrier, splintering into shards within a cloud of dust, and then how the shards of stone rained like hail on the heads of the people, frozen down below.

To their credit, all of the citizens had already hidden themselves in one of the central buildings after my first salvo. The windows over there were covered with metal plates, all the entrances and exits were stopped up, leaving just a few holes where archers and crossbow users were hiding. I was just guessing about the last ones, since I couldn't know for sure.

Soon a bright flame came flying through the cupola. Leaving behind a barely visible trail of many, many sparks, it slowly flew right at me. Plus that bastard could definitely see me, since as soon as I moved to the side, it change its course.

The Japanese down below started being a lot more active, pointing their fingers at the sky, and I set about getting away from that annoying hanger-on.

It was sticking to me like toilet paper on my shoe. And actually, as soon as it got close I could make out that it really was a little piece of paper flashing green. Was it some kind of artifact? In any case, my hand just passed right through it, and I was completely unable to pop the bastard into my inventory.

Well, just let it fly then. It's slow anyway.

Most likely someone had just used their Follow ability. And that someone was surely so proud of the fact that their ability had finally found some use in a real battle. Except I really couldn't even think of how else you could use something like that against me. Alright, yeah, Zorn could read my mind and see my intentions. But this paper piece of shit? Maybe it didn't just help you see ghosts, but invisies too. If so, then you could say it had at least some use.

But I could still fly faster. And even though I couldn't stay in one place anymore, there was in fact only advantages from this piece of paper. Without knowing my speed, the fighters would waste their mana, shooting off their abilities straight into the air. And with their arrows going wide, I would figure out what the local army was capable of.

A lot of the attacks looked boring and dumb. Ice arrows, fireballs, ball lightning... Even a direct hit from any of those would do me only insignificant damage that I could heal using energy with my Vampiric Aura. So, basically, you could say they were just doing that damage to their selves.

Only one of the mages gave me a bit of trouble. He had a full three active abilities in his arsenal, and most likely that same number of passive ones too. And from what I could see, he was dressed to the nines, everything high-quality and rare. Most probably he was either the local leader or just the head mage, or something like that.

The worst skill for me was the homing one. It looked like a fireball, about the size of a decent orange, but it flew as fast as an arrow shot from a bow.

But I hadn't even made any attempt to avoid it when the fireball changed course and flew into a building.

Wrong way.

Next they sent a long gout of flame my way. It also burned the neighboring building, making a little localized fire, then kept going after the receding leaf, nearly catching it on fire.

The third skill also ended up being a fire one, but much more typical. A normal fireball, a little bit smaller than a soccer ball. It went off into the sky somewhere and exploded into a bunch of smoking, burning sparks about a mile up.

From then on the fire mage stopped experimenting, concentrating on shooting small curvy shots. They all kept on hitting one spot, exclusively on the wall of the building, the leaf notwithstanding. So soon enough the rest of them also switched to attacking the empty building.

Huh, what did I mean empty? Shit! Eva was there!

I had to shoot off a quick return volley and then immediately rush off to help the girl. I just managed to catch out of the corner of my eye how a dozen fighters had been sent to go get her. Well, more like three fighters, since the rest were citizens armed with crossbows.

I have been thinking for a long time that that weapon really helps normal people become something like useful soldiers. At least you don't need any abilities to use it at all, I mean. Let them shoot each other as much as they like, just as long as they don't shoot themselves.

By the time I got to the place I was headed for,

dodging stray attack abilities shot off by those bumbling mages, the wall had taken some significant damage.

CRACK!

A pretty big crack appeared, then another and another. Man, there was two tons here, no less!

Okay, Eva could wait. She was a big girl, and even if a whole crowd of people broke into her room, she could just get away with her portal, wherever she wanted to go.

And if I don't drop this wall right on the heads of the Japanese, then all this work I've done with Eva will be for nothing…

PFWIT! I paid no attention to the magical shots passing by every now and again, even though I got some little burns sometimes, and started pulling out fairly good-sized pieces of the wall.

Even though some concrete bits were coming off of it sometimes, I had already set this goal for myself, and I wasn't about to give up. Maybe Gosha could have gotten me out of this with his cactus, or just growing daisies in the cracks.

Anyway, I did have to freeze them a little. Even though a directed aura would eat up my mana, my last level-up had really made me a much stronger wizard. At least I managed to freeze the frame that was holding the piece of concrete enough so I could break through it with a few hits from my hammer.

Or maybe that was due to Strength. Who knew? In any case, I had definitely gotten stronger, on the basis of my all-potato diet. I was afraid to even imagine how it was in Belarus, where they had such a special, friendly, warm relationship with those tubers.

GRAKH!

I managed it in the end. I ran into it, full force, and broke through the busted wall, flying down with it onto the street. I got a few moments of enjoyment, feeling the freefall, before the mages in the settlement began trying to knock away the wall flying toward them. I had to dematerialize and dash off to the side, but I still enjoyed the spectacle.

They couldn't manage to knock the wall away, unsurprisingly. They couldn't even break it apart, although the inhabitants sure did try.

It fell practically right on the center of the dome, so the hit came not glancingly, but direct with its full force.

I was pretty much sure that it wouldn't break through the shield, but turns out I was wrong. The wall, shattering into a bunch of fragments, continued falling and slammed into the smithy, turning it into ruins.

As for the shield?

I rushed down in. Even though the leaf was flying behind me, and the Japanese weren't standing around in shock, constantly shooting in my direction, none of that mattered at all. I was almost there!

Eva: Kasp! Help!

Somewhere behind me I heard a smacking sound, which meant the girl was trying to get away from her pursuers. I just barely caught the sound, right at the edge of my hearing, since I was flying down at full speed, trying to get to the stele as fast as possible.

It wasn't hard to find. A little wooden house was reposing in the midst of all this dense construction in the settlement, one built following ancient local customs. Super recognizable architecture, impossible to get it confused. And the System had duplicated it exactly down to every single detail.

As far as I could recall, their doors were whatever, since the Japs had put their stock in only their idiotic katanas since the olden days, and you could break into them just like that.

Eva: Kasp!

Oh, what is she shouting about? Did they get her? But there was definitely no reason to go back up, it would just be wasting more time.

BAM!

My spiked metal ball slammed full force into the security guard's back, protected by a cuirass, and he flew back a good five feet, somersaulting over the spacious veranda.

The next one got hit by my hammer, since I didn't have time to swing my main weapon around again.

Right after that a self-guided ball slammed into me, a fair-sized one. A fire mage had shown up nearby and used his signature move.

"Expelliarmus!"

In less than a second I had moved over to the

mage and smacked him as hard as I could in the groin. The Asian, screaming in a high falsetto, flew up a little and then fell like a lump on the ground, curling up into a permanent fetal position.

"That's what I thought," I said, waving my arms for some reason.

But I had to make a quick retreat, since the fighters were hurrying down from the walls towards the main building as quick as possible. The distance wasn't far, plus their reinforcements were coming closer every minute, so I rushed to the stele in all haste.

CRACK!

As soon as I got up to the door, seemingly made of cardboard, my class effect shut off and I broke through it with my head. But okay, the important thing was that I had gotten past the barrier. The rest was just trifles, including the three randomly-armed men inside.

It was possible they were already planning to rape Eva over there, so I had to hurry. You could say I was doing it for the lady's honor. And the future earnings in my treasury, of course.

As soon as I got to my feet, I tried to turn all my auras on. But not a damn thing! Nothing worked! I couldn't even use my dematerialization. I don't know how I lived without it before. I suddenly remembered how much I disliked talking to people. The only good thing was that even if they talked to me, I didn't understand a single word. Which was great.

A flame started burning on the arms of one of

the fighters. Within a moment it had moved to his weapon, but before he could throw it at me with a triumphant war-cry, a heavy, thickly-gloved fist slammed into his face.

That was the sign for the fight to start, and a defender and the head of the settlement came after me.

But their fate differed from that of the other Japs for just a moment. The reindeer leg flew at the ice chunk and ball of electricity that had been sent toward me. It stoically took all the damage on itself, with just barely singed fur. The Japanese, unable to dodge due to their shock at the reindeer leg, only saw the Warhammer flying straight at them at the very last moment, followed by my spiky metal ball.

You thought it would be that easy? They thought they could pull off some magic, those pricks.

But they shouted something, wanting either to come to terms, or demanding that I put up a fair fight. But I didn't see anything unfair about my hammer. Since I had been deprived of my trump card anyway, I needed to use something else.

Well, hello there, darling. So green and lovely…

The stele was situation right in the middle of the room, just like everywhere else, and there were some comfortable high-tech chairs around it. Even though they weren't giving massages now, it would still be nice to plop down in one of them after a long, hard day.

But they certainly weren't going to let me sit

around here. Any second now a whole army was going to show up behind me, and without my self-defense skills I definitely couldn't take on that whole mess. So, as soon as I got to the middle of the room, I put my hand on the cool, rough, green surface. Alright, let's go…

Do you wish to capture the stele of the Fuji settlement? Yes/No

No imagination. They could have thought of something cool, but the named the city after the city. So dumb. But what could you do? Yes, System, I do, thank you.

You cannot capture the stele of a vassal settlement without the consent of its sovereign.

Awaiting response from the sovereign.

Response negative.

Do you wish to declare war? Yes/No

Well, that was annoying. But what could you do?

It was annoying mostly because I had entirely forgotten the word "sovereign". But I had just remembered it, thank you, System. But really, why not? Let all of Japan unite, we still had a couple aces up our sleeve.

Okay. Let's declare war, my sweet System, whatever that might entail. And hurry up, because I have no idea what they're doing to Eva over there.

CHAPTER 6

JUST ANNOYING. If I had started the attack through the System, I could have chosen my goal. Like capturing all the vassals, or turning the army of my enemy into my slaves. Diversify the clay division, you could say.

But like this I would have to make a huge investment, without even a guarantee that there would be a battle. And I really didn't feel like wasting my hard-won resources, since who knew how much money the sovereign of this settlement had?

And I had no idea what kind of army he had. But that was the least of my problems, since I could, even though it would put my health at risk, use a crystal, my trump card. In the worst-case scenario, of course.

But the System was heartless, not like they could refuse. Either the sovereign would give me the vassal, or he would fight. There was no other choice, since, having personally touched the settlement's stele, I hadn't given my opponent one.

But the disadvantage was that I declared war, a situation that meant the defending side would be picking the conditions. That reeked of unfairness, since the last time, when a lone village had something like that happen to them, by which I mean the guys from District 9, they set their own rules. Pissed me off, since on that football field I could have turned at least a thousand Japs into my slaves. And the number really wouldn't matter, since my auras would hit pretty far.

But the main Japanese guy was going slow. He was thinking, choosing from the available arenas, trying to figure out which field it would be easiest for him to win on.

And I couldn't even see what he could choose from. I just had a short glimpse of a small list, but I totally forgot it. I hadn't been planning to attack anybody with my whole village, since that would take up my time, which I didn't have. I still needed to improve my vassals, and I was completely busy with Kaspiana.

Well, what I had seen among the Japanese had inspired me to embark on a building spree in the near future.

I had a Portal Arch, I had a Portalist. Just needed to level them up a bit, and I could get hundreds of tons of resources, and basically whatever ones. Open up a wormhole right by an oil well, and you got yourself thousands of gallons of rightfully gained System oil. Or diesel oil, just to make life hard for our enemies.

And what's more, soon I'd have a local vassal here, and that would be direct access to seafood. Before I broke through the shield I noticed that their kitchen here was fairly large and centralized. They didn't use potatoes, and the stores had long been looted out, so for the most part people ate things that swam around and bit hard. So their fishermen were quality. They got zombie corpses from somewhere and then tested their mettle with whatever crawled out.

So I had something to offer them. We had more than enough zombie corpses in our neck of the woods, and if that wasn't enough, I would ask Eva to take me to India or China. There that resource sure wasn't going to run out any time soon.

Then we would just dig up worms like before. Sure, they might manage to mutate and become the rulers of the planet by then, but we'll just hope we can take care of them too.

One minute, two minutes, three minutes... And I was still just hanging around in the darkness, waiting for the leader of the main Japanese settlement to make a decision. I didn't think that he had taken over absolutely everything around, so it was unlikely that the enemy army would consist of hundreds of thousands of people. And I also didn't think that those hundreds of thousands of people had managed to spread out over the whole continent, much less this little island.

You opponent has chosen the fight format. (Battle)

Familiarize yourself with the rules and confirm you are ready

Awful son of a bitch! Prick hole!

I shouldn't say that. He could be worse than that.

First off, if I lost, I would have to give him one of my vassals. An unpleasant fact, but not critical, especially since all of mine were within a stone's throw. If need be, I could talk to them and entice them to my side. Or just take them back, whatever worked.

The worst part was that I couldn't personally participate in the upcoming battle. I could only watch and give orders, nothing more.

But it was good that it wouldn't be a real fight. My opponent had decided not to risk anyone uselessly, which I had to commend him for. I mean, when you don't know who's attacking you, it's better not to set the stakes too high. Especially when you're only risking one vassal in the worst case. And moreover, nobody was planning on killing that vassal, just setting the flow of taxes to go in another direction.

The essence of the fight itself was simply. I would sit at the top of a tower on one side, and the leader of our opposing army on the same thing, just on the other side. That's all. Then we would command the armies we drew up beforehand, choosing their positions, sending them to attack or telling them where to defend.

The victory conditions were either to destroy the enemy's tower or climb to the top and take down the leader in an unfair fight. I didn't know how it worked on the tower, but they would have to take mine apart piece by piece, because I definitely wasn't going to give up without a fight.

It might be a good idea to just hide my army and wait for the opponent to come here. Then I could warm up a bit and show him that it would have been worth it to just give me the vassal. Without all this mess. But for seem reason, this battle seemed like it would be exceptionally entertaining. I was actually kind of happy that it had gone this way.

Everything was just like in a video game, except on the field there would be living people with their own fears and weaknesses. And also their abilities and strengths, which you would do well to not forget.

I would also have to use up my crystals here, since I couldn't take equipment from my own world. The System had taken that into account, since if we, say, put just one fighter on the field and won, our enemy would be annoyed.

I immediately imagined Grugg in a space marine outfit made by Anton. Sooner or later he would make something like that. If not, I would pump him full of crystals until completed our main goal. Because really, what could you do to an opponent like that? Even bare-naked he was unkillable, and like that he would become something terrifying, even for me.

Okay... There were so many rules, you couldn't get your head around them all.

The maximum number of fighters was a thousand. I couldn't field that many even if I took out absolutely all of them from every settlement under my control. And that included the craftsman and just worthless people with very little use. It was a good thing that I had at least managed to get my guys up to level ten, but I hadn't given them classes, and that might be a problem.

But at the first phase we would have to come out with just a hundred people each. I could separate them into three division, which would help me control that crowd, at least a little.

I could also choose three messengers for the first phase. Basically I would have to use them to control all my forces' movements. I would give an order and the messenger would head off to the division I intended and give them the information. Only then would the division start moving.

So I would have to put people into groups, since giving orders to everyone individually wouldn't lead to anything useful.

That made sense. The messengers run around, directing the forces, and they arrange themselves exactly how I say. We use the landscape, clever tricks, and stuff like that, and we can gain victory over our enemy.

But that was just a hundred people. I could pay for more, which would cost crystals from the treasury. Part of me really didn't want to do that, but the other part knew we had gotten together, to put it lightly, enough to wage war for multiple days, or even more. Something like four and a half thousand, including both blue ones and purple ones, whose worth was quite high.

Where did we get all this wealth from? I don't think my vassals had killed that many deadies by now. Probably that income had come from selling unique items, both the ones I had gotten and the ones we received during the last test. Plus, after that whole mess with the massive horde we managed to get a significant number of both crystals and rewards. Everything that did us no good was also put up for auction, bringing in income, which included my opponent's efforts, it seemed. The Japanese had a big problem with zombies, so it was simpler for them to just buy everything they needed rather than wait for mutants by the sea.

I had a bunch of questions about equipment. You could only have one kind of soldier in a single division. From cheap swordsmen or peasants armed with pitchforks, up to extremely expensive heavy inventory, or even battle mages. But of course, the System only answered a very few questions on that, so everything would have to be cleared up as we went along. For instance, the store itself would only be open after the battle started.

It would be funny if I got a whole bunch of peasants, and then they in fact had just magic classes. But that wouldn't make sense, since the equipment would significantly improve some of the people's abilities or others.

At the start I could make three divisions, but since they were all paid for by the System, I could only choose from the basic ones. Swordsmen, archers, spearmen, and that was all.

I couldn't find anything like jaegers or those space marines yet, more's the pity. So it made no sense to put the bull out first in the fight. I wanted to get him set up right.

Too bad you couldn't see the battlefield in advance. Then I could have figured out right away what kinds of forces I needed and how many. Now we're just guessing.

30 swordsmen, the same number of spearmen, and 40 archers. Even if those last ones are extremely near-sighted, if I let them get off a couple of mass shots, they'll have the desired effect.

There was another thing in the rules I didn't like. Even though nobody would die a real death here, I still couldn't summon those who had fallen in battle. That meant the numbers of my forces wasn't just constrained by the limit, but by how many subjects I had. I didn't think that would be a problem for the Japanese, which meant they could overpower us in numbers, at least, without worrying about losses. They would just buy a thousand peasants and overpower my bull with a wall of flesh.

And that meant I couldn't afford to make mistakes. I could, possibly, just refuse these hundred people and buy some for real money right away, but only the System knew how much time that would take. It was possible that my opponent would manage to tear my tower down brick by brick first.

Alright, okay. The window for choosing had opened, and now I was supposed to quickly put everyone in their divisions. But I couldn't remember names or faces. Out of all our people I only knew a couple dozen, and the rest were completely unfamiliar.

Oh! Awesome. I had to pick the officers first. That was nice, since the messengers would be giving my orders to them, for sure.

Definitely Igor would go for the archers. He would shoot, show the rest of the archers where to shoot, and help them with wind. And if our enemy closed the distance, he could just smack them with a fist of air.

I could put the elves with him, since those guys clearly knew how to use those weapons, but I didn't want to just waste them. I would buy them when I had the opportunity to make better divisions.

Who else would go with the archers? The girls! All of them, no exceptions. Besides Eva and the redhead, who I would leave for entirely different purposes. Yeah, let them draw the bowstrings to the best of their abilities, the main thing was that they didn't riddle each other with holes. But that would all depend on my orders and how fast the messengers delivered them.

I wondered how badly they would stink-eye me once they learned that I had offered them up to the slaughter. I mean, the first divisions would almost certainly die to the last man. Oh! I could put all of Amazonia there. But I recalled the dark-haired girl, who seemed to be using a sword and shield, so she would go in the next division.

I made the commander of the soldiers who had come to our settlement the officer of the swordsman division. He might be used to a different weapon, but mastering a sword and shield wasn't too hard, in my opinion. At least at a free-for-all level. I also put the rest of the fighters there, besides that girl, and made up the rest with villagers. They'd get along, surely.

The spearmen were a no-brainer. Bale in the lead, and I would get the rest from the store. That grocery store. They had so often fought off the deadies with just that weapon, so the job would be nothing new for them.

Even though there were less than 30 fighters there, I could still always take a bunch from the non-combatants. No big deal, let 'em train on the Japs, then it would be easier for them to fight deadies. See, even the craftsman could manage to take part in gathering crystals. But only on the weekends. Their main job was still just to make all sorts of System stuff over there. Oh yeah, once I got back I was going to give Brownie a beating. Seeing how these Asian islanders had developed all sorts of production so quickly, it was so shameful that it burned in the pit of my stomach.

The messengers were last. And they were very important, since how fast my orders got around depended on them. But I was unsure whether the System would allow Eva to use her portals. If so, it would make sense to use her as my messenger first and foremost. If not, that would be too bad. But I had to try.

The description only talked clearly about fighters. The System said that they all would lose their inventory and items, receiving the equipment of whatever type of forces they were in return. And so it would be worth it to make the most expensive divisions later, since we would certainly lose on numbers eventually. But if the fighters didn't lose their abilities and classes, didn't that mean the messengers would be unnecessary? Weren't they their own type of soldiers?

I was also wondering if I could use them as attacking forces. I would summon the bull and tell him to rush headlong to the enemy base and give our opponent my regards. And he would tear everything that he met along the way into pieces. He wouldn't even need a weapon for that, just a headbutt from his cow's head. Then he would come back and tell me that the Japanese leader had managed to say hi back, right before he got a slab of meat upside the head.

But they had some kind of emperors and shoguns here. I hadn't ever been interested in their culture, but you pick these things up. I was almost sure that that historical fact had now been completely restored, so most likely the leader would consider himself the messenger of god or something like that. He might even in the enviable position of having had the good sense to pick up a gold class. But let's leave that for after our victory. For now it was too soon to even think about parlaying with the local bigshots.

Okay. Eva will be the first messenger. She had no military potential, so even if she couldn't use her class, there would still be more use from her as a runner girl.

The second one would be Glash. Sure, she could be my air force, but sending my orders by air was also important. But here it would be pretty bad if her class ability wasn't working. Way, way too bad, since she could give our enemies what for in battle too. And nobody, except the archers, could do anything to her. Whatever. She would fly.

And the third... I don't know. It could be some young guy, we had more than enough of them. Like Cole, he could move around quickly and quietly, and was also a pretty high level with a bunch of stats that would keep him from getting tired. But I also had some plans for him. I mean, he was a Saboteur, and that class was definitely necessary on the field. I had no idea how big the arena would be or how it would look. But I felt like it was all going to be serious.

Probably the System would give us a square some miles across with forests, fields, creeks, hills, and other natural wonders. That way the leader could play to his heart's content.

And in conditions like that, a sabotage division would be absolutely necessary. Blowing up bridges, hitting the rear of the enemy's forces with long-range weapons, and setting up well-planned ambushes. Nikolai could do all that, so let's leave him in our back pocket, until the time is right.

Well, there was one more, a village boy. He was a firecracker, but just level 15. I had taken note of him when Zorn was helping us destroy his horde. The guy had dealt with the mutants assigned to him with gusto, not even asking for help. He wasn't overly strong, but he had passion, and that was appreciated, at least.

I decided to make a mental note of him as potentially useful but kept scrolling anyway.

Oh! I totally forgot about her. The girl who could train animals. There were quite a few questions about her, first and foremost being whether or not she could bring her pet here. As far as I could recall, her dog had shot up in size, and now it could easily carry around a full-grown person on its haunches. I had encountered that beast only once, and then just in passing. To be honest, my first inclination had been to kill it, but I held off, remembering how good the dog actually was.

Could she bring it here? Unlikely. But whatever, it couldn't hurt to try. The two of them together would really come in handy. Recently Olya had taken to going off into the forest with her dog and she almost always came back with a prize.

Although we had agreed on no attacks with the massive bear, nobody had forbidden us from hunting. Everything was understood, the laws of nature had been in place before the apocalypse, and they would continue long after. In fact, now it was the other way around, with the laws of nature being even more fundamental, even the only ones left. The strong eat the weak, predators always attack prey. And most importantly, nobody would touch and inedible ghost.

Alright. It would be bad if Olya came without her dog, but not the end of the world.

Why did I even think that she could get here with her dog? It was really just a guess, since I didn't actually have any idea how her class was set up.

Okay, the choice has been made. A little red button appeared for finishing my preparations and moving to the battlefield. If my opponent hadn't yet gotten around to picking his forces, I would have to wait for him there. But so much the better, since I could look around a little and set up my forces how I liked them. And people would have time to come to terms with the rule that said that if they died it wouldn't be permanent. And then they could get to spreading out, since it wouldn't be smart to just hang out in front of the Japs.

Prepare to be transferred to the battlefield.
Transfer will occur in 3…
2…
1…

CHAPTER 7

WELL, THIS WAS WHAT I expected. The battlefield really did turn out to be a nice size.

I spawned on a high tower, about a hundred feet tall. Right on the roof, so I had a sweet view in front of me.

I could spot a tower exactly the same as mine about a half-mile or a little more ahead. At least, in height and width it was exactly the same, just shaped a little differently. Mine was just a stone pillar with a door at the bottom and some simple outbuildings and little houses next to it, while my opponent's had some patterns, and the roofs of the houses were decked out, while the buildings were covered in traditional Japanese patterns.

Did this idiot buy a skin or something? Whatever the case, it made sense to take a look through the store. My enemy had made his choices much sooner than me and had managed to get everything worked out, and that could be a fatal mistake.

But still, standing on the place set aside for me, I set aside a few seconds to take a look at my surroundings. To my right was a tall hill covered in a thick evergreen forest. That was what we were used to, so maybe we could use it somehow. The hill was separated from the plain in the center by a shallow creek.

The creek flowed right out of the border of the battlefield, splitting it diagonally, hitting a thick wall of gray haze on both ends. I didn't think that you'd be able to pass through those barriers to get around to the enemy's rear. That meant all actions would be clear and open. For me too.

The battlefield itself was in the form of a square with each side about half a mile long. Besides the hill covered in trees and the creek, I could also see a swampy area from here. It was a little to the left of the center, as if it had been put there on purpose to frustrate any attempts to flank the enemy. Everything was against us. But going head-on was no good, there was definitely more of them, so we might not make it. Moreover, there weren't enough high-level Systemniks on our side. The majority of them were just lambs to the slaughter.

To the left of the swamp you could make out a narrow trail. It wound through a rocky area with a ton of massive boulders and crevices, connecting both of our towers.

Actually, if you looked closely there were three paths on our battlefield. All of them went from me to the enemy. Although it would be pretty hard to follow those roads, no matter which way you were sending your forces. The forest, the field, the rocks... All of that only seemed like places for a light walk from afar. In actuality...

In the forest there was very thick undergrowth. Really very thick. Nobody but Grugg could get through it. Huh, was I asking too much of him? No matter, only his bulk could break through the bushes and heaps of fallen trees so that we could blaze a new trail, so to speak.

It would be easier on the fields in the center, but still no cakewalk. The places there were comparatively flat, but only comparatively. Sure, the crags, hills, and forests were densely packed with uneven areas, crevices, and other obstacles, but the fields were also set up so that you couldn't pass through them in a straight line.

And that was because the whole field was riddled with a ton of pits and holes, but that wasn't the worst of it. The System had decided to make sure nobody would get bored, so now every once a while powerful geysers of white-hot steam, acid, or something like that would come shooting out of random places in the barren wasteland. I couldn't tell what exactly those hissing fountains were from here, but I knew for sure that you had better not be next to them when they erupted. Although maybe it wouldn't be too bad for Grugg. He might be able to run through it...

But the middle path split right between the swamp and hissing field, so you could easily go down along it.

All these attractions started right about 150 feet from my tower and ended the same distance away from my enemy's. So, no matter what, I would have to tell my divisions in advance where and where to go, and as soon as they got there, who to attack or to avoid. It wouldn't work to just tell them to advance and kill everything in their path.

Prepare for the start of battle in 1:00...
00:59...

Shit. I didn't have time to admire my handi-work. But my enemy so far seemed to have just a tower, no forces at all. Just like me, actually, and that wasn't right...

Place your forces in their starting positions.

Okay, that was the message. I feel so much concern from System-mommy. But first priority was the shop. Maybe I could buy all the forces I needed right away and just raze my opponent to the ground?

Nope, I couldn't purchase fighters before the fight started.

The shop was set up right in the middle of my command center. It looked like a little touch screen set on top of a small pedestal. It was quite convenient, since I could easily mess around with it and watch what was going on on the battlefield.

And though I couldn't buy any soldiers yet, I could still buy stuff for my tower and check out the available types of forces in advance.

Telling them apart just by looking at them was

pretty hard. But still, there were a lot of them there, and they all belonged to different cultures. And the range of prices wasn't too bad, from ten gray crystals up to three purple ones, which was 3,000 gray ones.

The System had finally set the values of all crystals here. The green ones were worth ten gray ones. The blue ones were worth ten green ones, and correspondingly, the purple ones could be exchanged for ten blue ones.

That made perfect sense, I would say. But not spending money on our image didn't, so I picked only from the most expensive ones. I could afford all of it, and demoralizing our opponent over again was always nice.

There we go, that's what the doctor ordered. For just a moment the tower and everything around it was lit up by a bright flash. Within literally just a few moments there were significant changes. White snow all around, flags hanging on the walls, and the tower itself changed from gray to red. And it was now crowned with a red five-pointed star.

Welcome to the Kremlin, mother*cker!

Despite the fact that there was a thick layer of snow to a radius of 150 feet, it was still warm here. It seemed like it was just visual, nothing else. And it looked good! Everything was totally white all around, with white flies hovering above it, and in the background rose the Kremlin tower. On the buildings there were red flags with a depiction of an enraged bear. I had chosen the picture in a hurry, but Brownie would definitely like it.

No regrets.

Okay, my minute's gonna run out soon, so I gotta take a quick glance at these forces' prices and then position my warriors. I think I can definitely do that.

Peasant — 1

The prices were shown in gray, but you could pay with colors too. If necessary, the System would give you change back.

For a single military unit you had to pay one gray crystal. In theory, that was fine. I had totally forgotten about our American partners, and seeing soldiers like that now, I suddenly remembered. Let them be for the slaughter. Right through the field of geysers. Maybe they'll get through. But there was no way to be sure, since it would depend on our enemy's actions.

Spearman — 2
Swordsman — 3
Archer — 3

That was fair too. Most likely the swordsmen had a little better armor, and the shield wasn't free either. But the archers could be a little cheaper. They didn't have armor or any special weapons.

And how many arrows did they have?

I immediately got the answers to all my questions. There was a question mark next to every kind of fighter, and if you clicked on it, you would get a drop-down menu containing all the information you needed.

20 arrows. Then they would have to come back

to the tower, to refill both the division and their ammunition. Which was also not free, I had to say, but much cheaper. The archers were also equipped with simple wooden bows, light leather armor, and perfectly fine shoes.

Next I checked both the swordsmen and the spearmen. My hunches were right. The former were also in leather armor, but with metal reinforcement. They had a cuirass, greaves, and pauldrons. They even had a simple-looking metal helmet with a short visor. Along with a standard sword, about three feet long, with a small round shield. That would definitely help them against archers.

But the spearmen weren't so lucky. I thought it would be too dangerous to put them in the way of long-range attacks, since the System had screwed them on shields. Like it was saying we couldn't afford it for you guys. So good luck, keep your chin up, here's your stick, hold on tight.

Otherwise, the armor wasn't too bad. And the spears were long, which would command respect. Plus, as a back-up, each of them got a short sword.

And those were all the gray level forces. To train each fighter I would have to spend not just crystals, but time too. One second each for peasants, and five each for the more advanced warriors.

But that was just the gray ones. Farther on in list we got the green ones, blue ones, and even purple ones. And the prices, accordingly, were completely different.

What did we have in the greens?

Grenade Thrower — 30

Now that was intriguing. They got three regular grenades each and could throw them. That was all. Then they would run back to the tower, refill their ammo, rush back and toss their gifts at our foe. Their range, of course, was just okay. But they could break through any of the enemy's ranks. If they worked together, like sending two divisions of swordsmen and grenade throwers right off, then they could defeat a division of the enemy with the same numbers and no losses.

But the time spent on purchasing them was a lot more. You had to wait half a minute for each fighter, and that could be a problem. But yeah, if you made a division of ten people, that wouldn't be too bad. They would throw their grenades, and then they could run right back, not getting in the way at all.

But that type of fighter did look a lot less defended. No armor, just a bag with their ammo. They didn't even have shields, so putting those guys in the line of fire was not a good idea.

It was complicated...

Crossbow Archer — 30

Spearman with Shield — 40

Catapult — 100

The crossbow archer was clear. You didn't have to be a professional to master that weapon. Just keep going, reload, and shoot anything with a pulse. Since what the hell was the use of a pulse here anyway?

I think those guys would have great accuracy, and the piercing power of their bolts was probably way better than arrows had. As for the rest of their equipment, it was the same as what the cheaper guys had, but in addition to light armor they got short swords.

The spearmen with shields seemed a lot more hopeful. Even though they cost quite a lot, the price was more than worth it. Their shields were fair-sized, their spears were about six feet long, and they had two throwing javelins in reserve. Like Romans, if I recalled right. Plus their armor looked much more high-quality, meaning they could survive under fire, so just in close combat we would have a lot more fighters.

The catapult... You would have to wait ten minutes for it, of course, but then what would get? An actual catapult! Here the number of people in the division was strictly delineated by the System. To use it you put up ten people, no question. And moving this technological miracle could only be done by hand, so it could only be done on the common roads. And you could run into an ambush there easy as you please. Buts still, what military power!

You would have to be clever so as not to lose the weapon without having fired off a single shot, but it was definitely worth it.

Okay, what do we have in the blues?

00:10...

00:09...

Hey!

I have to array my forces!

I quickly rushed for the edge of the tower and...

How do you even do this?

For a few seconds I tried shouting voice commands, but everything worked out right away as soon as I tried pulling up the interface. There was no trace left of the old one. Now it had turned into a specialized one for the commander. In it I could see my available forces, open up a mini-map, and see how many people were in each division and their status.

Now all three of them were represented by icons of a sword, a bow, and a spear in the lower left corner. And the buttons were blinking, which clearly meant it was time to press them.

I certainly wasn't going to be slow about it and clicked on the archer division right away.

Ah. Everything was like in a video game. Green lights appeared before me, glowing right on the ground. The lights showed me where each of the fighters would go, helping me choose the arrangement in advance.

I had no intention of being tricky, just putting them in rows of two people each. Let them look at the enemy's tower and if nothing else they could just shoot wherever worked.

As soon as I confirmed my choice, forty confused women appeared, armed with bows and led by that damn Igor himself.

"Hey! Hi!" I shouted at them and waved. They all turned as one at the sound, but for some rea-

son I didn't see any joy in their eyes. Strange...
This was going to be a shitload of fun!

I put the swordsmen in front of the archers
and the spearmen in the first row. Those guys
would be taken out first, but no worries. Soon
enough there would come new, much stronger divisions onto the field. I wasn't planning to be
stingy. If need be we could get a bunch more crystals, no problem. Now we had to win, otherwise I
would have to go looking for other settlements for
a long time.

00:02...

00:01...

Right as soon as the timer reached zero I was
able to see my opponent's forces.

Uh-huh. Exactly the same number as mine.
Maybe the enemy leader had already taken part in
battles like this before, so he knew what the deal
was.

It was too bad that I couldn't see any of the
faces of our opponent's fighters. But still, I didn't
think somebody would allow themselves to spend
three purple crystals on just the appearance of
their tower and their soldiers.

Minute after minute passed, but our opponent's forces still never moved. However, people
started coming out of the central tower and setting
themselves up. And it was an endless stream, one
every second!

Peasants? Most likely. What stood out was
that, while our forces looked more like knights,
judging from their outfits, our opponents were

more like traditional Japanese regiments. The peasants just looked like trash. They all had different weapons, their clothing was light and torn up, and that was saying nothing about their structure. While all the other soldiers were standing to order, lined up in rows, those ones looked more like a mob.

I didn't even know if that was good or bad. On the one hand, you couldn't flank a group like that, but on the other... Well, until I tested them out, I wouldn't know.

In the commander interface there were a bunch more buttons that I hadn't gone through yet, and I thought it was time for me to check them out. Especially since, even if our opponent won right now, I would still have about 20 minutes to get ready. And in that amount of time I could make a whole brigade of grenade throwers. It would be no problem to load them all up right here, next to the tower, which would be mayhem for the Japanese. But I believed that our enemy was no fool and already knew that.

Well, let's go. First off I needed to learn how to move our divisions. There were a few different ways to move them, but only one for joining them together. I was supposed to pick their end point and then drag the division however I felt like it.

"Igor!" I yelled to boy since he was located closest to me. But all three of the divisions turned at once. "What are you all gawking at? Look straight ahead!"

"Kasp! What the hell?" He was asking a perfectly reasonable question. "I can't move at all! I can only shoot!"

"Well then try to shoot!" I answered, watching how it would go.

It turned out he couldn't shoot wherever he wanted either. As soon as I separated the archer division, a barely noticeable semi-translucent field appeared in front of them, separating into cones in the front.

Ah. That was how it showed me how far they could shoot. The possible firing options also appeared right over the division. For example, I could simply stop them from shooting. I would hide in the forest and tell them to wait. The enemy wouldn't notice them, would just keep going, and then...

And then we could hit them right in the back, for instance.

Finally Igor pulled his bowstring, let it go, and... The arrow flew right to the farthest edge of the cone. I mean the widest part. It looked like the System strictly limited how far arrows could fly. Now I understand why it showed that when you were picking your units.

Alriiiiight... But that was for the best. I could manage both my own fighters and the opponent's better that way.

What's more, I could mark out the enemy divisions too! And I could also see how far their arrows flew, which was shown right on the battlefield. Very convenient. Now I needed to know how fast I could give orders.

To see our trusty messengers, I leaned forward, hanging over the edge of the tower. There they were, standing around, talking. The three girls were frozen by the entrance, just waiting for their orders.

But unfortunately, Olya did not have her dog. It looked my plan had just fallen apart at the seams.

Well, fine. Let them run around. It was good for their health. In any case, nothing's going on yet, and we'll have to deal with it as it comes.

While I was looking over my messengers' capabilities, figuring out just how I could relay orders, the Japanese forces had grown significantly. But only in numbers, not quality.

The first to move was a group of peasants. Right down the middle road, no tricks, nothing fancy. Next came the swordsmen, while the spearmen and archers chose to go to our left, through the crags. But like the rest they chose to go down the path.

As far as I knew, all the divisions moved by marching. That was a special structure, where the fighters arrayed themselves in rows of three people each treading the path simultaneously. If you attacked a division while it was marching, that meant victory over that division. While the soldiers were taking their steps, they would take massive damage, plus demoralization and all the bonuses that came from that.

I knew all that from a hint box that the System had so kindly given me.

Well, let's wait for now. Purchase some more people, since the opposing army outnumbered us now three to one, if not more.

But it did make since to give my first order.

CHAPTER 8

NO, I COULDN'T COMMUNICATE with the girls. All my commands were given automatically, with no verbal ones. I even leaned over the edge of the tower again to see how that worked.

First order of business was to pick a division. Then you set the structure, like in rows, in a square, or what have you. Each type of force had their own choices. The spearmen worked best in ranks, but if you got behind them they were toast. So you could put them in a turtle formation, then the enemy would run unto a wall of spears no matter what. But it that state the spearmen wouldn't be able to move, just stand around and wait for attacks.

But that was just an example.

So, I picked the formation the soldiers would move in, then showed them where to go, where to and stand, and which way to set their ranks.

As soon as I made the order, a scroll appeared down below, and the messengers chose amongst themselves who would deliver that message to the officer of the division.

The first one was Eva. Unfortunately, she was running towards the spearman division on her own two feet. Luckily it was only 150 feet away, which didn't take too much time. And as soon as Bale, shooting me a dirty look, received the scroll, it immediately crumbled to dust in his hands.

Then the whole group of them, spewing all sorts of curses and swears at me, moved directly where I had commanded. And I commanded a lot.

First the spearmen set themselves to marching, going 300 feet, then the turned off the road, arrayed themselves in rank and file, and headed for the woods.

Ha, that was the idea!

Next Olya and Glash ran off to the divisions. They were giving the divisions complicated orders, and the people, still hurling deprecations at their commander, moved off after the spearmen.

And once my starting divisions had started moving apart, I ran to the terminal.

Who would I get? Grenade throwers! Ten of them would do. I didn't think I needed any more. For that I set another half of the girls. You might need to be brave for throwing grenades, but our ladies would definitely be able to do it.

And if our opponent got cavalry, then I would get some more. I mean, who else was going to ride horses on the rocks? That wasn't a task for men, definitely not.

Oh hey. He fell for it.

The opposing divisions had made serious progress towards my tower, but once he saw how my fighters were bypassing the main army, and that I had quickly started purchasing more high-quality divisions myself, my opponent started panicking. And the messengers started running to catch the divisions, telling them to retreat home as soon as possible.

And the Japanese leader, trying to gain time sometime, suddenly started buying new groups of peasants.

The spearmen had gone 300 feet, turned around, and were headed back. The swordsmen did the same, then the archers copied everything as I ordered it. Excellent.

The Japanese were still wasting precious time, with all their messengers sent out, having to wait for them to come back to cancel their stupid orders.

Which meant I still had about 20 minutes to get ready.

It would be worth it to buy some more specialized divisions in that time.

Okay. Let's check out the blue ones. There were a lot more of them than the others. But they cost a pretty penny. Still, destroying a whole mess of Japs would totally be worth it. I mean, I would have to meet with them again after the battle. And our future dialogue would depend on just how badly they got beaten into a pulp today.

By putting the Kremlin in the place of the tower, I had given a vague hint as to where we had come from. And that definitely caused a visceral fear in the hearts of many of the fighters.

And yes, I was the one who attacked, not them. Simply because I could. You could see it as a bad thing, but oh well, those are the rules of this new world. I had to do it. I didn't intend to kill anyone and I still don't, so the old morals are still fully in place.

But if it comes to the real world... Well, I could quickly take a crystal. And then their little island, eaten up by sea monsters, would soon be razed to sea level.

On the other hand, I was fully prepared to pay a little bit for the settlement I took. I think that if my opponent is not a total idiot, he would agree to talk. And then we can have some fun!

Heavy Infantry — 100

One fight cost the same as a whole catapult and its team. Damn.

But those fighters' stats were way more interesting than the others. Impenetrable magical plate armor, a wide range of powerful weapons, the ability to heal themselves, and a lot more. They may not be supersoldiers, but one of those could still easily chop up a dozen regular swordsmen.

Maybe I could put Grugg as one of them?

Okay, he couldn't pull it off on his own. And our opponent had noticed that was starting to fall back on stronger types of forces and would soon start buying something to resist them.

Heavy infantry could be armed with swords, axes, war hammers, anything my heart desired. And my heart desires all of it, right now. What would happen if Brownie put the heavy armor onto his fur? Only one way to find out.

And so, once I finished buying the grenade throwers and gave them the order to advance a little, freeing up space in the purchasing area, I started producing a new, elite division.

Brownie would be the officer, and for soldiers I would pick his colleagues from the police station. They were military guys with high levels and they would be able to surprise the enemy with a whole barrage of attacking abilities.

What was nice was that I had yet to even touch my own store of crystals. Everything came from the treasury, which was excellent. Somewhere across the ocean the 9th District was constantly getting me both experience and loot. Those poor bastards just kept going all out in fights with hordes of beasts, sending half of their gains to the treasury. Extraordinary. It would be the same with the Japanese.

Horseman — 150

We got three horsemen. Obviously they would be riding horses, but the question was what they would have in their hands. Maybe it would be swords again. Or spears. Or bows, crossbows, whatever worked. I could even equipped them with grenades, if I felt like it.

I had noticed that the blue forces, if I could call them that, gave me a much wider range for my imagination. The soldiers could have different kinds of weapons, but they would still be locked into a single division, which was quite convenient, allowing a whole range of various possible tactics.

Cavalry certainly wouldn't be a problem here. Although controlling them would be somewhat difficult, since I would have to give all my commands in advance. The messengers just wouldn't be able to catch up to the horses, so I would have to think everything through carefully.

The horsemen would be clad in light armor, so I could still only dream about knights. I would leave them to be purchased only in an extreme situation. In any case, I knew that I could wait at least 30 minutes for any attacks here. And that was only if their forces come straight to my tower. But they were being cautious.

So far, as I was standing here, the Japanese forces hadn't yet made it back to their side. And peasant after peasant just kept coming out of the opposing tower. He might be hitting the limit for number of fighters soon, and then victory would be ours for sure. We would just wipe out their ranks with our better class of forces, and deal's done.

But while they're heading home and gathering forces, I can keep checking out the shop.

War Mage — 200

These guys would make you wait a while. And it was doubtful how useful they were. Unlike the rest, they didn't have any armor. But, then again, you could choose a magic weapon for them. Like a wand that would create and shoot fireballs without the owner having to use any mana.

Plus the choice of clothes would improve the wearer's abilities, but in our settlement we basically didn't have any mages at all. I would have to work on that. Find someone with a good class and destroy them. Then one of ours could take it for themself.

It would also be worth checking how much experience we had in the treasury. Then I could level myself up right away and also buff up some useful people. Like Anton. Even though so far the only things we've gotten out of him have been dangerous and useless trash, I still had faith in him. He would level up his skills, improve his abilities, and become a legend for us in this harsh new world.

Forget the war mages. An idiotic waste of money, nothing else. But the next couple of ones were more interesting.

Jaeger — 200

Saboteur — 200

The first one was armed with a crossbow or a regular bow. But what stood out was that the first one had a higher range, while the second had higher accuracy. And that wasn't all. These fighters didn't have any armor at all, since they weren't intended for regular fights. They shot from afar, then hid or ran away, that's all. So the jaegers wore cloaks that helped them blend into any location. Almost like an invisibility cloak.

Of course, that meant they couldn't go on a marsh or into normal military formations. Divisions like theirs had different methods of moving around. Although jaegers would move pretty slowly, neither the opposing leader nor his divisions could see those hidden soldiers as long as they didn't attack.

And even after they shot, there was no guarantee they'd be spotted. For example, if they shot you in the back from stealth. So they were definitely way more useful than a whole heap of those war mages.

The saboteurs were kind of like the jaegers. Except they attacked in a totally different way. They were armed with only light crossbows and knives, but the important thing was that they had a whole set of tricks.

After stealthily moving to a destination I picked, saboteurs would set up all kinds of traps, lay mines, destroy roads, or, most importantly, help one of my divisions camouflage themselves.

I felt like that was the saboteur's best feature. If it worked, I could slowly move a significant number of forces, one division at time, into the woods, and surreptitiously flank the enemy.

Neither the enemy leader nor his soldiers would notice those actions. The only issue was that a single saboteur could only help ten normal soldiers move in secret. It would be a slow process, but definitely worth it.

So, after the heavy infantry I would field ten saboteurs. I picked Cole as the officer right away. Especially since his class was the same. That meant he could perform the role at 200%.

But wouldn't our opponent do the same? How else could he fight against it?

No, no matter what, if my division ran into enemies hidden in the woods, I would also see them immediately. Actually, I could just send a ton of peasants running back and forth to constantly follow them. And if they got killed, I would just get more. I mean, I had more than enough rappers.

In addition to all the ones I had already checked out, there were a ton more different kinds of soldiers in the shop. In the blue ones there was also a ballista. It was different from the catapult due to its increased range and accuracy and also the possibility of making stronger ammunition for it.

Berserkers, assassins, healers, powered-up grenade throwers... I had to check them all out, but I didn't have the time for that now. And I hadn't even gotten around to checking the choices in the most expensive and most elite forces. Plus, the prices and wait times up there were so high that it would be easier to just make do with the forces that were ready to go. And I did, right before I headed off to the edge of tower, put an order in for 200 peasants. They may well come in handy, so let's have them. They cost peanuts, they're basically useless, but still, if need be, they might seal a hole in our defenses.

Okay. Our enemy has made a new move. And we definitely couldn't trick him like before.

So far I had only four divisions at my disposal, and the heavy infantry was about ready.

Then we would have to wait for the saboteurs, followed by the peasants. Only then would it make sense to attack our enemy, right now better to gather our forces and go on the defensive.

The Japanese were pretty impatient. That was somewhat unexpected for me, since it seemed much more worthwhile for them to take the defensive. Or were they just trying to force me to attack? Most likely. But I'm not falling for that. I'm sticking to my guns, just kept growing my forces. No need to hurry, for now we'll just calmly array our forces and have a chat with Brownie who just showed up.

"Let's go!" I shouted to the big guy before he even started transforming. "How's things with you?"

"Where?" Oleg didn't understand. He spent some time turning his head around, trying to figure out where my voice was coming from.

"I'm here!" I waved at him. "How are things in the village?"

"First off I was confused by this battle starting. What the hell? What is even going on? And where even are you?" It was not like Oleg to ask so many questions in a row, but he still wasn't holding back. Obviously he was really surprised and annoyed at what was happening.

"Well I'm... I'm in Japan, alright. But I'm coming back soon!" I rushed to calm the big dude down. But he was still a tiny bit surprised, as far as I could tell from his expression. His eyebrows were high enough to wrinkle his neck. "You got the rules, yeah?"

"What the... Japan? How?" More questions. But I just stood there smiling.

"Go ask Eva what the hell Japan. I was surprised myself, to be honest."

"And what's the matter?!" The girl was offended. "It was a mistake!"

"A mistake?" Brownie tried to turn around with all his might, but clearly his body was categorically refusing to listen. So the large man, clad in plate armor, had to crane his short thick neck at an unnatural angle. Plus, with his helmet on, he wasn't very well able to look around. Yeah, Brownie quickly took it off and held it in his hand.

They shouted back and forth for a while, the rest of them just listening, trying not to get caught up in it. Oleg also informed me that golems and chimeras had turned up in the neighborhood again. They were looking for Kaspiana, and sometimes they tried to bother the inhabitants of the store.

Maybe I had brought them here at the wrong time. But anyway, Grugg was still there, so all their attacks would be just dumb.

Plus, hardly any time had passed, so those two assholes simply wouldn't have had time to make a powerful army. So that was just reconnaissance, a sign of what was to come. We would see.

"So, have you read the rules yet? The System has given you your instructions?" Eventually I couldn't hold back anymore and stopped their spat.

As it turned out, all the other kinds of our

forces had been swearing at me in vain. Probably most of them had just skipped over the important information that the System had given them before transporting them to the battlefield.

Oleg summarized everything he had learned from the instructions, and his words calmed down a lot of the fighters.

At least the information that dying here was not permanent immediately raised the fighting resolve of many of them.

Dumbasses. Not all of them, no. As far as I could tell, some of them had been swearing at me just to fit in. I wasn't going to say that that was praiseworthy, but still better than doing it out of stupidity and lack of attention.

"What about Gosha? How's he doing over there?" I just remembered my friend. He had a serious task, being to grow that strange plant out of the iron. Redhorn or something like that. And I was very curious about whether the master of plants had managed to figure it out.

"Gosha? You know what. Don't ask. Just be quiet. That's it, just keep quiet." So saying, Brownie put his helmet on and started transforming into a frightening bear covered in metal. That was a clear hint that he didn't want to talk.

Would the bear understand my orders? I guess he should. But how would he get the scroll with the action orders? He only had paws...

A couple hundred Japanese peasants, armed with pitchforks, clubs, and other trash were moving through the forest. At first they were marching proudly, but then they scattered into a good-sized messy crowd and started breaking through the thickets.

The swordsmen were moving over the crags. They were protected from behind by a small detachment of peasants, which also scattered over the surrounding area right in the middle, next to the creek.

The spearmen were also coming down the center. Behind them were the archers, already ready to shoot in advance, not hurrying with their walk. They had gone through the swamp, and would start shooting as soon as their opponents entered their area of attack.

The archers had that kind of firing mode. I already learned that. They didn't move too fast, but they were still effective enough. On top of that, the archers would run away if the enemy got too close.

So what was there for me to do?

Eh, that's easy.

"Brownie!" I shouted out of habit, only then remembering that I had to send orders. "Get to the woods!"

Right after that I grabbed a small division of heavy infantry, immediately put them into ranks, and sent them straight down the road towards the 200 approaching peasants. I also made them run. That would use a little strength, but the results would certainly be worth it.

The fight might only last about 15 minutes, but I would give my right kidney and part of my liver to see the looks on the faces of our enemies who had been sent into the forest. They obviously knew already that they weren't there to pick mushrooms, but what they would find exactly they still had to find out.

Well, what do you want? Sometimes there really are bears in the woods. You can't get insured against running into them!

CHAPTER 9

WHILE THE HEAVY INFANTRY DIVISION was inflicting their own brand of terror on the mass of peasants, I turned my attention towards the other directions.

Pressing in all sides would be stupid, in any case. Better to hold off the enemy's onslaught, leaving open access for easily refilling arrows, even if it meant giving up the possibility of ending everything right here and now.

It was interesting how each troop movement still came along with loud swearing. People keep screaming things about freedom of choice, the constitution, and other nonsense.

"Hey!" I shouted at my soldiers, leaning over the edge of the tower. "I'm just as much a slave of the System as you, don't you understand?"

But nobody wanted to understand. They would definitely love me even more now...

Whatever, screw 'em. I had come this far without the benefit of human kindness, and I wasn't dead yet. Maybe even the opposite, since fewer of them would be getting to know me. Well, there was one advantage so far.

I set up the spearman in a line, cutting off the middle path. I also ordered the division to go on the defensive, by which I meant making a very dangerous spiked wall. Especially since the same kinds of soldiers with spears were coming in that direction, so everything would be fair.

The swordsmen headed down the left path, holding off an onslaught of the same kinds of poor suckers and a whole host of peasants. I thought they would perform admirably, especially since a defensive line of grenade throwers had taken position behind them to help out.

They were just 150 feet from my tower, so they could definitely throw out their full set of three grenades and get back to fill them back up as needed.

For now the archers were standing in the front ranks in the middle. That way they'd be able to start shooting down the spearmen sooner, and if anything went wrong, the girls would just hide behind the powerful guys in Bale's division.

Hmm…

So what now? Wait? Well look, the saboteurs are almost ready. And what should I do with them? There was an argument to be made for sending them out right away to set traps and maybe even lay some mines. But that was only when the whole division was ready.

Right after that I would have to wait 200 seconds for my army of slaves and then...

Alright, let's do it.

Horseman — 150

15 of them would be good. They could chase down the enemy archers or just hit the other divisions from the rear. The swordsmen, maybe. It would be stupid to send them against the spearmen. I would need heavy infantry for that.

While waiting for my saboteur division, I turned my attention to what was going on in the woods. What was nice was that once they got a certain distance away a little flag showed up right over the division showing what type of forces they were, how many there were, and their morale.

What was annoying was that morale sucked. People didn't really want to go to their death, especially when fighting with a division that outnumbered them 20 to 1.

Hey! Those are just regular peasants! Japanese ones! And you have a bear, goddammit!

Well, I would be running full speed ahead, especially since I knew that death wasn't permanent. Just intense and full of heady emotions!

Okay. There were only seconds left until the confrontation, so soon they would get a taste for it. Now a calm had set it below. Every one of my soldiers was staring at the forest, impatiently waiting for it to be over with.

And not just them. A messenger from the enemy base was running toward the army of peasants at full speed, likely bringing them the order to beat a quick retreat. Our opponent had also begun to quickly produce more powerful divisions. Clearly he had realized that most likely wouldn't be crushing us through force of numbers. Had he seen how our soldiers' plate armor gleamed and pissed himself? Good boy. Just a little too late. There were only minutes left till they made contact, so there was no point in orders now.

What was he buying?

Horses! Well done, I respect it. He wasn't pinching pennies. And the cavalry was exclusively armed with spears. That was exactly what you wanted for a fight with heavy infantry and a bear.

But I couldn't sit around watching how one horseman after another came riding out from the bottom of the tower. There were much more interesting sights to see. Even though it was hard to see through the trees, I still couldn't tear my eyes away.

* * *

"Motherf*cker!"

"What is he on about? Like I said, he's a piece of shit, hardly a person! And not even a ghost!"

"Alright boys! Look lively! Let's kick the Japs' asses!"

Ten men clad in heavy armor were trudging through the thick forest. And though a lot of them were throwing profanity around at their leader, perfunctorily, some of them were sincerely happy to be participating in a battle. Especially when you considered that death was not permanent here.

But still, some people were against it.

A massive bear was leading them up front. His fur gave off a metallic glow, his claws gleamed in the sunlight, and his face showed only determination.

Each of them also had an interface in front of them. They were, however, extremely simple, only allowing them to see two bars with data about the division. They also had in front of them a shining path that they had to follow, along with a destination that corresponded to the orders the officer had received.

The guys were most angry about being so strongly constrained in their choices. Sure, they could still wave their arms and their weapon, turn their heads, and shout profanity.

And they could pick the path they would go down, too, but only within the boundaries set by the System. They had no idea how it was controlling everything like this. It's like you're going along a line drawn on the ground, and you could avoid obstacles at your own discretion, crawling under fallen trees and breaking through bushes. But no matter what, you were still marching right where you were ordered to go.

That made everyone upset. It was like you were kind of free to do what you wanted, and kind of not.

But everything changed in battle. As the enemy got closer, one of the bars started slowly going down.

Heavy Infantry.

Quantity — 10/10
Morale — 48/100

"That's kind of scary, if I'm being honest..." admitted one of the soldiers. "There's an assload of them there! I can't even count how much..."

"A hundred, at least," came a low voice from the helmet next to him. "Possibly two... Oh, don't be a pussy, they're just bums, we'll take 'em in a second. And if not us, then Olly's got it. Look at those hungry faces!" He cackled, swinging his two-handed hammer so it whistled through the air.

Morale — 47

"Who's pussing out, huh? What happens when our morale reaches zero?" asked a fighter with a fair-sized shield and a mace to no one in particular. Although his shield just looked good-sized in comparison to him, since the man was pretty short, though rather stout.

But nobody could answer. Just thinking about morale caused it to lose two more points.

But it soon went back up! Once the enemy was just about 100 feet away, they could all see the sign of the opposing division.

Pitchforks in a circle, and underneath them the same two bars. One was full all the way up, but the second one was much worse off.

Peasants.
Quantity — 198/200
Morale — 34/100

"Ha! Two of them have been knocked off already!" guffawed a soldier armed with two one-handed axes. "And they're pissing themselves worse than us!"

RAAAAH!

50 feet from the enemy the bear let out a fearsome roar and started speeding up. The fighters had no intention of retreating, shouting rudely and rushing behind their commander. Only the ones who were running in the back could see how quickly the lower bar dropped to zero. But even so the, the enemy turned out to be not so simple.

Out in front came, although it sounds silly to say, the peasant officer. When the bear was just a few feet away, he waved his hands and a huge boulder flew out of the ground and slammed right into the furry brown face.

There was a cracking sound and the bear, groaning quietly, fell onto his back, passing out within a few seconds.

The morale of the peasants immediately rose, and shouting angrily the Japanese guys, armed with whatever they had on hand, rushed forward.

But the bear was not alone.

"Konnichiwa, f*ckers!" screamed a soldier carrying a shield covered in spikes, dashing forward and knocking down everyone in his path like a battering ram.

People flew every which way, and the soldier got deep into the enemy forces. A large number of hits glanced off his armor, but he didn't give up, starting instead to swing his short sword and cut down the short-statured opponents one after another.

The bums tried to break through to the fallen

bear, who hadn't yet come to his senses, but his comrades were standing like a wall around the fearsome beast.

The dense forest was filled with the sounds of scraping metal, shouts of pain, and harsh swears in both languages. People were locked in fights to death, and nobody wanted to retreat.

The armored soldiers were indeed holding their ground, not even considering giving up for a second, but the constant onslaught of enemy forces was pressing in on them more and more with every second.

At some point a soldier who had just rushed into the fray shouted out in pain. The Japanese had managed to knock him down and then someone was able to yank off his helmet. His death was quick and painless, and his friends learned about it only by the state of the division changing in the interface.

Well, they just weren't up to the task.

Fairly soon the enemy forces, outnumbering them ten to one, surrounded the meager division and started hitting them from all sides at once. Little by little the Japanese morale rose as they saw how they could absolutely deal even heavy infantry a beating. Especially since, even though they were weaker physically, every third one of them could boast of at least some sort of attacking ability.

In addition to hits, the armored men, covered in metal, also had magical attacks raining on them. Roots tore out of the ground, tangling up the soldiers' legs, and sometimes the defenders got hit with electrical discharges.

One man's shield was hit with a thick gout of flame. The Japanese man tried to burn his opponent for a good while, but with how dense the crowd was, he accidentally lit two of his own ablaze too.

They didn't suffer for long, though. As soon as his mana ran out and the fire began to die down, a heavy mace flew out from behind the shield, immediately ending the suffering of those two misfortunate fools.

Then the soldier cursed wickedly, and a bolt of lightning hit the mage right on the top of his head.

RAAAAH!

The bear leapt up, rising to his back paws, filling the arena with his roar. Within a moment Brownie had torn off, rushing into the very thick of the enemies, tossing aside any person he met along the way. His sharp claws easily ripped through soft weak flesh, and soon the massive monster's fur, fully tinted with metal, was covered in crimson spots of blood.

The pitchforks, clubs, small hand axes, and other trash that the peasants were armed with couldn't do any damage to the bear, buffed as he was by his armor and class skill. At least not any physical damage.

Now a magical one came flying down the way. And soon it became clear why such a meager number of attacking skills had come down on the soldiers clad in armor. They had been holding them back until now.

The bear managed to run forward only 15 feet, trampling a few dozen people and tearing them to pieces. But then, just like last time, a hefty boulder came out of the ground and slammed him in the face. This time, however, the bear was ready for something like that and was able to cover his face with his paws in time. But right after the boulder came a bolt of lightning from the sky, leaving a fairly large wound, burned all the way down to the flesh, on his fur.

But the Japanese didn't stop there. They were able to separate the main force of heavy infantry from the bear and began doling out weaker, but no less effective, attacking abilities on him.

Someone let out a stream of cold, and from somewhere else there came a fireball, burning his fur after exploding into a cloud of searing sparks. Even the trees and bushes were extending their spiked branches, trying to tear the brown body into tiny pieces.

But even despite that whole hailstorm of attacks, the bear just kept on swiping his paws. His sharp claws were constantly grabbing more and more victims from the crowd, and his teeth always pierced with an iron grip, sending the Japanese home in a single second.

But even so, the numbers were having the desired effect. Every second that passed the bear would take more hits, getting weaker before their eyes.

The eight surviving soldiers couldn't get through to their officer at all, since they were on their last legs trying to withstand the onrush of attacks coming from all directions out of the massive heap of peasants.

But eventually everything stopped. The Japanese suddenly ceased all their attacks and turned tail, rushing off somewhere into the dense forest. The fighters stood around in confusion for a short while, then, after a couple of seconds, rushed to their leader, but it was already too late. Nobody had any potions, and only armor could heal up the wounds he had received a little. But only your own self. The armor did not allow you to improve the health of your comrades. Plus the mana had dried up a long time ago, so there was no point in even trying.

Without magic there was no way to save the bear. He was bleeding all over his fur, and a deep red sticky pool of it was gradually seeping out from under his fallen husk. The beast's face was completely cut up, covered in fresh scars. It looked like the armor under his skin had indeed tried to heal Brownie, but it simply couldn't manage with so many injuries.

Blood was flowing from his gaping maw too, and you could see that half of his teeth had been broken off. Basically, the bear was done for, and within a few seconds he quietly exhaled and expired.

You have been designated the officer of the division.

Heavy Infantry.

Quantity — 8/10

Morale — 29/100

"Well shit. Boys, I'm the acting officer now..." The man with the war hammer scratched his head. He checked out the updated interface for a few seconds, but soon was forced to take the position given to him by the commander's order.

The bear's corpse, along with numerous bodies of fallen peasants, simply sank into the ground without a trace, and soon enough the field looked just as it had before.

The soldiers quickly closed ranks and ran after the retreating enemies. Their morale rose up with every step, since they could all see just how much damage they could do with just ten of them. So what would happen when their division got back to the tower and Kasp decided to increase their numbers? Then they would be able to pull off victories no problem.

Peasants:
Quantity — 101/200
Morale — 37/100

"Let's go, brothers! Press on! We've taken out half of them, now they're on the run, and we've got 'em for sure!" shouted the new officer, hurrying as fast as he could.

But no matter how much the heavy infantry tried to catch up to the scampering peasants, it didn't work. Their heavy armor, despite being worn by powerful Systemniks, simply didn't allow them to move fast enough, and slowly but surely the Japanese got away.

But nobody was able to stop the chase. Every

soldier could see the destination that their order was supposed to take them to. But the officer had much more information available. So he was well aware that as soon as they got out of the woods, they would immediately have to turn around and march back to their own tower.

He did tell his men about that, just so they wouldn't think they were being led to the slaughter.

"Boys..." The low voice of a soldier who had gone ahead of the division a few feet broke through the clanking of armor. "Up there is..."

He pointed somewhere ahead with his spear, and the rest of them all raised their visors together, trying to make something out through the thick fir trees and bushes.

And soon they managed it, since the greenery was starting to thin out on the edge of the forest, giving them an exceptional view of the retreating peasants. And the oncoming cavalry.

*   *   *

Too bad I couldn't fly off the tower and at least watch what was going on in the woods.

I saw a bunch of flashes, heard the sounds of attack skills and the terrible roar of the bear. The clanking of metal, the shouting of people, all of that combined into a single monotonous din.

I did notice that morale amongst the rest of our divisions fell immediately. And the heavy infantry's morale first crashed to the bottom and then shot right back up. I had no idea what was even going on, but judging from the losses in the enemy division a pretty bad drag-out fight had gone off there.

But in the very heat of battle a messenger was still able to reach the peasants and get them the order to retreat. The Japanese immediately ran for the hills, while my dummies dragged their heels, not about to give chase. But they could have taken down any 30 people or so...

Ah well. Soon they would get there and get sent back home, if it came down to it.

Oh, you sons of...!

The opposing leader could still pull something off. Not a total dumbass. Well, yeah, they had always had wise men here, constantly spouting off wisdom. Such as not underestimating your enemy and whatnot.

Well, that bastard hadn't held back, going and making a small cavalry division. Which would easily deal with the ragged remains of my heavy infantry division.

As soon as the clanking metal plates of my soldiers came out of the dense forest they were met with a wedge of 15 horsemen rushing at them. They set their spears forward, accelerating, breaking right through their own allies.

Even from here I could tell how the horses knocked down and trampled some misfortunate peasants under their hooves, but that didn't put any damper on the wedge. Soon they ran right into my infantrymen, hurrying straight at them, scattering them every which way.

Heavy Infantry:

Quantity — 6

Morale — 0

Well, now we would learn what this morale meant.

CHAPTER 10

IN THE NEXT COUPLE OF SECONDS three of the six fighters simply disappeared. But that same number were left on the battlefield to continue the fight. That included the new officer. I would have to reward him somehow after this, since I had never noticed the man before.

As far as I could tell, once morale reached zero, the System offered each member of the division the choice of returning home safe and sound. Each one was free to take the opportunity to not die in pain and agony, so I couldn't blame them. That was their fault and the blame was fully on me, so let them go back and continue their business.

The treasury had already gotten much lighter, so now I had to buy my army out of my own pocket, but that was no issue. I had collected a bunch of stuff in my inventory, so I could easily spring for at least a hundred heavy infantry who would handily crush any opposition and show the Japanese who was in charge here.

But that was after I repelled this attack on two fronts.

So I simply did not have the time to watch how my three infantrymen took care of those 15 horsemen.

First off I turned my attention to the center. The opposing spearmen were rushing ahead there, leaving the division of archers behind to break through the swamps. They had taken some casualties, which had had an effect on their morale as well as their numbers. That was the fault of a geyser shooting off steam, instantly burning two spearmen alive.

Then the poor bastards were hit with a hail of arrows. I had purposefully sent my archer division with Igor in the lead for that. To show them this wasn't going to be a walk in the park.

The Japanese had been given their orders a long time ago, so I didn't have to worry that they might turn back all of a sudden. They had been sent to take the tower, nothing else. They were trying to press their numbers, given that another 250 soldiers in two divisions were marching through the crags.

What's more, the opposing leader had also started making heavy infantry. He had stopped being stingy, realizing that he definitely might lose. I would be worried too in his shoes, so I got it. But this was a done deal. On the list of more expensive fighters I had managed to find a universal soldier, armed like both an archer and a close combat fighter. So Grugg would soon be making his appearance in the arena. But his coming would cost me exactly 1000 gray crystals.

While my archers were exterminating the opposing spearman, as planned, and the grenade throwers were getting ready to send their first salvo, I headed for the terminal. My orders had all been given, my soldiers shouldn't come to any harm, and so I didn't have to worry about anything.

Your treasury has insufficient funds.

Huh... What? System, I got cash out my ass! Take it from my inventory!

But the System wasn't going to. So this was all I had, completely unexpected.

Treasury: 301

Three hundred and one gray crystals. To be frank, I was hoping for a lot more, but it is what it is.

Nothing I could do. I could get a couple of heavy infantry, or 50 spearmen. But if it was like this then it would be much better to buy peasants. I mean, at first I was thinking that my major limitation was going to be in people, but this sudden surprise from the System had shown me that was not the case.

Alright, well, everyone's inventory was blocked. Along with the interface and other luxuries of life on earth.

"People!" I addressed my defenders. "Here's the deal. Reinforcements are not coming, so you will have to manage on your own somehow!"

"Why not?" asked one of the soldiers who was standing closest to me. "What's the reason?"

"If we win, we'll get crabsticks!" And really, what else could you get from an Asian market?

Sure, their city was more well-developed, but that was only because they had somehow avoided attacks from sea monsters and zombies. Plus they had so many resources that were easy to get.

Anyway, I would deal with that after we won.

The archers retreated step by step, raining arrows down on the enemy forces. Our opponent took losses, but their morale had stopped at ten, and their numbers were decreasing too slowly. The distance to them was shortening much faster, at least.

So once the distance between the opposing forces reached 100 feet, a large number of attacking abilities started flying at our guys.

Damn...

But no matter. I had given the order to retreat in advance, so without managing to inflict much more damage the archers ran off behind our friends from the store. And a host of rappers totaling 200 people was running up to meet them.

What surprised me was that they weren't really swearing! I had quickly explained to our peasant fighters their objective and that they wouldn't die for real. They swiftly came to terms and started obeying all my orders unconditionally, without any dissatisfaction.

I had to admit, that deserved respect. Even if I

were to joke about how they were used to doing what they were told and so on. Right now that would be out of turn.

I would have to meet that settlement and converse with the inhabitants more normally, not in an insulting manner. I might even let the clay division go. But I wasn't sure. Someone did need to get resources, and I certainly wasn't going to do it. But what I could tell from the history of humanity was that it was still better to pay your workers. They would break their backs to get just one more pound of clay and get a bonus for it. Absolutely inadequate for the amount of work they had done.

Alright. Expensive soldiers were no longer available to me. It would be stupid to get a catapult or something like that, so we had to make do with what was left.

The fighters had already started scrapping and were gradually putting pressure on the enemy, but that was just temporary. One after another proud Japanese soldiers, clad in heavy plate armor, were coming out of the opposing tower, and all of them were angrily staring right at me.

Brrrr... Ten of them would be worth 200 peasants. But there weren't ten of them there yet. And I could have a maximum of 300 peasants...

I had already sent the saboteurs into the forest. Although our infantry were still somehow fighting with the cavalry there, trying to make use of the inopportune landscape, but that wouldn't last long.

Soon ten stealth fighters would be sent to set

up tricks and traps for the enemy. I had ordered them to stay there until the end, laying mines in every corner of the impenetrable forest, making it so not even a mouse could get through that barrier. But I just didn't have anyone to send on the attack. Just a few horses that I had managed to get. And I happily cancelled that production order to save as many resources as possible.

My swordsmen leapt forward, shouting, once they received the signal to attack. They had been encouraged by the successes of the fighters in the center, so now their morale was through the roof.

Even though each of them would have to take at least three opponents, even that didn't sow fear the hearts of my people. I had gotten good guys for that division, so I wouldn't have any problems with them. Still, they had to go through a lot, often having to fight and losing their comrades. But here those losses weren't final, plus they could remind the Japanese what our people were worth.

And the matter didn't end with the number of abilities they had, although our fighters had them in spades. The main thing was who would retreat first. So I wasn't worried even a bit about the left front. The boys would do get it done and not allow a single Jap to get to me, no two ways about it.

Soon enough the enemy realized that too. First his swordsmen started losing their numbers and, under a hail of frag grenades their morale totally faded, sending them home immediately.

But then came the peasants. Their strength was not in their weapons, but their numbers.

Wooden pitchforks couldn't pierce metal armor, and small sticks were much weaker than sharp metal swords. But there were a lot of them, which meant there were some who could use abilities while the others covered the spellcasters with their bodies. They were counting on that.

But even so, our fighters could withstand it. They were protected by small shields and held out until the recharged grenade throwers could hurry back. After that I pulled my archers from the center, so they could help them stop any bastards from getting through the barrier from the crags.

The saboteurs had worked in vain. A division of 40 heavy infantry had been created, and were marching straight to the center. You didn't have to be a military genius to see that they would make it through. Even if I brought absolutely everyone over there.

Now the cavalry was rushing down the path through the forest, but soon their icon disappeared into the thick undergrowth. They had fallen into the traps. But they hadn't been able to do much damage, since Brownie's boys had managed to turn them into foot soldiers, with only four fighters left on their horses.

"Hold the line, boys!" I yelled to the spearmen. And a similar command for the swordsmen wouldn't go awry, since every second they were getting pressed in on, cover from the archers notwithstanding.

I had to do something. To shout "Release the kraken!" and release the kraken. Then things wouldn't be so fun for our enemies. Even now I could see how their morale was going up with every one of our citizens they killed. And I couldn't just let that go.

I could forget about the expensive soldiers. But I didn't really want to. Maybe next time I would be better prepared, but right now we had what we had.

It was definitely worth it to bring Grugg in. I could also bring in the elves, but was it worth it? What were they going to do with pitchforks and other items that weren't fit for the battlefield? I didn't think that was the most efficient thing. But the bull was already armed, and I wouldn't have any problems with him.

Only taking my eyes off the purchasing terminal and its range of fighters every once in a while, I could still catch the ever-approaching division of heavy infantry from the corner of my eye. Terrible, powerful guys. No argument there. But...

Well, this was interesting. It was really interesting, and I hoped there wouldn't be any consequences from it for my settlement later. But how could I not try it?

"For sure now, let's release the kraken." I muttered toward the enemy base, smiling.

Two people came out of the base. One of them had a wooden stick, and the other one was sporting a pitchfork at the ready. But those weapons were immediately trashed, since the boys tossed them away as hard as they could at glanced upward. Right at me.

I myself couldn't get to the edge to personally see our new military units that I had gotten almost for free.

"My deepest apologies, of course…" I shrugged. "I hope I haven't taken you away from anything important?"

But the only response I got was silence and glares. And though the big one always looked at me like that, the second new fighter stressed me out a little. But fine. No reason to stand around, let's go attack.

Peasants.

Quantity — 2/2

Morale — 100/100

*   *   *

"What do you say to that?" The face of the Asian person standing on top of the fancy tower was spread in a wicked smile.

As it should, since now he had a catapult at his disposal!

He could allow himself the luxury. He had an unconditional victory in the center, right now fighting was going on in the crags, and it wouldn't last long, given that soon his archers would be coming out of the swamp and then the inhabitants of the Kremlin would definitely be having a bad time.

Everything was quiet in the forest, and their enemy had absolutely no resources left to mount an offensive there. And even if the enemy did, he would just buy a couple hundred peasants, no big deal. You couldn't overcome the whole army of your enemy with them, but as cover they were exceptional. They could be purchased quickly, use abilities, and he had more than 10,000 inhabitants in the settlements under his control.

"Obey the will of your Emperor!" shouted the Japanese man as he approached the edge of the field.

The people going with the catapult bowed immediately, without uttering a word. They were extremely afraid of their leader, since he was rather cruel and capricious. But it was exactly that which had allowed him to become basically the only person controlling all the settlements on the island, crushing all opposition with his invincible might.

Everyone knew that no weapons could help you against a gold class, so some survivor camps had asked to be taken under the protection of such a powerful leader of their own volition.

And their discipline was completely in order. In the entire time the Emperor ruled, short as it was, not a single rebellion had flared up. Even though, to put it mildly, his taxes were sky-high.

But the most important thing now was that it had become possible to find and deal with camps that were very far away. Where there were zombies in abundance and you could get rewards day and night. Everything was much more difficult with sea monsters. It was rather hard to get them to leave their home region, but that was just the half of it. Then you had to finish off the monster, and the System only gave you one reward for it. Zombies were a different thing entirely, but they were pretty hard to find on the island.

Having sent another division into the fray, the Emperor went back to the terminal and decided to take a little break. His soldiers were ready to fight, he could see that their morale was high, and now the only thing left was to wait and rejoice in their achievements.

"And you beasts will be my slaves..." he hissed through his teeth, glaring at his enemy. "Or I will burn you to the ground..." A light flashed in his eyes, giving his already terrifying visage even more conviction.

*　*　*

The fighters calmly tramped down the path, joyfully clanking their armor and rattling their weapons in time with their steps. The morale of the heavy infantry division was almost all the way up, and the mood of the soldiers taken individually was also high.

They all felt like they were taking part in some important event, one which would bring another victory to their Emperor.

Among the people that man was considered the same as a god who had come down from the heavens to save the human race. The Japanese in particular.

And these soldiers were his personal bodyguards outside of the System battle. The most loyal, the most powerful, and the best. The other simply hadn't survived, since the Emperor could sometimes go out of his mind, and then a whole storm of the destructive magic that he had mastered could be unleashed on the heads of those around him.

"I think they're out of resources… Look, they're not making any new soldiers anymore!" The soldier, armed with a long spear, pointed off into the distance. He also had an uncommon class that allowed him to significantly speed up his perception of time. Rather, speed it up for him and slow it down for everyone else. That had saved him multiple times in battle, and in a one-on-one fight very few people could even touch him, to say nothing of killing him.

"Ah, how typical for them." His friend smiled and smacked his metal glove against his helmet. "They never learn."

"Hey! Look!" Another soldier nodded ahead. "There's two peasants!"

Their vision wasn't great, so nobody could see the peasants themselves. Almost as if on purpose, the field was covered in a light mist which had just exploded out of one of the many geysers scattered all around, so they could only depend on the data that the System had given them.

Now the division was moving at leisurely pace along the path. Nobody had any doubt about their impending victory, but the sounds of battle could be heard far ahead. The spearmen sent before them still hadn't finished and were trying to put pressure on their stupid opponent. Distracting him from the real destructive force of the heavy infantry.

"Huh... What the hell?" One of the soldiers frowned, noticing how quickly the number of soldiers in the spearman division off in the distance was decreasing.

About three soldiers per second. Then their morale hit zero and the division just saved themselves all at once. Nobody had stayed to fight to the death. They had all just given up, no exceptions.

"Cowards..."

"Traitors..."

"Well, screw them. Let's show them, brothers, how to destroy an enemy in the name of the Emperor!" shouted one of the Japanese men in the third row.

Soon they had crossed the river and arrayed themselves in two rows, ready to attack. The sounds of battle ahead had died down, and the highlight on the enemy divisions had disappeared, but that had no effect on their morale.

Even though the mist was still hindering them from seeing the enemy and their movements, the soldiers sincerely believed in the superiority of their leader. So, without any hint of worry, they kept on moving forward, obediently following their orders.

Soon a System icon with the sign of a pitchfork appeared through the fog. Under the icon there was also a message telling them that exactly two peasants were coming toward them. The sight of it made them laugh, and the Japanese started joking and shouting threats ahead of them, but soon there was a grave silence.

"What... What is that?"

"A bull? Or something? And what's next to it?" Their voices sounded worried, interrupted only by the clanking of plate armor and the clacking of hooves.

"A zombie?" said one soldier, surprised, as soon as the cloud parted, allowing them to see their opponent in detail. "These bastards have zombies fighting for th—" But he never finished saying it.

"Exactly." A soft, hoarse voice could be heard somewhere nearby, and the soldiers realized that the deadie had crossed a distance of fifty feet without being seen and was now grabbing their officer by the helmet.

One swift movement and he crushed the poor bastard's head like a jar of preserves, leaving him to fall to the ground like a soulless doll, clanking in his metal.

While the rest of them were preparing for the fight, loud footfalls could be heard. A massive horned beast, breaking through the fog, came rushing behind the deadie. Right before he hit the packed line, the bull fell onto all fours and set his horns forward, then...

Heavy Infantry.
Quantity — 11/20
Morale — 0/100

CHAPTER 11

PHEW... THAT WAS JUST BEAUTIFUL, to put it lightly.

I appeared in a now-empty building right next to the stele. This was right where I had come from, so everything was right.

The decision to use Zorn and Grugg in the battle was my best one in a long time. They were cheap, extremely angry, and tremendously violent, what more could you want?

The bull may have been enough, but even so, I was able to see how strong the zombie Overlord was. He didn't even use his skills, simply tossing whole divisions apart whenever they came up against him.

He didn't run and he didn't try to scare the enemy in any way. He simply ripped and tore, showing the Japanese, just as expected, that even alone on the field he was also a fighter. And much more of one than even three hundred hurriedly-summoned soldiers.

The bull was just having fun, or at least that's how it seemed to me. He roared, mooed, and ran from side to side, throwing opponents into the air and grabbing them on his horns. Why? Simply because he could.

But Zorn was not having fun. Even from the height of the tower and a distance of nearly a mile away I could tell how the silent deadie was hurrying. Unrestrained, exerting all his efforts, putting his all into dealing with the enemy as quickly as possible to get back to where I had so rudely wrenched him away from without any choice in the matter.

Perhaps I had made a mistake. Probably I had gotten in the way at the worst moment, and now he would have trouble achieving whatever his goals were.

But now that he was a resident of my village, communicating nicely with people and in control of his skills, didn't that mean I could write him in the chat?

Kasp: I didn't get you at a bad time, did I?

I could! The message hung in the little window, semi-transparent, which meant that its recipient hadn't yet read it. But no worries, he would figure it out and answer it, if he needed to.

I squinted at the hundreds of messages that had been sent to me.

But I was surprised that almost nobody was cursing me out. A lot of people had been swearing on the battlefield, and now they were coming to me with their requests like fluffy little sheep? How strange.

Ignatich: Kasp. If it's not a problem, could you return some of my old memories to me?

Maria Mikhailov: Kaspy, could I ask you for a favor?

Grugg: Uh!

Slob: Get him away from me! Why? Why are you like this?!

The second to last one was interesting. The last one wasn't really anything. I just didn't know what Slob was talking about. Who was I taking away? What did I do wrong?

Eh, whatever. I was still in this Japanese forest only so I could make contact. Now that the battle was done I could easily teleport back home for free and take care of my business.

Supervising the construction, seeing Gosha's successes in his gardening endeavors, talking with the elf girl, none of that would be unwelcome. Even feeding Grugg hay would be better and more interesting than hanging out in this crowd of Japanese people.

But no. I had big plans for these guys, and I needed something besides taxes from them. When else would I be able to take such an unforgettable fishing trip? The crab's claw had hardly fit in my inventory, which hinted at even stronger sea creatures. Or plants. Who knew what was going on there, under the water?

If we set up growing water plants, then we

could start making good System food. We might even be able to start cooking up some kinds of potions, whatever we could get there. In any case, we could and should get some money at auction, and I was making a mistake by not using that feature to its fullest. Right now I was just going there sometimes to get something.

Recently there had been less and less standard System rewards being sold there, and handmade items were becoming more and more popular. Plus you could find whatever you wanted, and all of it would be orders of magnitude higher-quality than the standard stuff!

But I was only interested in unique items that were specifically for my class. And I had never found any. It looks like the System had helped me once with the slungshot. Without it things would have been much harder, no doubt about it.

Outside the building an impressive crowd had gathered right in the street. Everyone was curious to see the new sovereign of the settlement, while I, in turn, was really not excited to experience that many unfamiliar eyes on me.

"Get out of here," I said, sticking my head out of the broken doorway and waving my hand at the leader of the settlement.

He dithered for a while, bowing slightly and saying something in his own language. He was either greeting me or offering me tea, I had no idea what their traditions were, to be honest.

"Don't go anywhere, I'll slip into your mind and be right back..." I nodded at him and disappeared into thin air.

That baffled him a bit, but he continued standing calmly by the green stele, waiting for me to reappear.

Hmm... Not a bad dude. I don't know why, but I had been biased against the leaders of settlements. As far as I could tell, to get power, especially in this ruined, post-apocalyptic world, you had to have a whole set of qualities that were not characteristic of people you would call "good." Basically, a leader had to be a piece of shit.

Then again, I was also a kind of leader... But whatever, it was a foregone conclusion.

Everything was a little different with this guy. I wasn't about to dig around too deeply in his memories, so I only glanced at his history. Before the apocalypse he had been a henchman in a gang like the Yakuza. Or maybe just in the Yakuza, what did I know about these Japs?

He had done a bunch of bad things, but he didn't enjoy any of it. He just didn't have a choice, since the gangs here were extremely brutal and merciless with those who decided to retire.

But everything changed when the people around him started turning into zombies. The bastard had had the fortune of being on a fairly busy street, and only his outstanding physical abilities had enabled the man to first avoid the newly-turned deadies and then set up a defense of a fairly large group of civilians. Women, children, office workers... He didn't know who needed help the most, but he tried to help all of them.

He handed out rewards and shared his food, even though sometimes he didn't even have enough for himself. Basically all you could say was that he was a slant-eyed Jesus.

He killed his first zombie quickly, at least since he was armed. But he didn't manage to pick his class quickly too, since he needed to save himself somehow and then protect the people around him. So he only managed to get a green one. By that time all the blue ones had been taken by people like Anton, so tough luck.

But still, much better than a gray one. His class was called Blademaster. Its basic ability allowed him to speed up the perception of time, improving his reaction time and letting him use sharp blades much better and more accurately. And just as well with two hands at the same time.

This class would be great to combine with some sort of skill for using one-handed weapons, but he had been too unlucky to get one yet. And he had no money at all to purchase one, since almost all of it was distributed to his subordinates or went into the city's treasury. The Emperor was very greedy and demanding. He had gotten a huge amount of wealth and easily could have destroyed us in the battle, but he was too greedy.

Although some metal giant, something like a military robot, had come out of the tower at the last moment. But Zorn and Grugg had only taken about 10 seconds on it, not more than that. I hadn't attached any importance to it.

Over time the man's camp had grown, then the

System had sent him to a test where he chose an easy difficulty and completed all his tasks with aplomb. The people loved him, and he loved the people, so here a feeling of friendship and an extremely calm, comfortable, cozy atmosphere reigned.

Had reigned.

Right up until the point when the fiery fool calling himself the Emperor showed up. And he had shown up in person. It never occurred to that idiot that you could issue a challenge from afar, so he personally, along with a small detachment of thugs, had started wandering over the island in search of even more camps.

According to the Emperor, he had decided to make Japan a great power once more, which was possible only under his rule.

I even smirked, mentally, seeing how this pompous idiot, threatening a bunch of peaceful people, was talking about how cool he was.

I had to respect that the leader of the local settlement immediately caught on to the fact that he had no way to stand against that kind of firepower and simply accepted all his conditions to avoid the loss of human life.

But even so, the Emperor had taken some extremely attractive girls with him, saying they were now his concubines, and they would all die if there were a revolt.

"Alright…" I appeared in front of the man, noticing that he hardly moved from fright. More out of reflex, since his class let him quickly appraise a situation and not look stupid, like Slob. "I don't even have anything to say…"

For a second it seemed like had understood me. At least the tone. Now it was completely clear to me that I wasn't oppressing my vassals with taxes. Not oppressing them at all, if we're going to judge it! These guys had paid through the nose and had been forced to get more than they even physically could!

As for me, I immediately wrote the guy in chat about the new conditions and promised to give the Emperor a good hiding if he came back. Using all my forces on the battlefield, which included Grugg, Zorn, and my ultimate problem solver, Cyrush. Nobody was safe from a martial cactus. Those pieces of crap would burn real bad if it came down to it.

For about twenty minutes we stood around in the building discussing our future plans, but in the end nothing came of it. Or rather, everything stayed how it had been, for now. They would keep fishing, looking for hordes of zombies in the basements, and sometimes giving us seafood. And our people would help them get resources, as needed. It would be dumb to steal the concrete and glass from here using the portal. I think I'll delegate that to our staff manager.

I opened a portal to the city, let one person through, and he took a couple tons of whatever he could get into his inventory. Beautiful!

Then I dematerialized and started digging around in people's minds.

But it looks like not everything here is as awesome as I thought. The camp was split in two, with the majority of people supporting their old leader and his decision, but there were some who wanted to go back to the Emperor. In this short period of time they had come to believe in his superiority and his aims, and now they were considering everything to topple both their leader and later even me.

Kasp: I will point out people to you. You get them ready to be sent through the portal to my settlement. I have to do some work on them.

MoonWind: At your command.

At your command... Moon wind... They weren't all there as people, that was for sure. But just how much? I couldn't even guess.

But if they were obeying, that was good. I wouldn't be able to find out all the potential separatists anyway, but I could at least send some of them off for brainwashing. My power only went up when I was next to the Kaspiana stele, so doing that here would be too hard and take too long.

After pointing out some people I nodded to Moon Wind and sent a message to Eva. The girl went home right after the battle, so now she should be waiting for my by the portal arch to open a passageway to that corner of the world.

And she was. I did have to wait about 10 minutes for her, but soon there was a crack in space next to me, and within a second a window leading home had opened up in the air.

"It gets me every time..." I shook my head, having appeared on the other side of the portal. "It's like doing a flip."

"Weird... It's not like that for me." The girl shrugged. "You still need me? If not I'll be over there with the girls..."

"Yeah, go," I waved my hand. I didn't want to know what was going on over there and with which girls. "Just stay online, we'll have a lot more work soon."

Eva nodded, smiling, and rushed out of the room.

Out of the room? Only now did I notice that I was in a building. Brownie hadn't been sitting around in my absence, so now the portal was now in its own separate little building, nice and durable.

They had built it better than it needed to be, since nobody knew if the portal would be dangerous for the settlement in the future. Or come undone and start sending endless waves of all kinds of demons right into the center of the city. Who knew what could happen?

So now there was a fortress here, just inside out. The walls were three feet thick, the ceilings were high, almost 15 feet. There was a massive door with arrow holes and other implements to annihilate anything alive inside the portal room.

Nah, let's get out of here while we're still in one piece. And before anyone notices me. Otherwise, judging from all the messages in chat, a whole bunch of people will want to see me.

I just screwed around for a while. What was

there to do? Everyone here was busy with some kind of work, life was in full swing under the dome, and there were small clean-up crews to take care of the deadies outside. Nobody needed my help, clearly.

I went over to Gosha. As it turned out, the inhabitants had opened up another couple dozen irons, and now my artifact's personal garden had begun to flower and smell.

Almost no time had passed and I could already see a lot of potential in those plants. Some could be used for food, to make all sorts of meals out of them, some of them would just stay there and please the eye, and there were also some that should be able to be used to make potions. At least their System descriptions said so. Although nobody had yet been able to figure out how exactly to cook up those potions.

It was especially nice to see a trio of big guys in bone armor carefully, and maybe with a sense of reverence and trepidation, digging around in Gosha's garden.

The all-important cactus walked behind them like a bodyguard, following the deadies to make sure they didn't make any mistakes and break the delicate stems of the Redhorn and the other young shoots.

"Pfaa! Bugger off! Go!" Gosha suddenly piped up, distracting me from my contemplation of these alien plant forms.

It looked like Grugg had come to graze in the garden. But he still couldn't understand our speech, so the head's cries didn't stop him.

CRACK!

It turned out that the Redhorn was a root vegetable. Or something like that, I don't know from plants. And absolutely nobody could tell me, since we had quite few gardeners. Anyway it was something between a carrot and a... bull's horn. The vegetable itself, which could be found underground, was about 15 to 20 inches in length, a little bent, and sharp at the end.

And judging by Grugg's face, it was also pretty tasty...

CRUNCH!

"Bastard! Get him away!" Gosha shrieked. "That one's name was Rudy, you horned monster!" The cactus started growing, and poisonous green spikes appeared all over its body, while Gosha's face broke out into a furious grimace. "You eat any leaves and I will end you right here, arsehole. I'll turn you into fertilizer!"

Now his voice sounded serious. I had never heard anything like that from the head.

And not just me. Surprisingly, the fearless, bloodthirsty warrior who could take on a whole regiment of the strongest Systemniks without any weapons or armor, opened up his mouth and let the rest of the Redhorn fall out.

"If you come near my garden, I will destroy you," Gosha whispered hoarsely, grabbing the injured plant like it was his own child. "Don't worry, Rudy. We'll fix you right up, lad. Were you frightened?"

He was definitely mentally ill. I had actually been starting to be nervous for Grugg and was about ready to put Gosha and the cactus back into my inventory. I had even checked to make sure I could I could easily fit 100 pounds in there.

But it was done now. The bull took a few steps back, and then headed off, mooing something in annoyance.

One question. How were we going to eat things from this garden? Only now had I noticed that people were giving this place a wide berth. And with every movement toward it, the big guys would immediately hit the uninvited visitor with their heavy, empty stares.

Well, whatever. When harvest time came, I would but the head in my inventory. Nothing else for it, we had to eat something. Otherwise we would soon be switching to beef from starvation.

Oh! I wasn't interested at first, but now I was dying of curiosity.

It seemed they had put up a few buildings in my absence. People were still working without a break, getting more and more resources, using both their inventories and the army of big guys to move them around, and now construction was moving along at a much more swift and frequent pace.

The System constructions also drew my attention. Among the many messages from Brownie, which I only rarely even glanced at, there had been a fair number of reports on that. I had given him freedom of choice, since for me, at least, there could only be positives from that.

Okay. They had chosen two men from those who had recently reached level ten, and they became the most basic builders. And even though that was a gray class, they still had much greater capabilities than normal people. In construction, I mean.

So their first order of business had been to construct a shared cafeteria, improved barracks for the inhabitants to rest more comfortably, the portal building, and to significantly expand the workshop, with a view to the future.

Now other craftsmen could work there too, as soon as the spaces for them were finished. Blacksmiths, leatherworkers, seamstresses, potion makers. All these classes had spaces set out for them already, and they were just waiting for me to give the go-ahead for people to pick their classes. Or once some green or blue class got freed up. In that case they would take it immediately, no hesitation.

There were a bunch of people in the cafeteria. The carpenters had already managed to make a ton of fairly comfortable System furniture, so now there was a place for people to spend their leisure time.

I also freed up my inventory a little while propping up the kitchen by unloading a whole heap of crab meat under the surprised gaze of the chefs. As a cherry on top, I tossed the reindeer leg covered in gore onto the stovetop. I should have gotten rid of that thing a long time ago.

I had to hand it to the ladies who worked in the kitchen. They were only shocked for a couple of seconds, then immediately started sorting out the goods. I even noticed that at least two of them managed to sneak a couple pounds of the delicacy for themselves into their inventories. What, are they being starved to death here?

But I wasn't about to punish anyone. I just put the fear of being caught in their hearts. On the settlement all of their thoughts were under my full control, so doing things like that was really quite simple.

I found Eva at a table with the elf girl, Olya, and Glash. Unsurprisingly, they were talking about me. Pretty stupid considering I could show up anywhere at any time. And listen in. But it was not good to eavesdrop. Still, even knowing that, I stayed floating right over the table.

"Yeah, no, you…" Olya waved her hand. "He's cool, for sure… But not my type… Kamanta over there is into him! I saw you!" The Tamer burst out laughing, winking at the elf girl.

As far as I could tell, they were translating everything for her using the chat, so in a few seconds she turned bright red… or rather, blue… Anyway, she was embarrassed.

"She says that Kasp is not her type at all." Eva smiled, realizing that was a lie, at the very least. "But really, he doesn't look too bad at all, but his personality… Ohh, I thought I was going to kill him in Japan!" She chuckled again, and the rest of them smiled sweetly in response, pretending that they understood her perfectly.

"Nah, I know him the longest out of all of us." Glash, the flying redhead, shook her head. "You better not get with people like him. Stay far away. Even if he asked me on a date, I would never ever say yes…"

Okay. I realized that there was no love lost for me here. They smile sweetly to your face, and here they say shit like this behind your back.

I hadn't thought that I would do this, but now my hand was forced. I simply had to slip into the mind of at least one of them. Or even two, just for the integrity of the experiment.

But who? I would have to use only the most scientific and serious method to make this choice.

Eeny, meeny, miny, moe…

Alright, Glash. Who was prepared to stay far away from people like me.

"You bitches, like hell you'll take him…"

Whoa! Chill! There was such an intense flow of thoughts in the redhead's mind that I needed a few moments to even understand what was going on. No, never going in her head again…

I didn't remember who was next, so I decided to see how things were going with Eva. She definitely wasn't lying. I could see it in her eyes. Honest, pure, and fairly nice. And she had also spoken sincerely.

"You snakes! No, I'm not giving up that easily…"

What is wrong with you? You sit there smiling at each other, giggling, and in your heads your making plans for destroying your competition. About ready to strangle each other.

Let me fly away from here and check the auction, please. I'll watch the construction, or go kill zombies in the forest. Anything was better than listening in on other people's secrets.

With that thought I floated upward and within a few seconds I was hovering right under the cupola.

Everything was in motion down below. And despite the sun already dipping towards the horizon, the people just kept going on building a bright future for themselves with their own hands.

There were some flashes in the workshop along with constant sounds. There was a truce and a fairly large zone of exclusion around the gardens, Slob was running across the area between the town hall and the portal building, shouting something, trying to swat away…

Oh, I got it. The spirit I had made hadn't died. Actually, it had gotten stronger and was now sticking to our Berserker for some reason. It was just sitting on his bald spot and getting warmed up.

If I looked off in the distance then I could make out some barely visible dots gathering above the city. They might be birds, winged zombies, or even chimeras. Maybe even some kind of golems, who knew?

I really didn't know what to do with myself. It might be worth it to track those two down and finish them off once and for all. Especially since that would immediately free up two interesting class that could then be used for the good of the city.

While I deliberated on where it would be best to start my search, the dark forest was lit up by a bright ray of light. Fairly far away, about a mile and a half. But every second the ray of light was getting closer and closer.

Soon I could hear the steady rumbling of a powerful engine, and people started coming out to check the sound. Some purely out of curiosity, while others had grabbed their weapons in advance, knowing that there were very few people coming around in these times with peaceful intentions.

But I knew immediately who had come to pay us a visit. I had to meet him properly, since he was no ordinary guest. And I had better not go alone.

But as soon as the rumbling transportation came into my field of view, I immediately spotted the problem.

Zorn, perched atop his chopper like a Grand Tsar on his throne, looked maybe not ragged, but pretty bad, at least. He had on smoking tatters of clothing and holes through his chest, with arrows sticking out of his body. But the most important thing was that he was alone, without his granddaughter. And judging from his facial expression, his granddaughter was definitely not in a safe place. And it was safe to say that he did not like that.

"Kasp, I know you are here." As soon as the roar of the motor died down, Zorn's hoarse voice resounded through the area. "I wrote you in the chat and have been waiting for your response. Are you ready to take me into your perpetual service?"

What? What did he write me there? I mean, we had agreed that he would come back and help us, but this perpetual service... That was almost like our overseas partners, but without any time limit? How much clay could he get?

But what had given him that idea? Well, I wouldn't know until I read the chat.

CHAPTER 12

"GRUGG, STOP. You don't have to kill him." Zorn had put up his hands, trying to stop my companion, but the bull hadn't seemed to notice it. "We have taken the tower! That's all, all done. The System will take us back in a minute."

And that was true. As soon as the zombie and the horned beast had broken through the sparse defenses and gotten to the tower, the System had informed them of their upcoming victory. They just had to hold the tower for one minute without letting anyone in and simply wait for the battle to finish.

"Ugghhh!" The bull bared his teeth, and his hooves clattered across the wooden spiral staircase that led upstairs.

"Fine, let's go get him." Zorn shook his head. Although was in a big hurry, but there was no way he could stop the bull, it would just take longer.

The deadie easily outpaced his companion, being the first to the top of the tower. But the leader turned out to be scrappy. A huge fireball flew towards Zorn, but the zombie easily avoided it, taking cover behind the hatch leading down to battlefield.

"Hmm?" A massive figure appeared behind the deadie, lost in his own thoughts. "Ugh!" A powerful paw pointed at the entrance, and Zorn simply stepped aside, letting the bull pass.

"Go, if you want." The deadie shrugged his shoulders and waited.

First he heard a crash and then a frightful roar. Within a few seconds a smoking, horned head could be seen through the entrance. But now he had a very satisfied expression on his face.

"Ugh!" The bull pointed at something down below and clattered his hooves back down the stairs.

"Where did they find this guy?" Zorn shook his head, hurrying after his military companion.

As it turned out, the bull had simply thrown the fire mage off the tower. And as soon as Zorn caught up to him, he started trampling the poor bastard into the ground with his hooves, stopping him from accessing his rich arsenal of spells.

But he didn't want to kill him. Rather to teach him a lesson, since the bull, to all appearances, hated when someone tried to burn him.

The man, screaming in panic, sometimes flew upward, received a flurry of damaging blows, and then made acquaintance with first the left hoof and then the right one.

"Alright, stop! Finish it!" shouted Zorn, seeing that a minute had passed. But they had all left the tower, so the countdown had stopped. "Hey!"

But the bull wasn't paying any attention to his companion's shouting. He just kept right on methodically torturing and destroying the morale of the opposing leader, never letting him die.

"Fine. I'm sorry, but I am in a hurry." Saying that, the deadie swiftly closed the distance, tore the groaning victim from the monster's paws, and... "You remember my face. I do not recommend that you try to get revenge."

CRACK!

The Japanese man did not have time to respond. His eyes were full of terror, and the crack came right as he opened his mouth. The powerful bony hand had simply crushed his neck bones into powder, and the body fell to the ground, flopping like a lifeless doll.

*   *   *

"Ahhh!" The Asian-looking man leaped out of the massive bed, awakening and frightening dozens of beautiful nude girls with his cry. "Get out! All of you!" he shouted, hysterically, grabbing his head.

He hadn't been able to sleep for a long time before this, and now he had had such a terrible nightmare. Dreams full of fear, in which what had happened to him not so long ago kept happening over and over again.

He could not get rid of the terror that had

seized his heart. No, instead with every passing hour it grabbed and squeezed his conscious mind with its long icy claws, causing the unfortunate man's whole body to shake, bringing the memories back to his mind again and again.

Not too long ago he had been an ordinary office worker. On the work days he devoted himself entirely to his useless and boring work, while his weekends were wholly devoted to computer games, anime, and wastes of time like that.

But everything had changed when the System had come. He knew immediately that he had been preparing for something like this practically his whole life. Plus, due to a happy set of coincidences, at the moment that everyone else was running out into the street, he couldn't get out of the toilet. Neither could his colleague. And that colleague become his first victim, after he slipped and fell onto the dirty wet tiles.

"I have a gold class!" shouted the Japanese man once everyone had left his opulent bedroom. At that moment his body became covered in flame which whirled up to the ceiling, carrying the spell-caster along with it. "I am the Emperor!" His roar resounded beyond the walls of the building, and within a second he himself had shot through the roof of the building like a comet.

He wasn't worried about the damage at all. People would fix it. That's why he had left them alive. What else were they good for?

The Emperor had long ago realized that fate itself, along with the System and universe, had destined him for greatness. The very greatest person, who would rule the world. He would make his own country great again, enslave the planet, and clear it of everything unnecessary.

The Emperor tried to chase away his terror with those thoughts, but it still crouched in his soul, sealing the deathly clutch in his mind. And there was nowhere else for it to go.

Every time the man recalled his own greatness, that scene from the recent battle would appear before his eyes. The one he should have one. He had to. And it had been so close.

At first he had wanted to play with the stupid Russian, in over his head. He had acted like he was not the great new leader of the world, but simply a pitiable pauper, incapable of buying expensive and powerful forces.

But he couldn't enjoy it for very long, and as soon as the Emperor noticed that his opponent was no longer able to summon strong fighters, he started making attacking divisions.

But the everything went wrong.

The Emperor was not used to losing. He wasn't used to retreating, sharing his settlements with someone else, or to showing his own weakness. Because he was the most important person on this damn planet! All people were supposed to either bow before him or die in terrible agony if they refused to do so!

Every single person... But this time that didn't happen to them at all.

The whole time he was flying like a comet over

his demesne, two scenes kept popping up over and over in front of his eyes. The massive jaws of the bull and the completely empty, yet still somehow soul-piercing eyes of the deadie.

And a shiver ran across his flame-covered skin once again.

"No… I can't let it end there…" hissed the Emperor through clenched teeth. His face was contorted into a grimace of rage, and a furious roar exploded from his chest.

The Emperor, who had been flying over his own settlement in the form of a flaming comet, turned toward the settlement seized by those bastards. He was picking up speed every second, intending to burn every single inhabitant and then all those who had done him wrong, but then… The terror, driven into him by the iron fists of those two monsters, made itself felt again.

"Goddammit…" The man shook his head and changed directions.

He had thousands of soldiers who could do the work for him. So there was no reason to risk coming face to face with any monsters in person.

"Convene the council!" bellowed the Emperor, slamming into the ground right by his own town hall.

The fire on his body immediately went out, and the man himself walked swiftly towards his throne room.

He didn't have to wait long. Hardly had the Imperial bottom touched the ornate gold throne when a troop of loyal soldiers rushed into the grand hall.

Mostly it was made up of commanders of his armies, but the leaders of other settlements could also be found there. All of them instantly bowed their heads, ready to listen to the orders of their, if not deity, at least lord, and he had no intention of beating around the bush.

"Fuji..." the leader of the world said, barely keeping the quiver out of his voice. "Our enemy has seized our settlement over there. You must raze it to the ground!"

One man, standing nearby, raised his head in surprise. He glanced out for only a moment, since the irrationality of the order had shocked him to his core. He said nothing, true, and he didn't intend to, knowing that would just draw the rage onto himself, but...

"You!" The Emperor pointed at him. "Are you opposed?"

"No, my liege!" the terrified man shouted instantly, falling to his knees. "I will do whatever you command, my liege!" His entire body was shaking, and he was unable to tear his forehead away from the floor to see his smiling ruler.

"I am merciful today. So speak truthfully how you feel about my plan," said the Emperor softly, all the while smiling and looking at his underling. "You have nothing to fear. Simply speak how you feel."

"M-my l-liege..." He began murmuring, but still managed to collect himself and raise his gaze. "I just wanted to say that we can just take the settlement back. If we don't burn it, then Your Excellency will only benefit greatly from it, just as before. I myself am ready to march against them, if you desi...

He didn't get to finish. A fiery whirlwind exploded out of the ground, swallowing the unlucky man whole within moments, carrying him upward. He never even got to cry out, turned to ash almost instantaneously, which then floated around the room and settled on the heads of the terrified people, cowering in horror.

"I. Said. Burn. It." The Emperor repeated coldly, and covered himself in flame, rising into the air to a chorus of frightened shouts. "Right now!"

At this shout all those in attendance rushed off to fulfill his command. The Emperor floated in the air for a while, then flopped down into his slightly molten gold throne.

But burning the village was only the beginning. A plan for revenge was taking shape in the man's head, and he had the total destruction of his enemy in mind. Both physically and mentally.

Emperor: No need to beg for mercy! You got lucky once, but I won't give you that chance again!

Emperor: I will burn all of your people, one after another! I will come to your home and leave nothing but ashes! You have but one chance to save yourself...

Emperor: Ten minutes have passed and you have not answered! Are you afraid? But I can forgive you your insolence...

Emperor: Last chance... It is in your interest to respond here as soon as possible, otherwise things will be very bad for you...

The man sat for another ten minutes, paying careful attention to the messages in chat. He was trying to enrage his opponent so that he would rush into a senseless attack, but...

Kasp: Ah, duh?

"AHhh!" The Emperor covered himself in flame once more, instantly melting down the throne he had just been sitting in. "How dare you! Find that bastard! Find him and destroy him! I will personally turn you to ashes!"

*Kasp: F*ck around and find out, dude :)*

* * *

Zorn: I haven't finished my work, and so I would like to ask for your help. If you agree, I am ready to pledge myself to you in perpetuity and serve you until the end of time.

Zorn: I will soon arrive. Be ready to meet me.

Emperor: No need to beg for mercy...

What an idiot, that Emperor of yours. Even the name he chose for himself is idiotic. But if I could trust the memories of the Japanese, that guy was pretty strong. Maybe even really strong. Both physically as well as in his abilities. And his class was not just gold, it was also an attacking class.

Ruler of Flame, or something like that, I couldn't recall the name.

Should I be afraid of him? Absolutely! And a lot. Like fire!

Would I be afraid of him? Well, you'll have to forgive me on that one. So I would have to answer the loser. Troll him a little. And once he was good and pissed we would catch him off guard. I really wanted a class like that for my own team.

The Emperor had started writing me something, but I simply didn't pay any attention to his messages. I had more important things to do now anyway.

At the very least the half-naked deadie on the chopper parked right by the shield. He looked cool and terrifying at the same time, but that was only if you didn't know his prehistory.

As it turned out, being summoned to the Battle saved his life. His enemies could have dealt with even such a powerful enemy and taken him hostage, using all sorts of abilities and tools for that. People had all along been learning how to fight with deadies, plus there were certain classes that could enable you to defeat even much more powerful zombies.

That's what happened to Zorn, I would say.

"Do you mind if I put my mark on you?" Through the rumbling of the motor I could hear the zombie's grating voice, dragging me out of my reverie.

"Yeah, sure, why not..." I waved my hand, materializing on the seat behind the zombie. "And I will just sit here for now. Hey, how much does it eat? How fast does it go? How much are the parts? Have you fell off it yet?"

Zorn was smart enough to stay silent at my

questions. Strange, what's up with him? I was just curious...

He had actually called me just for the mark. But at the same time I learned a bunch of valuable information that I would put to full use when I got back to Kaspiana.

The settlement's level was necessary and important. Extremely necessary and important, I would say. Much more necessary than I would have said earlier.

Up to now I had been ignoring the possibilities the stele had. Yes, you could build it. Yes, it had a cool shield around it. You could gather resources and use them somehow, and also my class abilities got ten times stronger. I had been sure that that was it.

I had a few vassals with gray steles, and they had just about the same functions. But it turned out I was wrong.

Zorn couldn't take out his enemy because he simple couldn't see him. Why? Well, because the stele in the settlement that was holding his granddaughter turned out to be a blue one. Which class it was you could only guess, but it definitely wasn't a simple one, but one designed to fight zombies.

As soon as the Overlord had appeared on the horizon, the settlement and everything that happened to be under its cupola disappeared into thin air. Poof! But only in his perception, since soon he was getting hits and magical attacks from all sides.

The untouchable enemy inflicted terrible injuries on the deadie, time after time, and there was simply nothing he could do in return. He tried to avoid them, tried attacking at random, but there was no use.

That kept going until he retreated. But his enemies followed him, trying to do as much damage as possible. Although once they came out of the dome, Zorn could hit them back.

The deadie was forced to hide for a time. He followed the actions of the people who went outside the settlement carefully. Soon he realized that using torture to get information from them was well within his moral standards.

They definitely weren't saints themselves.

To level up their stele as quickly as possible, those people had been taking over more and more survivor camps. Even if they had no desire to join anyone else, nobody was asking their permission.

The level of your settlement could be raised by the number of inhabitants or by crystals. And if you had a bunch of people and you didn't care about spending a bunch of resources to level it up, then it would grow by leaps and bounds.

So what did you need it for?

Well, here for example, Zorn wasn't able to even see the city or its inhabitants because of it. Just like other zombies which were no longer a worry for people at all.

And that was all due to the class skill of the settlement! Yeah, just like people, settlements also had skills. They were a little different, but no less effective for it. And the more powerful the stele was, the fewer levels you would need to get similar capabilities.

We had gotten a new resource already by level two. Some kind of souls, whatever that meant. How to get them and what they did, I had no idea, but they were definitely necessary to use settlement skills like that.

Zorn didn't tell me anything else. He just mumbled that eventually, when he tried to get his granddaughter again, they had stopped him and were about to kill him, but one second before his final moments he had been transported to a different and much safer battlefield.

In his place I would have tortured the informant better. He had just gone over it perfunctorily, and the zombie had missed out on a lot of valuable information, as far as I could tell.

We spent two hours in silence. I just sat, lost in thought, enjoying the fascinating trip. Zorn drove his iron horse masterfully, easily avoiding his brethren who occasionally wandered onto the road and maneuvering around obstacles.

We managed to hit a rabbit along the way. It had wandered onto the road to grab a crystal from an unlucky zombie, but Zorn steered his devil machine straight into the poor fluffball, instantly turning it into mincemeat.

"What the hell you do that for, dumbass?" All I could do was shout. I wasn't about to grab the wheel, but still I couldn't understand that act of heartless cruelty.

"To answer your question about how much it eats," hissed the zombie, "open your System window and you will understand everything." He nodded toward the place where the instrument panel was supposed to be.

And he was right. As soon as I concentrated some messages appeared before my eyes. They informed me that the motorcycle was now far from its ideal state and required the use of a repair kit. Which I immediately set about doing, literally feeling Zorn's uncontrolled wave of approval.

As soon as I finished fixing it up in motion, I set about studying the other tabs.

The tank was half empty. Or half full, but whatever the case, you had to kill innocent creatures to get it more full than half. So it worked for both pessimists and optimists. The motorcycle didn't care, it would eat anything. But the interesting thing was that the fuel reserves gradually went up. Slowly, yes, but nevertheless. Strange, for sure...

It also showed that there basically nothing left for it to reach level two in collecting souls. It would be interesting to see what new functions this miracle of technology would get.

We spent some time traveling along the highway, with me enjoying the endless fields, the black silhouettes of the forest in the background, the occasional coffee shops along the roadside, and burnt-out car chassis that were scattered around like mortal ruins almost every five feet.

But gradually the countryside was replaced with cityscape, and soon I could catch movement off in the distance.

People. Lots of people. But only I could see them. Zorn was still pumping the gas pedal at that time, not even suspected that we were getting closer to humanity.

"You put that mark on so you could screw up later on?" I slapped him on the shoulder and the zombie instantly came to, pushing the brake pedal.

"Sorry. I was lost in thought." He shook his head and pulled over to the shoulder. Even though we had already caught the attention of the guards, it would still take them quite a bit of time to get to us.

As soon as we got off the road, Zorn touched the motorcycle and just disappeared! Did he put it in his inventory? Or was that some kind of special function, to shrink to down as much as its owner wanted?

Well, whatever.

"Ah, my ass is asleep. And it's not waking up..." I immediately started stretching, feeling that my body wasn't really listening to me.

And my health and mana bars had fallen by about 10%. Soon it became clear where that damage had come from. That awful chariot sucked out life force. And that included from passengers. So I had shared some of my life force which gave the iron monster a bit of fuel.

We weren't going to wait around long. We had decided everything in advance, but as soon as we got there I suddenly had all sorts of plans. Zorn was in no position to argue, so he just waved his hand, not wanting to quibble.

Rushing in to attack and taking the role of the zombie Overlord's eyes was not what I wanted to do. Or to participate in this fracas at all, actually.

I could trust Zorn completely, but his mind could distort the truth somewhat. What if these people were actually decent? Okay, they pulled in everybody that they met. Maybe even by force. But if on the inside, under the dome, they treated people like people, then why not? I didn't see anything too bad about that.

So, asking Zorn to stay in a small park about a mile from our destination, I headed off to do some spying.

Soon I came across a small group of marauders. They had just cleared out some stores and were now marching home in high spirits, peacefully chatting with each other.

I spent some time trying to hear something useful, but they were mostly interested in girls, so their discussions were only on the topic of the weaker sex.

In just 15 minutes we were getting near the cupola, and I decided to just take the risk. It was really very large and soundproof, and we would never manage to figure out how the local inhabitants lived without getting inside.

If I took a crystal I could take any body under my own personal control. But a lot of time had passed since the last time, and had gotten much better at dealing with my own capabilities. So it made sense to try it.

Especially since, worst-case scenario, I could just rip all the information out of my victim's mind. And that would also be worth it.

CHAPTER 13

NO, I HAD TO FIND the stupidest one.

Every second it became clearer and clearer to me why you needed to level up your Intelligence. That stat didn't just affect your memory and speed of thought. It also made it harder for somebody to get into your mind.

Maybe if I opened up the Conduits stat I would find something interesting there too. But right now I was experiencing how hard it was to subjugate intelligent people.

So, first of all, I tried slipping into the mind of the leader of the marauders. First I quickly perused his thoughts, hoping to find Zorn's granddaughter, but no such luck. These guys had joined the settlement quite recently, so there was nothing I could get from them. They just wandered around, filling their inventories will all sorts of useful items, weighing down their bags with food, and then headed back. If they came across a zombie, which seemed to be pretty common around here, they just ran away.

And that's all. Day after day, same thing. They remembered what they had done yesterday, knew what they were doing today, and were well aware of what they would be engaged in tomorrow. Wander around, get stuff, resources, medicine, and any other needful things. And every once in a while they might get rewards too, if they came across weak enough deadies.

In the past this guy had been a security guard for a grocery store chain. And instead of catching shoplifters at work, he just did crosswords constantly. Well, he had trained his brain, so now it was hard for me to overtake his mind. Ah, it would have been so convenient to break into the dome using someone else's body.

I wasn't going to try too hard since I knew I just wasn't going to be able to do it. Especially since they had about five minutes till they got to the dome, and I definitely wasn't going to make it in that time.

So I just started for the most not dumb one in the group. And while doing so I read their minds and memories. I mean, that's what I came here for.

These people were not saints. Well, just like the rest of all the first survivors in this crazy new world. Saints died first.

These guys' inventories were about 20 to 30 pounds on average. And each of them had scenes of killing living people in their memories, no way around it.

Then again, I had 1500 pounds, what of it? These things happen!

One of the interesting things I learned was that there was a caste system in the settlement. These guys belong to the Worker caste. The only thing lower than them was the Useless caste, the lowest caste of all. Above them were the Warriors, Mages, and other very important people. The caste system was organized based on both your working ability and the color of your class.

The Warriors, Workers, and lower castes usually had gray classes. Among the higher ones you could find green classes, and those with blue classes were free to do as they liked, obviously.

A dirty, gross city… I could see why Zorn had decided to get his granddaughter out of there. You were allowed to do whatever you wanted there, as long as you could eke out a place in the sun for yourself. Anybody who wanted to could torment the lower castes. The only thing that was forbidden was to kill them. The leader needed to fill his treasury, and that was the only reason he kept the free-loaders around, occasionally tossing them scraps from the lord's table so they wouldn't die of hunger.

The guys that I had the fortune of running into were not especially knowledgeable. I could only see things from their point of view, and they knew comparatively little. I would only be able to find out more about the castes by getting into the head of someone from the higher social strata. However stupid that might sound. Whatever, I had to try. But first I had to find the right victim.

There were five marauders in total, including the leader. Four men and one woman, but I never set foot in her head. I had gotten enough of that in the cafeteria a little bit ago. And I wouldn't be able to take over her body. For that I would have to become one consciousness with my victim, attuning my mind completely to theirs and becoming that person, even if just for a short while.

So there was no chance of that. That left three people.

After the leader I hopped inside the mind of a boy about 20 years old. He had been a university student not too long ago, hoping to become a civil engineer. He had studied fairly well, so he was also out. Even though his level was low, and he hadn't managed to eat any potatoes, his Intelligence was nearly the same level as mine. Moving on.

Oh, no... this was just a dark forest. Some kind of mathematician, so let him go it alone. I wasn't gonna fit into that.

But the last one was good. He had written some little books before the apocalypse, fantasy mostly. This was the guy, matching all my criteria.

Yessir. It was not hard to get into his mind. And if I tried I could get him to slap himself. Awesome. But that took about 20% of my mana, which meant I could only spend five seconds in his body.

More than enough for my plan. I just had to hope that I would be able to trick the System.

After the slap my victim got some weird looks,

but still nobody suspected that anything was wrong. It seemed like this guy had been considered an idiot by them for a while now, so silly stuff like that didn't surprise them at all.

I flew ahead so I wouldn't bother anyone with my aura. There was no need to arouse suspicion early in this matter. Let them do what they normally did, hand over their loot, and each go to their own homes. I had other plans.

It turned out that, in addition to the shield, there was a pretty solid wall in this settlement.

It was made of concrete, and now I could see clear traces of damage that had been done to it recently. I suddenly had a vision of Zorn trying to break a hole through the wall by running into it with his head. And then, confused, putting a hole in it the same way from the inside. And all the way around it, since there were quite a few busted areas.

"Get to it, boys!" The guard perched above the gates waved his hand, "Open up the gates for these dummies!" he shouted down somewhere below, and a few seconds later the heavy wooden gates started creaking open.

"Which dummies you talking about?" the leader of the marauders asked. "We're just the sam—"

"The deadie's come back! The sick one! He was seen a few miles away!" interrupted the guard, and the marauders suddenly got a move on.

I had to hurry too. Getting level with my victim, I waiting for the moment when he was as close as possible to the shield and...

Piece of cake. The second I slipped into the poor man he froze. But I quickly took control, forcing him to all but leap forward. It was uncomfortable to be in someone else's skin, so he fell down, but I didn't need anything more than that.

Inside the shield! Once I realized that, I immediately left my carrier and rushed off to the exact center of the city.

Judging from the fact that when I got inside nobody raised the alarm, I had broken through completely unnoticed.

Now I could go look around.

The first thing I did was fly up as high as I could, carefully inspecting the settlement itself. I couldn't do that before since I was worried about losing my ticket in. And there would have been no point anyway. What good would it do me to know what was under the cupola if I couldn't get in anyway?

But it worked out. Turned out I could. And that knowledge would have saved me a lot of problems with the Japanese.

The city, as I had known for a while, was not that small. At first the stele had been set up at the very edge of the megalopolis so that they could get resources more easily. Plus there was a fair-sized food area there. The zombies couldn't see the settlement so they smacked into the concrete wall like crash dummies, then got taken out by soldiers who were also invisible.

So every seemed well and good. People lived,

developed, built houses, got resources. They talked to each other, established entertainment, and made their lives at least a little bit happier in this cruel, heartless world.

That was if you didn't take into account that a good half of the settlement was suffering because of it. The outcasts, the weak, and those who were merely terrified undercastes. They weren't even considered people here.

The next question was, was I up to the task? More than likely not. But I would happily take those misfortunate souls with me. But nobody was going to give them up without a fight. Not even one little girl.

The barracks were located in the center. Good-sized concrete boxes with thick walls, tiny windows, and solid gates. All with serious-looking guards near them. Big dudes, ready to attack anybody at their master's beck and call, utterly unstoppable.

Well, that was interesting. If you considered that the radius of the dome was about 1500 feet, then those barracks could contain upwards of a few thousand people. From what I had gathered, there was about a thousand inhabitants here, but in reality it could be much more interesting.

So how could they all have gotten to level 10? In my estimation to do that you would need... Well, a hell of a lot of time. Or a truckload of crystals.

Sure, for me, fine. I was capable of basically mining them, whole handfuls. But these were normal people, and they weren't getting that much loot.

There were four barracks in total, surrounded by a high fence. Although basically anyone could get into them to use someone from the lower castes however their heart might desire, but getting out would be a lot harder. Even from here I could see the observation tower. Yep, just like a prison.

That prison itself was located practically in the middle of the settlement, close to the town hall. That made sense. Even if someone managed to get through the fence, crossing over the whole city, crawling with people day and night, would be basically impossible. Life didn't stop here, come day or night, everyone was busy with something, getting drunk on alcohol from the city, or just having fun.

Alright, I knew all about the city. Even here the buildings were a lot bigger than at our settlement. But that was the least of our problems. I think that when I get back we'll also have a pretty good housing fund. I mean, as far as I knew, we had finished building all the necessary production facilities and social buildings. The rest was whatever, since we didn't even need that many resources for it.

Zorn: I am certain she is in the barracks.

Exactly right. I had completely forgotten about our dead friend. But he was watching, paying attention to my thoughts, the sign of his mark still flashing in the corner of peripheral vision.

Kasp: No rush. First let me read their minds, then we'll consider what to do...

That's it. Nobody here was going to execute all

of the undercaste right away. So it made sense to first figure things out, learn whether we would be able to get the girl out without a fight.

I hoped we would, of course. The Hindus had come up with castes like these though. They could have gotten use out of the Useless too, just spend some resources on them to make them useful. But nobody likes investing...

Whoa! A very important-looking old man had come out of the town hall and was issuing commands to the soldiers. Judging from his face, he was, if not the main leader here, at least very close it. So let's start with him.

I floated smoothly down to the ground and slid into the fat man decked out in quite nice System items. Not a set, no, but still they looked rare, at least. And all of them probably increased his magic power.

In order not to waste time, I lightened his pockets along the way. I was wasting my strength a bit, but this should make up for it somehow.

"You will be cleaning the toilets, worm!" I shouted at the guard. I hadn't paid attention to the conversation, so I could only guess what the soldier's failing had been. "Get moving!"

Hmm... It looked like this fatass had been chewing out the soldier for failing to bow his head and greet his master fast enough. Jesus, I could give a shit less how the world worked here. What was important was that the bastard had decided to have some fun and ordered that guy to bring him girls for that purpose.

I knew that they used the undercaste however they liked here, but this asshole's tastes were a little... Specific. He liked them, let's say, a little younger.

The fatty headed for his mansion to prepare for his pleasures, while I kept pulling all the information I needed out of his sick mind. He would soon be dead. For sure. So I needed to use the last moments of his life to the fullest.

Yes, a settlement's class was very important. This one had a rare class designed for fighting deadies. It was that which had allowed the leader to gather so many people around himself. Because he had been completely invisible to the zombies this whole time! What a class skill, a passive one at that!

But mine was still better.

"Lord! May I?" A voice could be heard on the other side of the door. I immediately forgot about the fatass and flew outside to check it out.

Well, it was as I had expected. The servant had followed orders and brought back a whole bunch of girls so the guy could choose the one that suited him.

In his mind I found nothing but fear and despair. Poor, frightened, unfortunate man. I was filled with compassion... I would hit him with my slungshot first.

"Let's go, dumbshit!" shouted the lord. "Goddamn retard, what am I here for, just to wait for you?"

In addition to young slave girls, there were also

a few soldiers here. Pretty strong-looking ones. Their weapons and equipment were no worse than uncommon, plus I didn't think they were less than level 20. They were like a home guard, or more like a Gestapo maintaining order in the settlement.

Plus the bastard had his own personal bodyguards here too. With their greasy faces and wicked, soulless eyes. Guys! What is wrong with you? When did you become such monsters?

Well, screw 'em. The important thing was that I had finally found what I broke into this settlement for among the slave girls.

I couldn't remember her name, but that didn't matter. These idiots had brought Zorn's daughter here, and the only thing I could do was feel bad for them.

The slave girls were brought into the living room where the guest of honor was reclining on a leather couch in the middle of the room. He glanced lazily at the terrified girls, standing all in a row, and pointed at three girls that took his fancy.

The soldiers grabbed them immediately, dragging them off to another room somewhere, while the rest were sent back to the barracks.

Were they being taken to be washed? Eh, it didn't matter. Zorn's granddaughter was among those three slave girls. I thought it would be better to wait for them to take her a bit farther away and then first take out the guard, silently, and then get to work on the main bastard.

Kasp: Don't you worry. I'll get this done real

good, nobody will see a thing.

Hmm... I waited for a response for about five minutes, but Zorn hadn't even read it.

Kasp: Operator, do you copy? You can read my thoughts!

Weird. Did he fall asleep? Unlikely. I was sure that he would be focusing on me and what was going on here now. Unless he was fighting with a group of soldiers at the moment. I mean, they had noticed us, which meant they could have sent a division to neutralize the threat.

GRAAAH!

A loud sound came from somewhere and then I saw the glare of fire through the window.

Then I heard screams, sirens wailing, and the wild roar of some kind of beast shaking the air. But who was it? I felt like I could guess. And that beast still wasn't responding to me in the chat...

Ahh... I had wanted to do everything on the down low, but alas. My zombie friend had turned out to be too impatient.

"Guys! Although, how you can call yourself guys after this, I mean, really..." I had appeared behind the three terrified girls being escorted to some unknown destination. A second later my spiked ball, appearing out of thin air, resounded across the floor, and my face spread out in a satisfied smile. "Shall we begin?"

* * *

RAAAAH!

Zorn dashed forward, slamming into the invisible barrier over and over again. A visceral roar exploded from his chest, and his eyes were shrouded in fury.

The deadie was eagerly following his ghostly friend's thoughts and intentions and knew that he wanted to do everything simply and easily. The zombie was also fully aware that Kasp would most likely get everything done.

But even so, he couldn't hold back his rage, knowing what they intended to do with his one and only relative, so dear to him.

So he went on the attack, throwing caution to the winds.

"You are all dead men!" He roared, slamming into the invisible barrier once more.

Pieces of concrete flew in all directions, and shouts of pain could be heard, but that just further impelled the livid deadie. He took a massive axe out of his inventory, chopping down everything that got in his way.

The people weren't just standing around, but rather tried to knock out their enemy with their abilities, but he seemed to be made out of cast iron.

His dead flesh heated up, melted, fell off, but all of that was immaterial to the zombie. He chopped and chopped, first the concrete wall and then the shield of the settlement itself until it began to quiver.

"Soldiers! To the front!" yelled an officer, focusing all of his mana at one point. Soon a powerful charge formed at the top of his wand, seeming to suck up all the surrounding light, and one second later he sent the attack at his opponent, going hard on the wall.

But he dodged, moving at an unbelievable speed, letting the fatal hit pass him by.

The black dot slammed into the ground, making a terrible sound, and the shattered wall was covered with ice and cracks.

Zorn simply went back and kept right on hacking out a path for himself to save the person most dear to him.

More and more people kept coming to the walls. The ones who were out of mana stepped away, and the new ones went all out on their insanely dedicated enemy.

The deadie took hit after hit. Soon he started attacking soldiers in melee combat through a hole in the wall.

A spear came right out of the cupola, piercing straight through the zombie's chest, then it began shooting off sparks, sending a paralytic shock through the deadie.

While Zorn was frozen, the soldiers came out and surrounded him, ready to deal the killing blow.

"You insufferable son of a bitch..." said the officer, swinging his axe to cut his fallen enemy's head off, but at the last moment he stopped and stared off somewhere in the distance.

And so did all the others.

The third phase of the System has finished!
The fourth phase is starting now.
The difficulty has increased...

CHAPTER 14

"SHHHH!" I TOOK OFF MY HOOD and mask and pressed my finger to my lips. "Don't shout, okay?"

That wasn't necessary. The girls were stock still in fear and couldn't even budge, much less scream.

It had been pretty easy to deal with the soldiers. They didn't even realize they were in a fight before the slungshot knocked all three of their brains out. I had had to work fast, just in case those idiots decided to make use of their attack abilities. I don't want any innocent bystanders to get hurt.

Zorn's daughter was called Masha. Yeah, okay, I needed to level up my memory. I needed specifically to find the tab about remembering names. Had this problem my whole life. There were lots of times at work that I had to call a co-worker "Hey," since literally three seconds after meeting them that information would just vanish from my mind.

"Do you want to go back to your grandfather?" I said, crouching down next to Masha.

She froze for a second, then a tear rolled down her cheek. There, she's coming to her senses now.

"He... He's alive?" she whispered, hope in voice.

"Uh... How do I say this..." realizing what a pickle I was in now. "Let's just say, yes, mostly. Does that work?"

The girl was just confused and only nodded in response.

"Yeah, that's nice. Now just stay here and wait for me to come back. Hmm... No, you better hide." I pointed at the restroom. That's where they were taking them anyway.

My newest, fairly strong enemy had an uncommon class. Paralyzer. And the name was completely accurate.

I had looked at the bastard's memories in advance, seeing how he used his abilities and came to a couple of conclusions. His class skill allowed him to paralyze either one opponent or a whole army at once. That was how he had gotten such a high position here. It definitely was easily to take prisoners if you paralyzed them first. Then you didn't have to kill all of them, you could just set them up in the barracks and just get some good out of them.

I also learned why they weren't worried about overpopulation in the settlement. It turned out that they hadn't set up the stele here just because it was right by a large city. There used to warehouses with provisions right here, so feeding a thousand people in the "undercaste" was no big deal. The reserves would last for a long time, so they wouldn't have to start wasting their potatoes any time soon. Or growing their own food. There was no point in doing that now, so the locals weren't hung up on problems like that at all.

But I wasn't scared of paralysis, since I could easily go and punish that asshole, reclining on his couch, without using any tricks.

I waited for the girls to hide inside the restroom, dematerialized, and headed downstairs, right through the floor.

The freak wasn't so relaxed now. The dick had heard me cracking his henchmen's skulls. He had also called in two security guards from outside, hoping they might help him somehow. And he was brandishing his wand in front of him.

"It won't help." I shrugged, appearing right behind him.

But in the next moment I felt like my body was no longer listening to me. But dematerializing brought everything back to normal.

"There's nothing you can do, prick!" shouted my victim, hysterically. Ha, I didn't even have to activate my Aura of Fear. He had just pissed his pants.

"You think so?" I whispered in his ear and disappeared once again.

Soon after my spiked metal ball slammed into

him between the shoulder blades, knocking the bastard off his feet.

"Ahhhh! Do something!" he screamed, trying to get away using his other class.

A green cloud exploded out of his hands, heading straight for me, but I easily dodged it. One of the security guards, however, breathed in the poison. He turned pale, and the skin of his face started breaking out in blisters. Within a few seconds the unlucky man fell onto the fluffy carpet, seizing.

THWACK!

Inventory Increased +50 lbs.

"Waste not, want not." I smiled and winked at my opponent. "Keep going, I won't get in your way." I raised my arms and dematerialized.

"Stop!" he shrieked, once the second security guard fell down dead, having taken a hit to the head. "Stop! What do you want?" He threw his wand on the ground and raised his hands, kneeling. "You see? I'm not fighting back! Although I could!"

He started looking around in a panic, while I floated right behind him.

"If you go, I will give you..."

Inventory Increased +275 lbs.

Inventory 1865 lbs.

I couldn't help it, had to check how much I had. Not too bad, I have to say. My goal for tonight now was to get a whole ton. I thought that was totally possible. Then again, on the other hand, I had to get the girls out of this city, all afret from the zombie Overlord's attack.

From the sounds of things, everything was going well there. Zorn was yelling so loud that I could hear him from here, even over the sounds of abilities being used.

And he himself was making a racket. As far as I could tell, he was trying to break through the wall with his axe. And then the shield. But that wasn't going to happen. At level ten the shield was just too durable. He would have had to wander around for a while, gathering an army of deadies and attacking with their cover. But he had gone nuts, and now...

Something was wrong. The sounds seemed to be dying down, and the air was full of tension. A familiar feeling. Just like it was right before...

The third phase of the System has finished!
The fourth phase is starting now.

* * *

The knight and his clanking plate armor had been wandering over endless fields for two days now. Sometimes he would come across small cities filled with the walking dead. He had also met many people along his way, but each time they had parted ways peacefully, without the use of weapons or abilities.

A fair amount of time had passed since he appeared in this world. And gradually his hatred had died down. But his compass continued stubbornly northward, forcing the knight to continue onward in that direction.

Eventually a massive city strewn with tall buildings rose into view. The knight had never seen anything like that before, so he couldn't just pass it by, and deviated from his path a bit.

"Stop!" As soon as the knight, armor clanking, approached a nearby building, a frightened voice shouted at him.

"I intend you no harm!" The large man put his hands up, showing he was unarmed. "I come in peace!"

Silence hung for a time, broken only by gust of wind on the steppe. Soon he heard another voice.

"What the hell did you forget here? Take your helmet off so I know who I'm talking to!" roared someone out of the window. This was followed by a crossbow pointed at the iron warrior.

"I am a Warrior of Light! I am the Right Hand of Justice, come to this world to punish evil!" shouted the knight in response. "If thou beest on the side of darkness, gird thyself to face me in honorable combat!"

FWIT!

At that moment an arrow whistled past the warrior, sticking into the ground behind him.

"The next one goes in your visor. Got it?" shouted the same voice, and a loaded crossbow appeared in the window again.

For a moment the knight stood there, staring into the dark opening of the window, then he shook his head and stepped forward.

Last time, when he had been attacked in the

mountains, the battle had lasted a rather long time. First they had shot a large number of arrows and attack skills at him, and then the fighters had rushed him in close combat.

They had traded blows for many hours, but nobody could get the upper hand. And once the people and the newcomer had fallen in exhaustion, they had no choice but to start talking.

In the end everything was concluded with wine and delicious fried meat. The knight had never tried such delicacies before. Especially since alcohol never existed on his world at all, so the System wine immediately loosened his inhibitions and he spend the night in unrestrained joy. Breaking all the rules of his own world.

Now the knight was ashamed of his behavior, but in the depths of his soul he knew that, should someone offer him to drink again now, he would certainly not refuse. In fact, that was why he had decided to stop in to the city. Maybe he could get another cup or two...

"I may not remove my helmet before strangers." The man tried to shrug. "But if thou shootest again, or thou speakest ill, I shall attack."

And that's what happened. As soon as he took one step forward, another arrow flew from the window. This time it landed right in the narrow gap of his visor, but then ornamentation on his armor flashed bright gold and the arrow was deflected away.

"That was dishonorable. Thou shalt pay for thine insolence!" roared the warrior, speeding up and taking a massive golden hammer from his inventory.

But the archer had no intention of getting into a real fight. He managed to get a couple more shots off, and also dropped an icicle that had appeared right in air onto his opponent. The ice exploded into a thousand pieces the second it touched the shimmering armor, and everything around was clouded with thick steam.

But once the knight ran out of that could, nobody was left in the building.

"There is nary an ounce of honor in thee!" shouted the large man into the emptiness, but the only answer was a soft rustling of wind.

But soon enough the first guests came in response to his cries. A small horde of deadies was shuffling through the area, trying to find food for themselves. So very soon their teeth were trying to gnaw through metal.

But the golden hammer easily smashed the skulls of even the armored big guys, leaving the whole horde lying on the concrete within just a few minutes.

"This world is rich with rewards..." the warrior said to himself once again, collecting the potatoes, spheres, and books of skills. He was overjoyed, since what he had gotten here was more than enough to buy him an estate on his own world and to acquire a fertile wife and also some slaves for himself.

But first he needed to fulfill his obligation and avenge his honor. There was no other way.

In spite of his hurry, the knight continued exploring the enormous metropolis. There was nothing like it on his own world. There were tall buildings all around, and strange metal carts were strewn about the streets. Even just the streets themselves aroused only fascination and admiration in him for a long time. It was as though they had been carved from rocks, but there were no cracks at all.

All of this, the whole world astonished the knight over and over again, and every day that he spent here he was left with an indelible impression that would last the rest of his life.

After the mass of deadies, people appeared again. Again the knight rushed after them, hoping to get satisfaction for their dishonorable actions. But eventually his pursuit led him to a System settlement.

The town hall, which looked like a wooden hut, was located between two tall houses, covering the entrance to the yard. It wouldn't do to go around them, since it had been placed there on purpose. The shield abutted a durable-looking concrete wall, so you would have to attack it head-on in any case.

The knight was glad to see that. Twenty armed people were arranged in a row, taking cover behind the semi-opaque veil before him. They stared at their insuperable opponent with malice in their eyes, prepared to fight to the end.

But he...

"Harumph..." The iron warrior, a head taller

than any of his opponents, took a gander at the settlement.

In addition to the fighters, staring daggers at him, he could see dozens of frightened faces.

Women, children, a pair of old men... They were entirely dependent on those men who were ready to lay down their lives to keep the stranger from getting through the shield.

"Hmm..." muttered the large man, taken aback. "You profaned me and fought dishonorably." He took another look at the terrified faces of the peaceful people and scratched his metal head. "However, I shall forgive your first offence. Act not so again. If you fight, then as is right and proper." He pointed a threatening finger at the defenders, then turned and walked off.

Though his soul was craving battle, his honor would not allow him to leave defenseless people with no chance of survival. Without fighters, that settlement would eventually come under attack from zombies, and then they would all die.

"They did fight dishonorably. Perhaps it is acceptable among them..." the knight murmured to himself, wandering through the empty streets. "And I came here completely... My father spoke truly, and I was a fool not to listen..."

The large man headed onward, towards the direction his compass was pointing. He occasionally encountered zombies, killing all of them with gusto, filling his inventory with mounds of rewards and crystals.

"Hmm. I could take some victuals..." He

sighed, stopping into the first building he passed. There he collapsed onto a couch, and a blue potato appeared in his hand. "Bon appétit to me!" He recalled the well-known phrase and opened the reward.

Saliva started dripping out of his visor. To be expected since a number of delectable dishes had appeared before him all at once. His ancestors had spoken of such thing, but the knight had been able to try such delicacies for the first time in his life only once he had come to this world.

His metal hands immediately grasped his helmet to tear it off his head. And soon a massive green face came into view. Long fangs poked out of the knight's mouth, with an unreasonably large jaw and no nose at all.

Anybody would have called him an orc. But the orc himself had only learned about that when he was talking to the people in the mountains. He was in disbelief that they had heard so much about his race and it flattered him quick a bit.

Licking his lips, the knight prepared to dig in to a large, still-sizzling piece of meat, but before he could sink his teeth in the tidbit, a message popped up in front of his eyes.

The System in this world is updating to a new phase.

Do you accept the update or will you return to your home world? Yes/No

Warning! If you should accept this phase, returning to your home world will become impossible using the standard method!

"God's wounds!" swore the large man, leaping off the couch. "Oh Light, incinerate my soul!" he cursed, understanding what the message implied. "May God strike my genitals! What do I choose?"

* * *

Yoshikezu: Emperor! We have surrounded the traitors! Do we have your order to attack?

"Ha!" exclaimed the man, jumping off of his new throne. "Got it! And now..."

Emperor: Attack, but not at full force... Wait for him to come to their aid.

According to his plan, the soldiers would act like it was a raid, and the new sovereign would be forced to appear in person to help them.

Then the Emperor himself would appear to execute the unlucky foreigners. Or maybe take some alive, and find out where their capital was and burn it to the ground!

The man broke out into wicked laughter, terrifying his servant, then covered himself in flames and shot into the air.

The comet rose to about 200 feet and rushed toward the mountain off in the distance.

At first the Emperor had simply wanted to burn the traitors and forget about this unfortunate situation. But his enemy's insulting messages had forced him to be clever. He would trick him and personally burn him alive. And he was even happy about getting to take part in the battle himself. To punish that asshole.

It didn't take much to get to the settlement. It took the man just about an hour, and in that time his forces had managed to deploy fully. Precision strikes rained down on the shield, not even letting the defenders leave their hiding places.

The Emperor, to inspire fear and horror in the hearts of his enemies, flew around the settlement a few times. That way every one of its inhabitants could see his majesty in its full glory. And he took indescribable pleasure from it.

Terrified faces staring up into the sky were his favorite sight, after all.

"You can beg for mercy! But there won't be any! HAHAHA!" He proclaimed, pausing right above the dome. "No one can help you now!"

"F*ck off!" came a shout from down below, causing the Emperor to lose his cool and nearly diving down there.

"What? You dare?! Who sa—" But the System interrupted the furious man, covered in flames. The attack suddenly stopped and silence resounded. Absolutely everyone stared off into space, attentively reading the message before their eyes.

The third phase of the System has finished!
The fourth phase is starting now.
The difficulty has increased...
Chat has been improved...

CHAPTER 15

The third phase of the System has finished!
The fourth phase is starting now.
The difficulty has increased...
Chat has been improved...
Auction has been improved.
Language pack has been installed.
The level cap of 30 has been removed.
A level cap of 40 has been instated.
Preparations for the next phase have begun...

THE SOUND OUTSIDE had stopped. But only for a couple of minutes. Soon the furious, soul-piercing wails of the maddened deadie could be heard again, and I quickly recalled my unfinished business.

"Get behind me!" I appeared in the room where the girls were hiding. "Quickly!"

The froze in surprise for a few seconds but

pulled themselves together and soon realized what was happening. And followed my orders to the letter.

We had to get out quickly, but as straight as possible. Even though a lot of the inhabitants were hiding in their homes, still there were somehow a bunch of soldiers outside. They didn't pay any attention to three girls dressed in rags, however.

But where was I gonna put the other two? It was silly to take dead weight. But putting them back in the barracks could cause problems too.

"What's with you?" I asked the two girls tagging along behind me and my charge.

"Uh, we..." The braver one of them stammered, but was distracted by a soldier running past.

We had stopped in a dark alley, where I wasn't visible at all. Plus, my Shadow Set effect was working right and nobody could focus on me unless I was under a streetlight or a flashlight.

"Okay. You got someone to go back to? Family in the barracks?" I asked, right in their faces.

They just shook their heads in response. Orphans, then. There were a lot of them now, among us too. What would they have to look forward to, if they stayed here? Most likely exactly what I had just saved them from.

Ah, screw. I would take them with and then figure it out. The motorcycle was big, Zorn would only have to make one trip. If he survived, that was. But there was so much sound coming from the wall that I was really beginning to doubt that.

"Hey! You all get in the barracks! Right now!" I

heard a voice say somewhere behind me.

Shit. We got caught anyway.

Not me, but my charges. But that was just until...

Three guards came up to us, and I took a step back, watching their actions and unfurling my slungshot.

But I wasn't expecting to see this. I thought they would try to grab the girls, frozen and staring at me with hope in their eyes, and carry them off, but the first soldier to approach immediately raised his hand to slap the disobedient slave girl.

Inventory Increased +30 lbs.

But he never got to. My metal bar, flying at incredible speed, slammed into the idiot's head, tossing him five feet away. Well, what do you expect? You have to keep your wits about you!

"Aaaah!" shrieked the girls, the second I activated my Aura of Fear. Good, they were getting their senses back, little by little. A bit ago they would simply have frozen in fear if I had used that skill.

"W-w-w-who are y-you?!" shouted the soldier nearest to me.

I wasn't going to answer. Not even in rhyme, though the thought did occur. I simply slammed my spiked ball into his temple. Nice and easy.

Inventory Increased +20

The last one didn't even scream. Simply turned around and rushed off into the dark narrow alleyway somewhere. I dematerialized, and, as was fitting for a ghost, first scared him, then, jangling my chains, sent him towards the light.

"One sec," I smiled at the former slaves, appearing before them for a bit. "Don't go anywhere."

I almost forgot. I had to go back to the Paralyzer's mansion. I had left some very valuable stuff there, not to mention the crystals that every person had in their chest, which I had totally forgotten.

I had already carefully looted all the soldiers down to their skivvies, and their equipment was safe and sound in my inventory. It didn't take long to find their crystals either. They were in the same place that the zombies' crystals were, around the solar plexus.

Wise old Asians had already informed the world long ago that somewhere around there was the focal point of spiritual power or something like that. It didn't seem too farfetched now, since the System certainly wouldn't have put such an important thing right in that place for nothing.

All in all I managed to get one green one and six transparent ones. They looked completely different from those that zombies had, or even animals. Transparent, pure, and...

With a fire inside? Yeah, actually. If you looked closely you could make out a spark flickering within. I had never seen anything like that before, probably cause I hadn't been paying attention.

As soon as I finished getting the crystals, I led the girls toward the exit.

It wasn't hard to get through the city. Right now the guards had better things to do than deal with slave girls running off somewhere unknown. They could deal with that later, but now the slaughter at the wall was ramping up. And more and more forces were being redirected over there.

Once in a while I fly up to let Zorn know where his enemies were hiding. But eventually I stopped, realizing that the deadie was so far out of his mind that he wasn't paying any attention to the mark.

He was simply rushing back and forth, trying to do as much damage to the enemy as he could. Not caring at all for his own safety.

Along the way I had to finish off two groups of overly-curious guards, and even five workers. We ran smack into them, and they wanted to call for help, but never managed to. Seems my slungshot can work pretty fast, especially if it was already out and ready to go.

I wouldn't have even touched them, but why the hell were they calling the guards? We would simply have run right past them, no harm no foul, but no. They just hadn't liked the black figure that appeared as if out of nowhere in the light of the fire blazing right in the street.

I needed to reach level 30. No. I needed to reach level 40. My class skill would gain two additional features at once, which meant I could wreak much more havoc. Like giving someone else the ability to dematerialize. Then we could leave this settlement no problem.

But for now I was still level 20, and I had to think of a way to get through the wall in corporeal form. Right up there were a whole lot of armed people, and it would be pretty rough to beat them in a fair fight.

Good for me that I'm just not very fair.

Frag Grenade (rare)

My face broke out in a smile in spite of me. Especially since a little pomegranate the size of an ostrich egg had appeared in my hand! It was chilling to imagine how much this thing was going to blow.

But why imagine? We had to try it! Especially since the description was completely clear. Throw it, and wherever it lands it will leave a crater about 15 feet wide! And more than that, thousands of pieces of shrapnel would fly out all over like bullets, damaging anything in its path that hadn't managed to take cover.

And only my charges were going to be taking cover.

BLAM!

The powerful explosion echoed throughout the whole settlement. Shrapnel whistled through the air, tearing out sizeable pieces of stone from the walls of houses, overloading the dome so much that it began to ripple, and tearing apart the living forces of the enemy in their path. Each piece ripped out significant chunks of flesh as they flew towards their destination. I just floated in the air, enjoying the sight of it.

Yeah, it was a cool thing. I would only throw things like that. It was pretty heavy, sure, but thanks to my dematerialization I could easily use it without endangering myself.

"Now get ready..." I appeared by the former slaves and stared into space.

Kasp: Eva! Can you open up a portal by... Oh, who the hell knows. About 10 miles north of us...

Now I realized that I couldn't explain where we were. Plus, I had been sitting in the passenger's seat and couldn't remember the way. I could get back, no problem, since I could fly straight there, but opening a portal...

Eva: Just share your coordinates, what are you waiting for?

Share what? If I were eating or drinking right now, I would have choked on it. But lucky me.

Eva: Right, I forget that you... You're no good with technology. It's a new update in the chat. Find the button, everything makes sense.

She was right. There it was, the button. And next to it there was a whole bunch of new functions that I hadn't checked out yet. I would have to do that, but for now...

Eva: Alright! It's ready! You'll have your portal in three seconds!

Clever girl. She could pull it off when she wanted to.

The space right beyond the hole in the wall started cracking at the seams, and the fires of our own city suddenly were visible in the darkness of the night.

"Run!" I pointed the girls in the direction of portal, taking out my weapon, prepared to fight off any attacks. We had spent too much time messing around here, and the sound of the explosion had started to draw in divisions of soldiers. "And you come right here, darlings." A nasty smile appeared on my face as I disappeared into thin air. Everything but my metal ball, rotating one turn per second.

Inventory 2265 lbs.

That's done. And with no effort, since I still had 30% health left. Turned out our enemies weren't stupid. And the enemy's mages quickly shot back at where the danger was coming from. I did withstand a few hits by attacking abilities, but then it got too dangerous. Anyway, I have a ton in my inventory, a couple dozen pure crystals in my inventory, and I could head home with no worries.

But I should check on Zorn. I could still hear the sounds of battle over there, even though I had distracted some of the forces away.

* * *

The third phase of the System has finished...

The deadie, run through by a spear, noticed that everyone around him was distracted by the System message. He paid no attention to it and, taking advantage of the moment, leapt to his feet.

"ARRRRGGH!" The monster teeth sank into soft flesh, tearing through the nearest opponent's neck.

Blood spurted everyone, but his victim didn't die yet. As if he had gotten his second wind, Zorn dove into the thick of the fray, taking out people with his own bare hands.

His finger sunk into flesh, tearing out whole chunks of meat. The deadie tossed those chunks into his mouth, swallowing immediately, not even bothering to chew. The holes in his body slowly began to close up, and he became more and more active, taking down anyone who got in his way.

The soldiers quickly realized that they had gone outside the walls too soon. So their whole crew rushed back under the shield, although only a few of them made it back. The rest were simply torn to pieces by the rabid beast.

"What kind of monster even are you?"

"Kill it!"

"Keep up the pressure, brothers!"

At first shouting could be heard, then a whole gamut of attack abilities came crashing down on Zorn's head. The air literally exploded with so much charge. Chunks of ice, massive boulders, fireballs, and sparks of lightning flew from the walls.

But none of that bothered him at all. His dead flesh was smoking, covered in ash, but steadfastly resisting every attack, and the zombie himself just kept on tearing at his enemy's shield, once again completely forgetting about everything else in the world.

But the deadie did not forget to dodge the strongest attacks. Somehow, even though his eyes were shrouded in fury, he still wasn't going to get himself killed over it. Somewhere in the depths of his soul, the fires of reason were still lit, constantly reminding him of his ultimate goal. To save his granddaughter, any way possible. Even if the price were his life or soul, the zombie was ready to pay it.

His axe had long turned to dust, and he had no other weapons in his inventory. But there was no need of one, when you yourself were the most powerful weapon for annihilating everything that was alive.

Sometimes small groups of zombies would come running to sound, and the Overlord was not above taking them under his control. Sometimes it even allowed him cover from the majority of the humans' attacks, although the groups of zombies were finished off pretty quickly that way. Not even getting to attack the shield.

Over time he got more and more distracted by constantly annoying notifications about chat messages, but Zorn just brushed them off. His sight was focused somewhere in the center of the settlement, and his only desire was to kill. Everyone.

He had read the conclusions that Kasp had come to. And now it was impossible for him to think about anything else. Just because they had the intention of harming his granddaughter, Zorn was prepared to destroy every living thing within a 10-mile radius. To punish everyone involved, making them suffer before he finally ended them.

Eventually his enemy's attacks began to slacken. Something had distracted the defenders, forcing them to divert their forces, but even so, the rest of them were able to continue fighting back.

That was much easier to do when your opponent couldn't get past the shield.

The effect of the meat he had eaten had completely disappeared by now, and his wounds were no longer healing quite as fast. And so Zorn was gradually becoming weaker, taking more and more damage.

At some point the zombie got a hard hit to the head, throwing him 10 feet back and knocking him into the ground.

He tried jumping up to his feet, but they wouldn't let him get up. His invisible opponent hit him once more, sending the Overlord flying for a short time, his back slamming into the nearest building. The concrete cracked, but even after that Zorn found the strength in himself to get back on his feet.

He kept on trying to get to his invisible foe, but the foe just waited him out, damaging him only when it was most convenient for him. The deadie roared, knowing how powerless he was against an enemy like that, but never stopped trying until another hit pinned him to the ground. This was followed by his chest being pierced through by spears in multiple places, and after that he could no longer rise up.

Only now did he feel his death approaching. Every second fear was coming closer to overpowering his soul, causing every muscle to tremble. Then Zorn was hit by a wave of cold, finally losing the ability to move entirely.

"No! I won't give up! Fight me, you beasts!" Despite his mounting fear, the deadie bared his teeth and sought his opponent with his eyes. But there the attacks stopped. The enemy, as if to taunt him, remained invisible, but was in no hurry to end the dead monster's suffering.

All the while his numb flesh began hardening, covered with a coat of ice, and his consciousness sank into darkness.

* * *

"You're supposed to be sentient, but you're so dumb..." I came up to Zorn, making sure that the System notes were still over him, then turned to look at his opponent. "But you know some tricks. I respect that."

"Who the hell are you? And what kind of monster is this?" The man was about 40, dressed in a gray cloak and armed with a long spear. He was staring at me in surprise.

His hands were starting to shake more and more, and his frightened gaze, which didn't really go well with such masculine features, gave away his true feelings. But what else could you expect, since I had activated all my auras to the full? And now it was just a matter of time before our opponent either ran away or froze.

"He's the monster? You go look at your guys over there." I nodded troops the mass of troops gathered on the wall. "Pedophiles, the lot of them, nothing else."

After I said that a throwing knife came flying

at me. I had never seen anything like this before. A new weapon? Or handmade?

Throwing Knife (uncom.) (Bleeding) 37/100

Description: Made by Master Kozich. Mana 10/10. Bleeding is an active skill. Upon hitting the target, it causes serious bleeding which can only be stopped using healing or local application of a health potion. Damage is variable. Costs 10 mana.

So it was handmade. And pretty tricky. But only if the target couldn't dematerialize. I, as you know, can. And I do.

"You an idiot? We were talking just fine." I picked the knife that flew through me just a few seconds ago up off the ground. "Or did I offend you?"

The man stared at me in shock for a moment, then collected his strength, charging forward, but there was no trace of his former speed left. He was frozen, you see. How sad.

"Arrrggh!" He waved his spear, ready to stab me in the chest. The tip started glowing, but I de-materialized at the very last second.

CRACK!

The steel ball flew right into the man's nose, breaking the bones of his face and leaving a deep dent. He flew backwards, falling to the ground, croaking, but I didn't manage to get off a second hit.

The fighters leapt out of the settlement and rushed toward us. A few people, quickly crossing the distance, covered their leader with their bodies, and the others headed towards Zorn, splayed out on the ground.

Damn. Well, screw it. We'll deal with it now. I only had to call for a portal...

Kasp: Give me another portal. Sending the deadie back to you.

Eva: One sec...

MoonWind: Kasp! We are under attack! We can't hold out for long!

I saw that last message by accident. Turned out he had been sending me messages like that for a while now, and each time the texts got more and more intense.

Never rains but it pours... Okay, screw these pieces of shit. I wasn't planning to get revenge on anyone, so let them live. We did what we came here for.

I flew over to Zorn and cranked my Aura of Fear up to full, chasing off the idiots running up to get their free experience, and one second later, once the portal had opened up, I tossed the unconscious body of the deadie through it.

"Watch yourselves, now." Finally, I smiled at my new enemies and, winking cheerfully at the terrified soldiers, disappeared into the hole in space.

CHAPTER 16

"OPEN ONE UP FOR JAPAN," I said quietly, stepping out of the portal arch. "But... give me three minutes."

Having said that, I disappeared into thin air and flew off to the garden. At first I was intending to put Gosha in my inventory, but I stopped myself in time. If I took him now, the big guys would start doing what they love most. Smashing up the place. And if they trampled the garden... No, no point in awakening the inner demons of that brainless head. Although I could trample the plants and say that the Emperor did it. Then I almost certainly wouldn't even have to join in the defense at all.

"Get the big guys out of here. Hurry, we're gonna go fight the Japanese!" I appeared behind the cactus, catching the head who had fallen towards the ground through force of habit.

"Errm? What? The hell? The Redhorn will

flower soon! I can't now!" shrieked the head, but seeing my harsh face he gave in. "Give me half an hour to finish tilling…"

Tilling? The Redhorn was a darn carrot! It needed tilling? Oh, whatever. I didn't have half an hour, but ten minute's rest wouldn't get in my way, since it made sense to take some time to get ready.

"Ten minutes, no more." I shook my head. "Get ready."

"One green crystal," Gosha answered shamelessly, and the cactus shrugged his shoulders. "Give me a blue one and I'll be done in five."

Greedy prick! I wondered how he would be tilling if I gave him a purple one.

"Here." Seeing his face change gave me an indescribable feeling of joy when I handed him the epic gift and stepped back a few feet.

"Th-this is for m-m-me?" Gosha's lips were already trembling. "Cyrush, take me." His voice cracked there at the end, and I nearly broke out laughing.

"You got three minutes."

"Oh, I'm ready!" The cactus set the happy head in place. "Who are we killing?"

"What about tilling?"

"Sod it!" He waved dismissively at the garden and tromped off towards the arch. The big guys followed after him, heading for their pen. "Come on, let's go!"

Good thing he hadn't snorted it right away. Otherwise I would have had to calm him down.

Leaving Gosha and his desire to move mountains, I sent a few messages and warned the soldiers that they soon would have to fight. Possibly to the death.

According to our Japanese guy, a few hundred enemies had come to raid the settlement. And not just some weaklings, but locked-and-loaded Systemniks.

"Kasp! Is everything okay?" I heard a sweet feminine voice behind me. Which would have been whatever, except when I turned around I saw the elf girl.

"Kamanta?" was all I was able to get out in my shock. Only then did I remember that the System had mentioned something about this.

Language packs had been installed, it said. So now I could understand aliens? Or just everyone? Well, I would check that in Japan soon. Now I was interested in talking with Grugg. I was pretty sure that his "Ugh!" just meant "Ugh!" Most likely translation won't do us any good there at all.

"Kamanta. Just get ready to take a gold class. Or tell your brother if you don't want to be a fire mage. Got it? Do not follow me." I got close to the girl, making her blue skin flush. I didn't even think she could do that.

"Uh-huh…" the embarrassed elf girl squeaked and took a step back.

Exceptional. We could really use the fire.

Our people gathered pretty quickly. Brownie showed up, then soldiers, then Glash flew in, then the Trainer galloped in on the back of her gigantic dog. Ah, what a fearsome beast! The dog looked like a killing machine. But that didn't stop it from coming up and licking my face, leaving a gallon of spittle on it.

"Enough! Stop! Olly, get her off me!" I had to materialize, but the dog didn't even consider standing down. Honestly though, deep down, I was pretty happy. Cats might sometimes be the biggest f*cking pricks, but with dogs I had a completely different relationship. They were straightforward. And that meant something. You could never have a relationship like that with human beings.

"*&$*!" At some point the portal activated and Grugg stepped out. His face was stretched out in a satisfied grin, and he continued to greet us in some language that we all understood. "Cocksuckers!"

"You've been swearing this whole time?" Brownie was surprised. "I thought you were moo-ing..."

"That's cause you're a dumbf*ck!" Grugg smiled. "But that's normal for people like you."

"This beef-ass motherf*cker..." Slob had crept up unnoticed. Judging from his face he hadn't slept for at least two days straight. His eyes were twitching and his face was gaunt. A small dragon was sitting on the back of his head. It was the spirit of heat that I myself had made not too long ago. It was stuck to his bald spot and seemed pleased as punch. I wasn't about to get between the lovebirds and, pretending I hadn't noticed the spirit, simply nodded at the Berserker.

"And you're a piece of shit." Grugg shrugged and immediately got distracted, forgetting about the bearded man entirely.

Oh, how I missed this. When everyone is swearing at each other, your soul sings. It's like there's a cozy, homey atmosphere all of a sudden. I wasn't about to stop anyone and just watched all this affectionate profanity that the bull had started.

But we couldn't wait. In theory we could go now, but I still had one thing left to do. The level. Our treasury had been significantly cleared out after that battle. I mean, I had cleaned out the crystals entirely. But we should be up to our ears in experience!

Now everything was so much more complicated... How many experience points did I need to level it up? I couldn't even estimate that!

Treasury:

Experience — 24867

Crystals — 536

The numbers looked great. Amazing, even! But I wasn't sure. I mean, maybe that much experience was only enough to get a couple of levels, who knows? I knew the people were killing a bunch of zombies. Sometimes even a whole lot. By myself I could never kill anywhere near that much, no doubt about that. But my slungshot mostly picked just powerful opponents, so it was up to the rest of them to take down the normal deadies.

I knew they were killing mutants too, but they were definitely not doing that alone, which meant the experience was shared amongst the whole group.

So...

Found it! There happened to be a tab in the interface for distributing experience from the treasury. Doing it for the whole settlement was completely normal, plus the System had just had a new update literally one hour ago, so everything should be working without a hitch.

Kasp

Level 25

Experience 40131/41000

Not too bad, I must say. I would like to know where those numbers came from and when I managed to get so much, but... Now I had another question in mind. Let's say I spend a thousand now. Then what, would I need even more than forty for the next level?

Well, there's only one way to find out.

Level Up +1

Kasp

Level 26

Experience 41131/44000

Alright. Thank you, System, for not screwing me over here.

As far as I could tell, every level required me to get three thousand experience. That was totally fine. It meant I had to kill three thousand normal level one zombies. Or a couple of superpowered ones. Everything was totally fair, no need to scream and shout at tech support.

Hmm, they did redo the chat, so maybe they

added that feature, along with the others. I wouldn't mind flooding the System with complaints. Let her sort it all out.

Alright. Here we go.

Level Up +1

Level Up +1

…

Level Up +1

Ah, that's good! The treasury is empty, but now I'm a bit stronger. What level are we?

Kasp

Level 32

Experience 64998/68000

The next one definitely wouldn't be for a while. But that was only if my vassals kept lazing around. I couldn't let that happen. I would have to get them hunting, plus I could work on getting stronger myself. Soon enough we would be getting some rare classes for those who hadn't managed to get any yet.

A couple dozen people were sitting around waiting for the right awesome class to show up on the list, and they had all been warned that we were going to clear it out.

Okay. Level 32. I put 40 stat points into Conduits immediately. I mean, even without them I would be doing just fine, but you can always be better! I know that for sure.

The stat rose to 58 but, recalling that long-ago test where I buffed it up to 100, I already wanted a lot more.

I closed the stats and set my attention on the

list of skills. I already had some points there, and they were just enough to get Energy Vampire up to level 30. And it got a new additional effect!

Energy Vampire (rare) (30)

Description: Passive skill. Steals mana and power from all those within a 30-foot radius. The speed of siphoning is from 0.3% to 3% of their reserves per minute.

Additional Effect. Range Regulation allows you to regulate the radius of the activity. The range extends from 30 to 120 meters. The effectiveness of the skill depends on the extent of the range.

Additional Effect. Single Target allows you to concentrate the effect of the skill onto a single target. The range of the effect is 100 yards, increases the effectiveness threefold.

Additional Effect. Reverse Flow allows you to regulate the speed of siphoning, even into the negative. That means you can give your energy to all creatures in the surrounding area.

Regulate... That was much better than if I could only toss out all my juice willy-nilly.

I immediately tested how it worked. Although we might be in a time crunch, as long as our enemy had not moved to an active phase, I could allow myself the time to get familiar with my new capabilities.

Plus, the army had come to the city a long time ago. The Emperor himself had been flying around over the dome for about half an hour. Spells and shots would come flying at the shield every once in a while but still it was all so... Half-hearted. That led me to the conclusion that they were just trying to trick me.

Was it a trap? Eh, whatever. The important thing was that I had time to prepare and spend my points, everything else was irrelevant.

I couldn't manage to fully stop the effect of the aura. No matter what, I either had to draw out of the surrounding forces or give them back my own. Many just the tiniest amount, but I would never be able to stop the process ever again. But it was a completely different thing now that I could drop the speed pretty low. Nobody would even notice. The only thing was that they might have to eat and rest a little bit more often, nothing more than that. So I was pretty happy.

What now? I still had 40 ability points left, so I could level up the rest of them, but was there any point? Sooner or later I would find something really cool at the auction or after fighting a powerful monster.

So cool that all my earlier abilities will seem like nothing more than child's toys. So, let's save them, alright? I'm already a lot stronger, and I'll be able to beat that Emperor in a completely non-traditional way. Like nobody has ever beaten him before.

Name: *Kasp*
Level: *32*
Class: Ghost
Stats:
Body (42): Strength (12), Dexterity (13), Consti-

tution (13)

Mind (51): Intelligence (18), Reaction (17), Perception (16)

Spirit (87): Repository (29), Conduits (58)

Available Stat Points: 0

Skills:

Active: Appropriation (epic) (20), Aura of Fear (rare) (1), Aura of Ice (epic) (10)

Passive: Energy Vampire (rare) (30)

Additional: Dematerialization (Class Skill)

Available Skill Points: 14

Abilities:

Martial:

Craft: Concentration of Energy (10)

Available Ability Points: 36

Auction

Inventory 2430 lbs.

Oh, the Auction was gone. That was unexpected. But the System clearly had seen that there was some work to do there. Probably it had become its own feature and now you could find stuff more easily there.

Before I wanted to hit the designers in the head with a chair for the awful interface and the many examples of their obvious loathing for their users.

And I was right. Now the auction was with the basic functions of the interface with its own dedicated button. Right between the inventory and the settings.

Kasp: How are you over there? Have they attacked yet? You all alive?

MoonWind: The shield is at 50%, no casualties yet. Two wounded, but they were still outside when it started. Are you coming soon?

Kasp: Right away.

I checked just to make sure. They could wait a bit.

The auction had changed entirely. Now you could separate items into groups, arranging them by price and popularity. You could also rate the seller and, most importantly, make your own trading platform!

I wasn't about to fiddle with the settings, but it was clear enough. You could now open up a System shop and put the goods you made yourself up for sale there, for a small fee. I would have to ask the Manager what features it had. Probably the same ones, just in a better format.

But that wasn't the most important thing.

System! I know you can hear me. Now I'm 100% sure of it...

In addition to the regular auction there was now a special one for settlements! There, in addition to handmade goods, you could also purchase resources! They would immediately be sent to your storehouse, and you wouldn't have to put any effort into it at all. Pay, get, and build to your heart's content!

And didn't just have to use crystals to pay for things! At the settlement auction, although I would prefer to call it a market, you could buy goods and resources with experience! It would be taken from your treasury and sent to the new owner.

Of course I wouldn't be buying anything with it. But I was definitely going to be selling. I would level up myself and others. I mean, just Anton could bring us massive profits if he just started churning out normal power stations and lights. No matter how far I flew around this world, everyone was still using shitty torches. Only very rarely would you come across a System lamp or flashlight, and even those mostly came from irons. No way you could ever mass produce them.

Shit. Fine, they could wait a little longer.

Okay, what could I offer?

I headed straight for Anton in his lair and found him, as expected, hard at work. What did surprise me, though, was his new apprentice following at his heels, a cute-looking girl as well. And she did her work exceptionally well. I was thrilled to witness how that girl finished her tasks with such aplomb.

Without a word and still smiling, she smacked our head engineer on the back of the head, and he immediately turned away from his work.

"Ah!" The boy dropped some small bits off the table. Some normal-looking circuit boards with tons of wires sticking out all over them, something like a soldering iron, and other junk. All of that scattered across the stone floor, some of it rolling under the table and other furniture. "Why so hard?"

"You won't get it otherwise," purred the girl, never dropping the sweet smile. "Would you like another?"

Anton immediately started taking his coat off, and then they took him off to get lunch. Looked like he had forgotten to eat again. That coat had some serious side effects, but the positives clearly outweighed the negatives.

"Wait!" I appeared in the passage connected to the exit. "You, darling, go make some food for now and set the table. We need to have a chat."

The girl really was complex. She threw an angry glance at me, but couldn't look too long.

My gaze was even more angry. You're barking up the wrong tree, sweetheart.

"Get on," I waved her out of the production area and she, realizing she wasn't going to get the better of me, looked over at Anton. Then a few seconds later headed off for the exit.

"Alright, I'm done for," whispered the boy, miserably, as soon as she disappeared behind the door. "You've basically just got me killed."

Laughing heartily, I made the boy show me all his latest work and productions, ready to pick the most useful ones. And practically all of them were, except one, of course, which was just strange and incomprehensible.

"Just don't tell her. This is my secret project…" The boy tensed up, taking a device out from under a mountain of junk, one that looked like a cross between a megaphone and an electrical kettle.

Healthifier (not) (norm.)
Description: Made by Master Gnominumbus. Requires an electric current. Upon activation creates a wave of health that positively affects the general

state of the body (description is fundamental incorrect, refer to the inventor)

Okay. That meant you could make a misleading description. And if you tried to trick future users, say by making a bomb and calling it something else entirely, the System would add its own edits.

"I didn't know that that would happen with the description. I wanted to give her a present, but it didn't work out..." Anton looked down in shame.

"So what does this thing actually do?" I had a hunch it was nothing good. But Anton was a decent guy. No way this thing was lethal or could harm you. I mean, maybe it would scare the girl, the but it couldn't be that bad...

"She can't handle it when the air is dry. And when it's hot. She came here from the north somewhere, and she makes it like she wants it..."

"This is a drier and a heater all at once?" I burst out laughing and the boy nodded yes.

What a trickster this is! Ah, I was impressed. He had tried to get one over on her at least, and I respected that. I do that stuff too, love it, good at it.

In the end I took some lightbulbs, three weak power stations, and a couple of new inventions from his workshop. A paralyzing collar that he wanted to put on his overseer. The nice thing about it was that you could activate the paralysis from a distance using a remote. That would definitely come in handy for somebody.

And a rare class of energy knife. You could use

it both as a weapon and in your daily life. If the description was to be believed, it even cut through steel up to two inches thick. Because the length of the blade wouldn't last more than that. Just for ten seconds. Then you would have to charge it with a blue crystal and wait for it to cool down.

That wasn't for sale, certainly not. I put it right in my inventory. A weapon like that could turn out to be interesting.

I finished up with the trading platform pretty quick. It was no problem to deal with, and within a few minutes all the items were in the System store.

Done and done. All we could now was wait. If everything got bought I would get a few thousand experience all at once. I wasn't considering lowering the prices since there were very few objects like the ones Anton made on the market. I might even say there were none at all.

On the way back to the portal I send the boy a few messages, outlining the devices I wanted to see in the near future. I also advised him to delegate some parts of his work to other people. I mean, once you made a thing basically anybody could copy it. Let him focus exclusively on invention. If we needed resources then we would get them. At least I could grace him with a bunch of crystals, not like I was hurting on that front.

"Hey, what the hell are we waiting around here for you for? You're screwing around and I have to stand around with this dumbass?" Slob greeted me in his usual manner.

"Ignore him. Numbskull." Grugg waved his hand. "But yeah. When are we getting our asses outta here?"

"Same question over here!" Gosha said, joining the conversation. "I'm dying to snort that crystal, with relish and right now!" The purple crystal was still lying in the cactus's hand, and the head was unable to tear his eyes off it.

"Take me with you!" I heard a high-pitched man's voice. I looked around, surprised, and caught sight of a chubby man of indeterminate age. "I have a rare class! I'm a Healer!"

Ah, level ten. Without thinking I shook my head, telling the newcomer no. He tried squeaking something about how useful he was, but as soon as I vanished into the crowd of people waiting for me, the man immediately gave up. He couldn't get past Cyrush and Grugg. Even I couldn't have.

But we would have to speak later. A blue class, healing on top of that... I recalled the old man who had been trying to save everyone around him. But he should have saved himself. Only I can trust people that much, and I don't do that even when I can read their minds. Just a little bit has to change in their minds and there you go, the person is having second thoughts about being loyal to me.

"Can you open the portal outside the settlement?" I asked as approached Eva. "But just for me. In secret..."

The girl first eyed me suspiciously then looked over at the milling crowd.

"Where do they go?"

"We might not even need them." A wicked smile was coming to my face, making Eva flinch, just a tiny bit. "Eh, what's wrong? You know I'm a good person..."

CHAPTER 17

THE EMPEROR HAD BEEN FLYING around the settlement for some time, quietly swearing to himself. The curses were mostly directed towards me, but he also went over his officers and even had a bit left to give the inhabitants of the settlement a few choice words.

I didn't understand it, to be honest. What was he so pissed about? What the inhabitants have to do with it? Okay, I beat him on the battlefield, so what? I was the one who won. My actions led to his defeat, it was my wishes and my goals that were the source of the conflict. And yeah, I would try to come to agreement, if only the Emperor wasn't such an idiot.

So all we could do now was get rid of him. I couldn't leave messed-up people like this skulking around in any case. Especially since I couldn't even read his mind!

The flame covered his whole body, and as soon as I got close it started damaging me. The flame didn't cause pain in the normal sense, but definitely an unpleasant feeling. One that was even worse than pain. It was like your soul was being burned away.

For a long time that idiot just flew around in the sky, so I stuck to him, gradually drawing off all his available energy.

Eventually the Emperor started to feel tired and landed on the edge of a tall building, staring downward.

"Bastard! Prick! I'll burn you! To ash!" Everything he was fantasizing about. Some more swearing, "Freak!" And that was insulting!

"I'm a perfectly good-looking young man, at least!" I appeared behind him and aimed a powerful kick square into his backside. The solid hit caused him to lose his balance and fall screaming downward.

The Emperor was completely out of mana, and he shouldn't be able to do any real damage to me. The important thing was not to let him get more than 300 feet away, otherwise the thread drawing his mana to me would be broken.

"Oh, no way!" Eventually the Emperor came to his senses, adjusting his flight and regaining his equilibrium. Then he took a blue vial out of his inventory and was about to down it, but...

"Ghaa!" The spiked metal ball flying into his solar plexus caused him to choke, and all the contents of the little bottle flew right back out. If he had any mana then I would have a bad time. Especially if you factored in how much I had been able to get out of him. That was more than twice as much as I needed.

It should be said that he didn't mana either for flying or for maintaining the flame around him. It seemed like that was an additional feature of his class skill. Nothing but gold, and he was a gold class. I could also turn into a ghost in practically any situation. All I needed was one speck of mana and there you go, I was a ghost.

My slungshot started spinning again, but the bastard could dodge a controlled hit. I had to hand it to him, he sure didn't have any issues with his stats.

"Ha! You thought you could defeat me that easily? I AM THE EMPER—"

I didn't let him finish. I had no mind for chit-chat right now. I had to finish this nonsense as quickly as possible and figure out the System update.

But this time too the man was able to block the hit from the slugshot, pulling a shield shimmering with multiple colors out of his inventory at the last moment.

Sparks flew from the hit in all directions while my opponent tried to attack back. For that he had grabbed an uncommon sword that sliced through the air where I had been just a second before.

I felt that that thing could definitely damage me. It wasn't just a sword covered in flame. I had to act carefully.

The Emperor knew that too. After blocking multiple hits with his shield in succession, he realized that nobody was intending to play around here. So he finally shut his trap.

After blocking one more shot he pressed the attack and, having observed how the metal ball moved, struck a blow with his flaming sword.

And the son-of-a-bitch hit. I wasn't able to block that terrible blow and my health bar went down by about a fifth. It was a massive hit, no argument. But right after that I shut off my class skill and appeared right in front of my opponent, throwing a flashbang right at him.

He covered himself with his shield to block it, but the off-white egg exploded, lighting up the whole area with a blinding flash. The sound echoed through the whole city, attacking your ears, and for a second my enemy lost his spatial orientation.

I let out my slungshot and started raining blows on him, while he covered himself with his shield and flew backward, trying to put some distance between us.

No, he won't get way... Especially since he quickly ran into the wall of a house and was left with no avenue of retreat.

CRACK!

He couldn't cover his legs. Too bad. The metal ball breaks bones quite nicely, and I couldn't pass up the opportunity.

His knee cracked loudly, causing the Emperor to let out a muffled whimper. Only now could I enjoy watching the fear in his eyes. The terror. He had realized that he might die.

The fear and pain had given him strength. The fire covering his whole body began to explode with tongues of flame rushing straight at me. I had to put some space between us, and that was when the Emperor, covering his shield with fire and sending it flying, got out another vial of blue liquid.

And that trick worked. Now my opponent had stopped shouting threats and raging. And that meant he had become much much more danger-ous. With his mind was working at full throttle, the Emperor carefully calculated how much time it would take for me to dodge and managed to take a revitalizing gulp.

At that moment the flames around him began burning even stronger. Very soon the fire started swirling into a funnel, forming a real whirlwind, slowly dragging me into it. Even though I was an incorporeal spirit, the pulling power kept getting stronger every second.

A smile appeared on my face. I had almost been upset that killing the Emperor would be so easy. But he had in fact shown me the value, the power of a gold class. Mine was one thing, but his power looked much more epic and impressive. But nothing more. No matter how strong the chain, there was always a weak link. Same for any ass-hole, but then you would need a different tool. Luckily for me, I had one on hand.

BOOK FOUR

*   *   *

The two armies stared into the sky, the sepulchral silence broken only by the sounds of hits followed by bright flashes. Everyone without exception was simply waiting for the duel to end, having chosen to take no action.

The whirlwind of roaring flames, however, was gathering momentum. The Emperor's fighters were well aware of how destructive their leader's skills could be, especially when he was out of his mind. And he was well out of it now.

Only the most inattentive could fail to notice how strong his opponent's attacks were. While he himself seemed to be elusive and untouchable. A few officers had even wanted to damage him some-how, but it wouldn't work. If they started shooting abilities into the sky, they might hit their leader too. And that would just ensure them a slow and torturous death.

But they also knew that if they admitted to the Emperor that they had chickened out or been neu-tral, their deaths would be much more...

So some of the fighters sincerely wished their enemy would win.

The defenders had similar feelings. Many of them absolutely hoped for their former ruler to be defeated. They wanted to be free of his yoke and the appearance of the foreigner had been like a sign from on high. More than that, some of them still believed that Kasp was some kind of messenger from the System. If not a part of it himself.

He was a man who nobody could call just a regular one, so people started going from house to house, spreading rumors and gossip.

"He's going to burn us all..." a woman who had been watching the course of the battle since the beginning said, emotionally, resigned to her fate. "We're all going to die..."

"Oh, come off it!" Her friend placed her hand on the woman's shoulder. She was wearing a coat covered in fish guts and it smell like it, so the panicking woman immediately pulled her shoulder away. But it was too late. The smell had transferred instantaneously.

"I think you're worrying for nothing," Another fairly plump middle-aged woman came up to the two of them, smiling. "You heard who that ghost was, right? He's a messenger from the System! I'm telling you!"

"What are you talking about..." the woman, already dripping with fish, waved her hand and shook her shoulder. "What's this about a messenger? He's a normal Systemnik..."

"What?" The one who believed in the ghost was offended, but she quickly calmed down, since more sounds could be heard from above. Part of a building broke off, unable to withstand the extreme temperature, and pieces of glass, concrete, and other trash clattered down onto the defensive cupola of the city. "Judge for yourself," she continued, once the noise died down. "Where is he from?"

"Uhh... Somewhere up north, probably? So

what?"

"And how did he get here? Where'd he disappear to? Why did he show up again right when we were in danger? He's like the protector of our town..." the woman had started babbling, gesticulating emotionally.

She didn't stop even when the next explosion boomed, not even getting distracted by the Emperors shouts. She just kept going on, finding more inconsistencies in the behavior and actions of the new "Protector of the Settlement."

The rest of them listened and agreed. Only a few soldiers standing a little ways off and ready to start the fight at any moment looked askance at the rumor-spouting woman. There were some curious ears among them too, though, greedily sucking in the delusional information, taking it all as fact.

But suddenly the sounds of battle went silent. To everyone's surprise, the Emperor was still alive. He went over to his soldiers and they started loosing a host of attacking skills into the sky, and right after that the metal ball gleaming in the rays of the sun simply disappeared.

For a while the Emperor's soldiers could not believe that they had won. The fire mage himself stared dumbly into space, waiting for another attack to come at any moment. But after a couple of minutes it still hadn't come, and then his face twisted into a terrible grimace of wicked joy.

"The day of reckoning has come!" roared the Emperor, rising 30 feet above the ground. "Your defender has shown himself to be too weak and now you will all fry!"

He addressed those words to the inhabitants of the settlement, at which some of them immediately fell to their knees, trying to beg their true ruler for forgiveness. Some of them frowned, getting ready to make a brilliant last stand, taking at least a few of their enemies with them, while other fell into despair, knowing that the Emperor would never forgive any of them, and death was unavoidable.

But only one person was smiling, staring at the approaching army.

The man, staying here behind the leader, was not about to tell his terrified companions that the icon of the sovereign of the settlement was still active. And Kasp himself was still constantly sending dirty jokes to the arrogant Emperor in the chat.

The ghost also was aware that he shouldn't get involved in the fight. His people also needed to increase their inventory size.

"Ugh!" The extremely fragile paper door couldn't hold up against the attempt to open it from the inside and fell to pieces. Then a massive face with horns appeared in the doorway. "Not sh*t..." quipped the bull about Japanese quality, glancing at the pieces, then his heavy hooves clattered across the floorboards.

The Japanese, who had not been expecting the arrival reinforcements, ran away in terror, allowing the new army to get to the dome. First they were shocked to their core by the gigantic hairy bulk of the bull. Next a massive bear squeezed with the doorway, just barely, followed by a stocky bearded man who did not pass up the opportunity to swear at everyone there. Just because he could.

It didn't seem like there was anything else that could surprise them. But then a green body of a cactus came shuffling through the door, with a whole pile of sharp points rustling across the floor.

"Oh, I'ma snort ya... I'ma snort ya!" said the zombie head attached to the cactus's shoulders, gazing starry-eyed at a purple crystal.

After that freak show basic, normal people started filing out. They were all dressed in decent armor, holding high-quality, no less than uncommon level weapons in their hands. And on the whole you could tell from their faces that these fighters were confident in their own strength.

At the end was the zombie. At first glance he was entirely average, no different from the billions of other ones wandering and moaning right now through basically every corner of the globe. But not a single one of the locals had the slightest doubt that this deadie was in no way normal.

It was his eyes that gave him away. Piercing, precise, and tenacious. Capable of reaching all the way into your soul.

One of the local soldiers was about to express his objections about the presence of a zombie under the dome, but received a hard smack from one his officers.

"Shut up, you idiot..." the man hissed to his subordinate. "They are on our side. And pray that they stay that way."

"I wasn't going to say anything, I just..." muttered the soldier, then immediately gave up when he caught the deadie's gaze on him.

Although he looked tired, wounded, and worn out, the feeling of terror he was radiating out sank deep under the skin of everyone who was unlucky enough to standing nearby.

The stream of fighter exiting the town hall stopped, and they all started trudging for the shield. Behind them followed the local soldiers, also silent. Every second the belief that they would win got stronger in their hearts, since now they at least had a chance. Even against such a powerful and seemingly-invincible fire mage.

* * *

Bah... Tired. That douchebag really is something, no wonder everyone's afraid of him.

And he had done a number on me too. Although the base damage had been done by the Emperor's soldiers. He had only been able to drag me in with his whirlwind, which got him a slungshot in the side. Broke a few ribs, and I was able to pull myself out of the tornado sucking me in, taking care of my health right after. To do so I had to spread out my Aura of Vampirism and perch right behind the Emperor.

A large crowd of Japanese people were there to attend to all my needs.

My mana bar reached full in a matter of seconds, but restoring your health in this way was not so fast. Oh well.

While the Emperor was showing off some more special effects and threatening the settlement with the pain of death, I was reading the minds of individual soldiers to determine their fate. I mean, there must be some people here who didn't support the Emperor at all and were just acting out of fear. Or maybe this was his own personal Secret Service, all of them gotten for just things like this.

Anyway, there were two different mindsets. Only a few of them happened to be here by chance. They stood apart from the rest, afraid to even get close to the rest of the soldiers. They had been summoned here from the next settlement over so they could curry favor with their ruler. And they were not seized with a desire to punish the peaceful inhabitants of this strange little seaside town.

But the rest were. The believed that the will of their Emperor trumped all else and that it was necessary to fulfill anything he desired. And to kill and torture people with impunity.

Kasp: Alright, go, increase your inventory space.

Grugg: Ugh!

Slob: It's been less than a year!

Gnominumbus: Maybe we don't have to? I have enough, at least...

Ah, this unfamiliar interface! I had sent it to everyone at once. Well, at least it didn't go to my vassals, just my own people could read it. I hoped that Brownie had had the good sense to stop the flow of volunteers, otherwise I had no idea how we would stop the onrush of fishermen when we were dealing with the bodyguards.

All this time the enemy's forces were advancing. Inspired by the words of their ruler, many of the soldiers rushed into battle. Their souls were filled to bursting with a lust for blood, each of them imagining scenes where they murdered these defenseless traitors.

They were really in a frenzy. It would be child's play to trick them. Although it was good that the soldiers in the back were still in reserve. Either the Emperor wanted to show off how powerful his army was, or he had simply forgotten about the reinforcements. But that played into my hands, since I wouldn't have to lose innocent people.

But they really believed that someone from their forces had killed me. They hadn't even checked if someone had gotten a message telling them their inventory space had increased.

But there was no need to mess with their heads. Or anything else. The soldiers had advanced and were now starting throw all their forces against the shield, all while the Emperor stayed right where he was. Simply floating 15 feet in the air, covered in flame, just watching.

And that meant the fun could continue.

A new item appeared in my hand. I had never used anything like it before, but everything was telling me that this little baby was going to become my new favorite weapon.

Firecutter (uncom.) 10/10

Description: Made by Master Gnominumbus. Press the red button to activate. To deactivate, let go. Costs 1 mana per second. To recharge, place a blue crystal in the handle of the Firecutter.

C H A P T E R   1 8

2 seconds remaining until detonation
1...

HE HAD A BLUE motherf*cking class! A blue one! Rare! And still what an idiot!

The only thing I could do was fly back a few feet. Most of my time was wasted on materializing and jamming the partially-functioning knife into my unsuspecting opponent.

Partially, since it did still work. A light sword, like something out of Star Wars, about 8 inches long, came out of the handle. A tester sword, I would say. The blade looked pretty short and dull, anyway. Okay, we'll stab it in a bit, see how it works.

But I had to admit, it was more effective than I thought. I managed to jam the blade into the Emperor's side and it easily passed through the light armor and then into his flesh. And without even dematerializing! The dagger worked even in my incorporeal state!

Harsh smoke rose up into the air, and then the System warned me that the device was malfunctioning.

"I will burn your so—" his frightful voice boomed, but the flaming Japanese man didn't have time to finish his thought. True, it wasn't hard to imagine what he meant, since he had suggested the same thing to me multiple times before. I got it the first time.

BRAAAH!

I will burn your "so." Interesting. I could write that on his tombstone, and the phrase would make passersby wonder what he meant. Might even go on the list of famous last words or something like that. Quotes from famous Japanese wise men and all that.

Both me and the group of soldiers hiding behind the Emperor were caught in the blast, and they couldn't understand what was going on at all. It took half my health, and that was a few feet away!

The more time that passed it seemed more like Anton was just trying to kill me. In the dirtiest way, too. I would have to read his mind, check if he was really bearing a grudge against me. Maybe he thought I had set that girl on him, something like that. After something like that I would be trying to get revenge however I could too.

The Emperor was blown a few feet back, his

body slamming into the wall of a building, his bloody body slumping down it.

Kasp: Let's get started.

As soon as my message reached the group chat, I could hear shouts, the roaring of the bull, and Gosha's loud swearing. The shadow of the cactus, swollen up to an enormous size, fell over me, and sharp spikes flew toward the attackers. Harsh, for sure. But what could you do?

It was too bad that the Emperor was unconscious. I was still hoping that he would come to so I could read his mind. So I could understand where all this aggression was coming from, and why he was such an idiot. And to find out how he got so many people to follow such an admittedly powerful but exceptionally unstable dumbass.

Inventory Increased +1890 lbs.

My inventory was already at two tons! Now I could fit a small car or even a whole crab in there! That bastard really killed that many people? It really was a pity I never got into his mind. That flame surrounding him on all sides had really got in the way, no way I could have gotten past it without taking damage.

But it wasn't that important now. One thousand eight hundred and ninety. And he was no Manager, so you could really feel something different here.

Okay, fine. I needed to make up half my health, otherwise I could just be taken out in my corporeal state. Spiritual pain was much worse than physical.

And the soldiers from the neighboring settlement, left behind in the rear, would help me with that.

You have killed the leader of the Flame Capital Settlement.

Do you wish to take the stele of the settlement?

Thankfully the System had had some foresight and indicated the color of the stele in the name of the place. Blue. I was afraid that might mean a settlement test at a high difficulty level would happen.

So here was my dilemma. There was no way I could turn down a blue stele. Taking it in a full-on assault would be difficult, at the very least getting through the shield would waste up a bunch of products made by our great Gnominumbus. I didn't have such high hopes anymore, so we could safely consider all of them to be bombs. They blew up quite well, doing a lot of damage, so it would a shame not to use them. The only problem would be if you threw them and they actually worked right. Especially if it was like a cannon, for example.

So I would take it. It would be useful. What about the inhabitants of the settlement? The majority of them had supported the Emperor. So they were in this now too, let them figure it out themselves.

If nothing else, I could fly there later and offer for them to join us. And if they refused, to hell with them. They couldn't do anything to my vassals even if they really wanted to.

A little blue figure appeared in my hand, and I put it straight into my inventory.

A survey is being conducted amongst the vassals of the settlement you captured.

I had hoped something like that would happen, but I hadn't been sure. But it made sense. Your sovereign is gone, and you are free to choose whether you want to switch to the conqueror or separate and become independent.

I wondered if the Japanese would willingly switch to a foreign leader.

Designate the Sakura Settlement as your vassal?

Designate the Nakamoto Settlement as your vassal?

...

Designate the Unizaki Settlement as your vassal?

Seven in total. What kind of populations were there? I couldn't even imagine. But no matter what, it meant food. I went down the list, pressing yes for all of them, happily imagining how much tribute was now flowing into the treasury...

I didn't have it in me to spend any more time getting distracted by the interface, dealing with the new vassals, so I flew up a little and watched how the battle was going. Or more like the slaughter.

Yeah, our opponents were strong. Or at least there were a lot more of them, something like 200. They were all Systemniks, with a whole set of powerful skills and weapons. Each of their inventories was more than 20 pounds, and even though the

Emperor had been a greedy bastard, he had still decked out his guard.

I didn't even consider getting in the fight. My health was slowly going up, the Japanese weren't planning on going anywhere, happily giving up their energy, so I had nothing to complain about.

Especially considering that my guys also need additional inventory space, plus sometimes they just needed to stretch their legs.

Grugg was the first to pass beyond the shield. With a wild roar and terrible swearing he flew right into the middle of the enemies, and then a massive hammer appeared in his hands.

One wide swing and multiple members of the guard flew shouting in all directions, knocking over their compatriots with their bodies and landing on their heads.

"Moo moo, f*ckos!" The horned beast grinned and kept slamming into the row of enemies, completely ignoring the hits and small wounds.

All the while the unfortunate invaders were being met with another problem just ten feet away. A large brown bear, his claws covered in metal, his massive bulk covered by solid fur, strengthened by System materials. He stepped confidently out from the shield, moving forward with undisguised boredom and fatigue, taking up more and more enemies with his body.

But eventually a fighter came against him, one with an uncommon class and skills. They allowed him to confidently stand against any blow, not matter how powerful. Brownie rushed forward, but literally three feet from the opponent an invisible semi-circle appeared, fully protecting the Japanese man. The massive bulk tore into the defense, cracking and crashing loudly, then the bear, sighing heavily and shaking his head, fell to the ground.

Immediately spears jabbed into the brown fur, and the Japanese, encouraged, began surrounding the bear on all sides, gradually tightening the circle.

"Winnie!" came an icy roar or shout, followed instantly by a furious naked sonuvabitch slamming right into the crowd of enemies that had piled up around the bear.

Nobody knew why the Berserker always lost his clothes, but that's how it was. Once he activated his unique ring he definitively lost the last remaining shreds of his already meager sense, got naked, and ran off to destroy the enemy.

Just like now. Refusing to take a weapon, he exploded out from the shield, flying straight into the flabbergasted Japanese. They thought the bear was already done and were ready to skin him, but within a few seconds five of them had been sent flying to the air like sacks of broken bones.

Slob screamed, roared, swore, making all sorts of weird sounds. Soon after the fighters crowding around the bear were heaped in a pile, and the Berserker stopped only when he hit against the invisible shield. But now it could be seen. And that was because after being hit by the massive body, it had become covered in faint, thin cracks. Like glass after being hit by a pebble.

Seeing that, Slob started pounding at it with his fists, not once considering that he could just go around. Why use your brain when you have brawn?

"Raaaaah!" roared the Berserker. But that was more a cry of joy, since his fists had turned into bloody mush. And the man clearly loved pain.

Just a few seconds later the defensive semi-circle shattered into a thousand tiny shards that fell to the ground, giving the man some insignificant cuts. His whole body was covered in little scratches, and the blood oozing out seemed to give him a second wind.

But the Japanese man waved his arms, causing a loud bang. A flash flew out in front of the berserker and a powerful shock wave pushed him back a few yards. Before he could get back up on his feet, the crush of Japanese men shouted fiercely and made for their fallen foe.

"Oh-ho! Look at that, you knobheads! Ha!" The next second the attackers' way was blocked by a massive green leg covered in spikes.

"Oh," was all the first pursuer managed to say. He slowly brought his gaze upward, seeing Gosha's malicious grin for only a moment before the second green leg slammed down on his head.

Within second all hell broke loose on the battlefield. Watching from the sidelines, I wouldn't even have called it a battlefield. Not at all. The gigantic cactus was playing football with the Japanese, with the bull acting like a goalie. But baseball was going on too, with his hammer. All the while the bear was watching it all, biting the Japanese for humiliating him, as Slob, per usual, was simply smashing faces with wild abandon. A couple of times he couldn't stop himself before jamming his fists into Cyrush's green flesh, but a few spikes in his ass helped him to pick the right target.

"What a circus," muttered the wounded Zorn. There were still no fresh places left on his body since the recent battle. Well, it's not like his body had really been fresh before, but the number of injuries was really intense.

He stepped calmly past the shield, which hurt me to the depths of my soul. I hadn't even called on him. I was sure that he would need some time to recover, plus I thought he would want to spend some time with his granddaughter.

The girls had been taken straight to kitchen, fed to full, and given all the conditions necessary to rest. I didn't actually witness the family reunion, but it was none of my business. I just wondered how Masha had reacted when she found out her grandfather had died but wasn't planning on passing down her inheritance for the next couple hundred years. Or thousands. If I were her, I would be annoyed, to say the least.

"What a circus," hissed Zorn, shaking his head. "Get it over with, you idiots."

He was talking to all of them, but he couldn't care less about the rest of them. Grugg was still just mooing, trying to break a new indestructible weapon. Gosha was cackling and kicking the Japanese who were running away from him, and only the bear turned to look at him for a second.

"Finish it yourself, if you're so smart." Brownie shrugged, once again diving on his opponents who were trying to burn his fur with weak fire skills.

Zorn stood still for a moment, choosing the right target, his gaze landing on one of the officers. He was standing behind the soldiers, watching the fray, making no effort to join the fight.

The deadie walked casually toward him. He ran across some random Systemniks along the way, but they died almost instantaneously. The zombie simply applied his deathly grip around the neck of his opponent, tearing pieces of flesh out with his teeth, and then continued walking right at his target.

The occasional hit on the death flesh notwithstanding, Zorn was looking better with every second that passed. Every death healed the wounds on his body, and the light came back into his eyes, with him moving more confidently. Although he was already fairly strong, by the time the zombie got to his chosen opponent, his body was all but rejuvenated. That was apparent under his ripped and torn clothing.

But the officer had noticed that a rather strong opponent was coming toward him a long time ago, so he was ready. The soldiers arrayed themselves in a semi-circle as if they were a single organism, setting their mass of spears forward. And as soon as Zorn approached dozens of attacking spells headed for him all at once, whistling, buzzing, and booming.

Chunks of ice, gouts of flame, lighting and stones, some unknown sparking balls, and blue waves of pure energy... All of that slammed into Zorn, throwing a cloud of smoke and ash into the air.

"You sheep..." the hoarse voice could be heard behind the soldiers, and they turned to see a whole and unharmed zombie.

One second later the deadie, moving faster than the eye could see, tore into the line, ending one life after another with his powerful blows, breaking right through to the officer who nevertheless stood stock still, staring into his enemy's eyes.

When less than two feet separated them, the commander of the attackers smiled and winked at Zorn. A black cloud appeared out of thin air behind the deadie, then, taking the form of a human being, the creature attempted to sink two long daggers into the back of the zombie.

But a moment before Zorn had stepped to the side, damaging the magical being with a swift hit, simply tearing it into shreds with his boney hand.

Now surprise could be seen on the officer's face. He tried once more to use his dirty tricks. He summoned another cloud of smoke which turned into a large spike, hitting the zombie right in the side of his head. Or rather, it would have hit him, but Zorn, as if he had predicted the trick, nimbly dodged the attack.

"How..." whispered the officer when the deadie

came right up to him and grabbed him by the throat, effortlessly lifting the body, trembling with fear, off the ground.

"The Mark of Overlord Zorn," answered the zombie quietly, piercing the officer's soul with his gaze, and closed his hand. A cracking sound could be heard, and then the lifeless body flopped to the ground like a soulless doll.

With that the battle came to an end. The zombie had chosen the only correct target. That officer was the last person who allowed the soldiers to believe they could possibly win. The right hand of the Emperor, quite powerful with an epic class. He had been at least as cruel as his ruler, if not more. And so, with the fall of the last pillar of power in Japan, the people finally lost any reason to continue this mindless slaughter.

They ran. In panic, leaving behind their wounded companions.

Where was your lust for killing peaceful civilians? You just got here! Where you going? That's all? Just giving up?

"You have a choice. Either you are with me, or you are against me." I appeared in front of the group of terrified soldiers that had not taken part in the attack on the settlement. Although, really, what kind of soldiers just pissed their pants?

I mean, I would have pissed mine too. When the Imperial guard is literally torn to pieces right before your eyes, and by just some...creatures. And then more and more soldiers join them and start making their way right at you.

Yeah, that was quite a sight.

"W-with y-you..." A muffled voice could be heard a few seconds later. "Right, guys?" The man turned to look around, trying to find some support among his companions.

The rest of them all nodded, agreeing with their hesitant comrade and a general murmur of agreement came up from the crowd.

"Then go and kill those assholes." I smiled, opening a path and pointing toward the retreating members of what was once the guard.

How quickly can people switch sides? The really quick ones took only a few minutes. Some people need a few hours or even days to think it over. Some people drastically change their opinion about this or that thing slowly and unwillingly, over weeks or even months.

Those guys didn't even need one second. As soon as I set forth the condition, they rushed off to attack. They weren't even afraid of having to fight against elite Imperial troops.

Because otherwise they would have to deal with me.

The execution was over in minutes. Their opponents soon realized that they couldn't run away, and some of them even tried to surrender. But their former comrades, driven mad with fear, had no respect for that decision and soon reduced the remnants of the once-mighty Imperial guard to nothingness. Brutally. Even by my standards. I mean, Zorn wanted to eat. The bull wanted to play. Cyrush didn't have a mind at all, and it was the same with his companion Gosha. The crystal had taken whatever was left of it away.

Brownie and the rest of the army simply stood by, watching the distasteful business from a respectable distance, refusing to take any part in it. Only the Berserker was off somewhere.

"Well, it's done," shouted the bear, coming toward me. "I'm gonna go, okay? I still have an assload of stuff to do…" He waved his paw and loped toward the settlement, followed by the rest of our forces.

"Oleg! Where's Slob?" His icon was still active in the chat window, meaning he was alive, and possibly even healthy. I just wondered where our weirdo friend had disappeared off to.

"Well, uh…" Brownie slowly turned around. "He went to wash off."

CHAPTER 19

"LET GO OF THE DOLPHIN, dumbass!"

"No! He's my friend!"

"I'm not your friend!"

"What??"

What was wrong with this world? A talking dolphin, seriously? What's next, a singing fish? Or a novel-writing toad?

We had clearly taken a wrong turn somewhere. There was nothing for it, we lived here. And that meant we had to get used to the new reality.

But it just made no sense. How could the Berserker beat a dolphin in its natural element, drag it on to the shore, and still survive? It was nothing less than a miracle. Or just the element of surprise. Really, no living thing could expect that in its right mind.

"Slob..." I put my hand on the shoulder of the panting, crazy-looking man. "That's enough. Calm down. What the hell you drag it out for?"

"Why not?" He was surprised, but still hadn't let go of the dolphin's tail. "I was washing off, and this guy swam up to me…"

Washing off. The dumbass was lucky, I'll give him that. The last time they put a zombie in the water when I was around, there were carnivorous fish pecking at in within two seconds. Or did they only eat dead flesh? I needed to check that with this talking sea creature. He would be able to clear things up much better anyway.

"Uh-hem…" the dolphin coughed politely, interrupting the conversation between me and the Berserker. "Am I bothering you? If not, please know I will dry out in a little bit. I can't be up on dry land…"

He immediately acted like he was sick, sending me a look as though he was suffering dearly.

Slob just shrugged and headed back to the settlement. His warrior rage had begun to subside, so normal, decent human thoughts were starting to pass through his mind. While his class skill was active there were just emotions in there, and it was only them that mad his muscular body do this or that thing.

"Tell me a little bit about what is under water and I'll let you go." I shrugged. "And sorry about my friend, he's not always so…"

"Dumb?" The surprisingly intelligent dolphin finished my thought. "But I won't be able to tell you enough unless you let me go back in the water."

And there was that deathly sick look again.

"Well, tell me a little." I smiled. "I'm not greedy."

"Fine." The marine creature sighed. "What do you want?" He gave up surprisingly quickly. "To know why he was messing with me? I wasn't going to kill him. On land it would be too late. And we, unlike you, don't make fun of other sentient creatures. We don't kill them unless they attack first, and even then, we protect—"

It turned out that the Berserker hadn't eaten any fish only because Kilin, which was the dolphin's name, had been swimming by hunting them. Noticing that there was a man in the water he had simply swam up to see the suicidal person. Purely out of curiosity.

He could have used his water magic right away, but what would have been the point? But it turned out there would have been a point. But the dolphin realized that too late, once he had been slugged on the head and ended up on land. And he was just afraid to use his skills there or maybe hadn't had time before I arrived.

"Enough. Please. I swear to you on the Mother of All Dolphins that I will tell you everything I know... Just let me back in the water, I beg you..." He was visibly drying out, his eyes rolling back, and there were notes of panic in his voice. Clearly he was telling the truth that he couldn't be on land long.

His body was pretty heavy, but I had expected it to be more. I mean, our gray dolphins could reach weights of over 600 pounds before the System came. This one was young or even just a child. Even so, I did have to drag him, scraping his skin roughly across the rocks on the shore.

PLOP!

"Okay? Talk." I wiped my hands on my cloak and sat on the shore, ready to listen to a long and entertaining story about the world underwater.

"F*ck you!" shouted Kilin and immediately dove under water.

How annoying.

"You swore to the Mother of All Dolphins!" I jumped up. But that looked more funny than angry.

"Go f*ck yourself!" He poked out of the water again just for a moment and then headed deep in the water, waving his tail in parting.

I just laughed. Honestly, I could care less what was going on with them. Well, not that much less. If I wanted to, I could head underwater myself and see it with my own eyes. So this wasn't the last time I would see Kilin, I was sure of that. But I just wasn't into it right now. My job was to get Slob back to the village, so we wouldn't have to open the portal multiple times and waste our precious energy for no reason.

Now everyone was all together. I caught up to the Berserker right outside the dome, and had a good time watching the soldiers tell him what they thought of him. And they thought quite a lot, unlike him. Even Grugg was smarter than him. And that was given that he was in a warrior rage 24/7.

Even on the toilet, judging from the sounds of it.

Speaking of which, the bull had appreciated the wonders of civilization and assimilated into our planet in a flash. He knew what a toilet and a shower were, had tried using cutlery, and even appreciated our food. Basically he would soon be a full member of our society. Maybe a little weird, but hey, weren't we all? I didn't need anyone on my team who wasn't.

The Japanese had lived through the attack with aplomb. I could see that some of them had been upset by the death of the Emperor, but the majority of them seemed perfectly decent, and now they were just pretending to go about their business, trying to make it look like all their problems hadn't been caused by me being here, of course not. Well, okay. If I were in their shoes I would take a day off. There was no danger around at all, all our enemies had been defeated. And if anyone came, they could always call on me for help.

I informed my vassal with dumb name of Moon Wind about that. I didn't forget to remind him that his name was really dumb either. But, as it turned out, that was just a translation error. After the patch the names of my new acquaintances were no longer translated, and most likely Moon Wind was actually something like Hayebuka or Herowato. Which were fine, I guess.

Anyway, about names. I knew that this country was called Japan. But what was the island where most of it was located called. Ah, I would have to ask someone…

BOOK FOUR

Okay. First things first, on my way back to the settlement I picked up all the crystals from the bodies of my enemies. Waste not, want not. I mean, I couldn't use them as bait, but I could get this stuff at home. Collecting worms, as it were.

I managed put more than 100 clear ones, about 10 green ones, a blue one, and even a purple one in my inventory! That last one looked like it came from Zorn's opponent. I hope my guys managed to take the newly-available classes and nobody else got them. Especially since they were all martial classes here, very interesting ones at that.

The only thing I didn't get was the gold crystal. But I would pick it up later. The Emperor's body was comfortable stored away in my inventory until I could use it for a completely different purpose...

After dealing with the locals and settling all the basic questions, I promised to stay in touch and immediately headed home.

Home sweet home. How long has it been since I ate? Constantly being in my incorporeal state was causing me to forget about my human needs more and more. I mean, when I was a ghost I didn't need food, sleep, air... And I was starting to look at girls in a completely different way. I might enjoy and appreciate how they look, but that was more from contemplating beauty, rather than having sexual thoughts about them. It was like looking at a beautiful landscape, a work of art, or something like that.

I would have to fix that and be a regular person more often. If I did, then I would of course have to tolerate more unnecessary human attention on me, but what could I do about it?

The first thing I did was go to the cafeteria. As is right and proper, I appeared right in the middle of it, took of my hood and mask, and sat at a table with a group of workers from our corps of future craftsmen.

"Oh! Kasp! Hey!" A man clapped me on the shoulder and held out his hand for a handshake.

Nah, I can't do this. Of course I shook his hand, but I really didn't feel like talking. So I was forced to extend my Aura of Fear enough that my table was empty within a few seconds. The rest were all full up, but now they thought twice about sitting near me.

Are there waiters here?

A few minutes watching showed me that no, there weren't. Everybody went to the kitchen and got their meals. But they looked pretty weak, with almost no meat, basically just the contents of a gray potato on their plates, just a little warmed up and spiced a bit so you didn't throw up from the stuff.

By the time I was getting to the point where I was about to get one of the mess of purple potatoes out of my inventory, I decided I would just try it. I didn't feel like going to the kitchen, so I just raised my hand and soon a girl was standing next to me, her whole body quaking. So there were waitresses, if you needed them. How nice.

"Bring me your finest food, if you would." I muttered shortly, and the girl dashed off.

In order to avoid waiting around for nothing, just wasting time, I open the logs. I hadn't been able to check the updates recently, so I hadn't gotten around to dealing with them at all. Sure, I had learned that the chat changed a little. It had gotten a lot more interesting and functional, with new capabilities and an updated interface. But only in broad strokes.

There we go! Found it!

"Alright…" I muttered under my breath, staring into space. "The fourth phase has begun… Blah, blah, blah… Difficulty increased! And what does that entail?"

And so on. I didn't spot anything critically important. Last time the System had taken away our electricity, heat, and guns. It had truly become much harder to survive, with so many human accomplishments gone that had once been taken for granted. But we could get them all back.

But what about now?

Lost in thought, I glanced around. What had changed. It seemed like nothing at all. People were still chatting with each other, although they now had a common language. If you listened closely, it didn't sound anything like what we had been speaking. It was some kind of System language, totally different and foreign, but understandable, to our surprise.

They were eating… Eating only System food. The dishes and cutlery were also from the System, and the food was obviously taken from potatoes. It had to be.

Where were our stores of dried food? Where were the grains taken from the city or mountains of canned meat? All of that should have lasted for a while. Plus we could always just open up a portal to any city camp and grab some more…

"Hey," I called over some guy who had dared to sit at the next table over. "What are you eating so bad for?"

He tried to pretend to be absorbed in a rag for a while, but realizing that I was talking directly to him, he finally decided to answer.

"I mean, it's…" the boy mumbled, looking all around, trying to find some support from his friends. But they were slumped in their chairs, trying their absolute best to express the smallest possible intellectual ability. "Well… Uh… Why do you ask?"

Son of a bitch!

"Why is there so little food?" I really wanted to add a couple of choice words, but I remembered in time that this was caused by my Aura of Fear. I would have to shut it off if I didn't want to wait around for answers.

"Well go and try to find some more System food. That's easy for you, but for now we have to share it equally, and it's running out."

You, us… There was nobody under level 10 in my settlement. Could anyone else claim an achievement like that? I didn't think so. Even if you took the big city nearby where we had saved Zorn's granddaughter. More than half of them there were the so-called Useless caste, and all of them were between level zero and three. And they were really the majority there.

And we didn't have an Us or You. Everybody should be on the same level. Except me, of course. I was a step above, because I deserved it.

"And your religion doesn't allow you to cook normal food?" After that question the boy's face scrunched in surprise, and I finally got it. "Oh... I understand."

And here was the difficulty increase. Now food could only be from the System. The rest of it was all useless. I did not envy those who had been surviving on their large stores of provisions, saving it all for a rainy day... I was sure there had been more than a few of them. In any case, the desire to put things off for tomorrow could come over any of us, especially in the apocalypse. Take me, for example. I loved saving stuff up too. But just a little, for sure, and I would say pretty weakly, not getting distracted from the task at hand... Right.

Well, there you had it. We had lost our food, but the rest of it was the same as before, no change. Honestly, it would just make life a little bit harder.

Having figured out that part of the new phase of the System, I moved on to the next one. They still weren't bringing me any food, and I had nothing to do. But I could just open up a potato...

The chat had been updated. I could tell that immediately, but I still hadn't had time to look at see what those changes meant.

Since I didn't have anything else to do, I

opened it up and started looking through each and every tab, button, and icon.

You could share your location. That was quite convenient when you had your own personal portal. Eva would now be stuck tight to that damnable portal and would be forbidden to teleport anywhere at all. She teleported once and all hell broke loose. We didn't need any more of that.

Sharing photos? Nice. I tried it out right away. To take a picture you just had to click on the camera icon and a picture would be sent to whoever you were talking to. So I could send whatever I was looking at right now.

I looked at the waitress's ass, squinted, and sent that beauty to Slob. He would enjoy it. Now the best photographer would be whoever had the highest level of Perception. There was also a zoom function, higher-quality pictures, and at night you could even see stuff.

That last one would really get some use! For example, when you were working in the dark. Someone with really good eyesight could take a picture of their surroundings, send it to everyone else, and then they could figure out where they were much better. Especially since you could take short videos in addition to pictures, and if you spent a couple of crystals then your recording could go as long as a few minutes and you could send a soundtrack too.

There was a social component in chat now too. Before you could put users into groups, like making a general chat for the settlement, but now there were groups based on interests. For example, there was a locked group called "Best of the Best." There they accepted only those who got lucky enough to get a purple class. I couldn't even imagine how the administrator determined what class the users had. I guess they were forced to show their abilities in a video or something like that.

Basically, the chat was now a social network. A real one, with a ton of groups, the ability to donate, and other luxuries. The System had stolen all of that from our social networks, no doubt, so all the features were extremely familiar, what we were used to.

The first increase in difficulty had been much more boring for people. Our devices had disappeared, our connections, our familiar entertainment, but now we had the possibility of pissing our time away again.

Of course, I wouldn't be doing that. As if I didn't have anything to do. I could check out the auction, but like hell was I going to get lost in there until morning. I would rather deal with the stele we had gotten, or even level up the settlement a couple times. In any case, there was always something to keep me busy.

"Where the hell is my food?" I couldn't hold it back any longer, having realized that I had been sitting here for half an hour already.

"Up your ass! Sit and wait and shut your mouth!" I heard a furious roar from the kitchen followed by every sound in the cafeteria going quiet. You could hear a pin drop. If a mouse farted outside, every single person here would hear it.

I didn't even know what to say. If that Emperor were here now he would simply burn everything to ground. And in some warped sense he would be right to. But I was not him, and I realized that the woman just didn't know who she was talking to. Plus, she was probably tired, there were a lot of people here, and we only had a couple of Chefs for the whole settlement.

"What'd you go quiet for, dummies?" the middle-aged woman shouted again, displeased, and stuck her head out of the little window in the back of the place. "Hey, you. What'd you go quiet for?" she demanded of a man standing by the window. But he just slowly turned to look at me and slouched down, trying to shrink into a dark corner and not stand out. "Oh…" the woman said, much quieter now, and started slowly disappearing back into the window.

Yeah, oh. But whatever, I could see from her face that she was completely out of mana. And so far as I could tell, this was far from the first time that had happened. The bags under her eyes, pale skin, and haggard-looking face told me that the woman was running on fumes.

"Is that better?" I scared away all the cafeteria staff, disappeared from the table and reappeared in the kitchen in a fraction of a second.

The woman stared at me in horror for a while, but slowly her face broke out into a blissful smile. Oh, now I definitely knew how to please a woman.

Although all I did was use my new additional Energy Vampire ability to give her a couple percent energy back. That was enough to refill the chef back up to full, and a couple minutes later she set about performing her magic on my meal.

She had not forgotten to apologize. Many times, actually, but I wasn't listening. Watching the cooking process was much more interesting.

Her apprentice had cooked a steak in advance, and the cut off a piece of meat, frying and seasoning it a little. It was about ready to eat, but the most important thing was still left.

As it turned out, to make System food, the Cook had to use her class skill. That cost mana and energy, sometimes quite a lot. But after a few seconds a System message appeared over the meal saying that the food was now uncommon and had some new features.

"Oh..." She was shocked. "It's not usually like that..."

Steak (uncom.)

Description: Sates hunger exceptionally well, containing all the nutrients, microelements, and vitamins to maintain the vital activity of the body. Also has a 90% chance to buff Body stats by 10 points for 3 hours.

Not bad. I dug in right away, without waiting for permission. Delicious! Enough to make you lick your fingers. I can confidently state that hand-made food was much tastier than even food from a purple potato. There everything was also presented beautifully, with delicacies and what have you. But this... This was food with soul!

"Where do you get the System meat?" I asked after getting the bonus to my Body stats. "Do we have hunters?"

"No... You brought the reindeer leg yourself..."

Suddenly remembering everything that had happened with that leg, I was very surprised, wondering why the meal made from it was only uncommon, and not epic.

CHAPTER 20

A DILEMMA. IT WAS DELICIOUS. But I still felt like throwing up. I had a clear picture in my head, remaining in exquisite detail how that unlucky reindeer's leg looked before. I hadn't forgotten about the chunks of rotten brains sticking to the shit-smeared fur either... And that was what I had just eaten.

No, I had given them the leg with the best intentions. I knew they would treat it, wash it, and cook it right nice. But the idea was that the meat would feed those who had no idea what had happened to it. Which was everyone except me.

But I had an iron will. Inner strength, spiritual energy, and all of that good stuff. So I tried to swallow the chunk stinking in my throat.

Now I would have to live with it. And so much the worst that I was the only one around whose memory couldn't be wiped. Anyone else, but screw me, huh?

"Thank you," I said, almost under my breath, pushing the plate with the unfinished steak away. "You can give that to whoever you like…"

"You didn't like it?" All the workers in the kitchen were staring at me, waiting for my opinion. I felt like a restaurant critic, all the attention was making me feel a little sick to my stomach.

"Exceptional." I gave them a thumbs up then, looking at the meat again, barely held back my gag reflex. Just drink a health potion… "Now tell me why our people are eating shit."

Honestly, I already knew. But I wanted to hear why it was so bad directly from those whose job it was to make the food.

The System had pulled a dirty trick. All the food, all the alcohol and every drink besides water had become unfit for consumption. You grab a roll, bite into it, and it's like there's a piece of rubber in your mouth. If you swallowed the thing anyway it would come out unchanged.

Thankfully, water at least had stayed the same. If the System had taken that too, this world would be doomed to extinction. No doubt about it. I would be flying around as a ghost, watching how the last remnants of humanity fought over the last gray potato. And finally how candy dropped out of it. I hoped the System wouldn't take it that far. She needed something to watch, right?

"Okay, I got it." I sighed after heard their detailed response. Everything was just pretty bad.

There were two hundred gray potatoes and

thirty green ones left for the whole settlement. Half a potato per person? And that was just enough for one day, at most. And if everything was so bad with us, how was it now for everyone else?

Loot was slowing day by day, since there were fewer and fewer deadies in the woods. The animals were taking back their territory, clearing them out of their home, and only lone zombies came by our dome now and again.

I needed solve this issue with food production. I felt like Gosha would soon be getting another crystal, and all I could do was hope that he wouldn't get hooked on it forever. He was already tweaking hard. But what choice did I have?

Disappearing into thin air, I flew towards a large table and pulled a thousand gray potatoes out of my inventory, then crowned the pile with a hundred green ones for good measure.

Now we had a little heap that couldn't even fit on the table, with most of them falling on the floor.

At first the Cooks couldn't believe their eyes, then suddenly they started whooping and shouting, all of them throwing my gifts into their inventories. I wondered if they would steal them.

No. The thought hadn't even crossed a single one of the ladies' minds. Being able to read them was almost better than dematerializing. When you can trust your people, life is much easier and calmer. That Emperor, despite his invincible power, could not sleep peacefully. He would constantly have to toss and turn, afraid of his underlings and burning anyone who was so much as suspected of treachery.

And judging by the inventory space I got, he had been a mistrustful character.

"Kam... Uhh..." I appeared behind the elf girl. I had wanted to call her by her name, but at the last moment I realized that I couldn't remember the name quite right.

"Kamanta, that's right." She smiled, showing her long, sharp teeth. Brrr... What a bite she could give, if she wanted to.

To my dismay, she, like the bull, was also gradually assimilating into our settlement. Dismay because on her world there had been two types of clothing. Military clothing, which covered the whole body and included a thick cloak, and normal, everyday clothing. And the everyday clothing consisted of two strips of cloth that barely covered just the most intimate places.

But now she was wearing a baggy t-shirt and long pants. What asshole gave her those? I was sure it was one of the girls. Even so, her figure was a sight for sore eyes. It had probably been out of envy.

There was also assimilation in the fact that her brother was no longer tromping around the settlement in the loincloth that one of the local idiots had given him as a joke. The elf had liked the outfit, so he wore it happily without ever taking it off. So now the positives more than outweighed the negatives.

"Kamanta..." I tried to get her name down once again. No use! I had to write it down. "Did you become the Ruler of Flame, Kamanta?" The smile instantly disappeared from her face and she averted her gaze in shame.

"No..." she whispered guiltily.

"Hmm..." I intoned. Annoying. We could have gotten a truly powerful fighter. I would have levied a 90% personal tribute on her and sent her off to cut down hordes of deadies. Ah, one can dream. "I hope you didn't take anything? We'll find you a rare class, don't worry."

"I did," she squeaked, even more guiltily. But before the veins in my forehead could pop in frustration, the blue-skinned beauty raised her hands and kept talking. "An epic one! I managed to get an epic one! A really strong one, one that on our world not all leaders could claim—"

Master of Shadows. It didn't sound bad, to be honest. The only thing stronger was a gold class, but you could only guess what that could actually be. And what Kamanta had was not bad at all. At level ten she could already make a double, just like coat. And also slip into the shadows, moving through darkness at double speed, attacking from afar, and a lot more.

Next to that my dematerialization looked pretty weak. No, really. The rest of the martial classes had so many abilities. That Ruler of Flame or whatever the Emperor had been, could use a vast number of abilities, just by using one class skill. He could light himself on fire or burn a whole crowd. He could turn into a comet, fly, or shoot fireballs. He was only limited by his imagination and how much mana he had.

But me? I could disappear into thin air and swing my slungshot.

Huh...

But I was alive, and he wasn't. And that wasn't even a one-on-one fight. He had been helped by his army, while I told mine to take cover under the cupola.

Turns out that swinging a slungshot isn't too bad.

But I was happy for the girl. Even if there was a new, extremely powerful fire mage somewhere else in the world, we now had in our settlement a very tricky and subtle killer. If you took her racial advantages into account, we would definitely find a way to use her.

Group: Kaspophiles

Kasp — Ghost

Kamanta — Master of Shadows

21:57:35 until a new test...

And this was something else entirely. I had noticed the new button purely by accident. It had a few little people on it so guessing what it referred to wasn't too difficult.

The first thing I did was leave the old group. I hadn't wanted to be in charge of people before, so I delegated those responsibilities to Brownie. He still did have them now, just in a completely different way.

It wasn't hard to make a new one, and as soon as I sent the invention to the blue-skinned beauty, she smiled sweetly at me and her name appeared right away in the list of fighters.

This group looked so much nicer. There was no gray in the list at all. No weak fighters who would die in a dangerous situation or just hide behind me.

Brownie couldn't hurt… But would he want it?

"There will be a test tomorrow." I reminded the girl as I was leaving. "And you have to work on mastering your skills. They will definitely come in handy for me."

Clearly wanting to show off her abilities, the elf girl winked at me and turned into a black cloud that rushed off somewhere outside the dome.

Huh. I wondered why that guy hadn't done the same thing. Most likely every creature or person's class abilities came up differently. I had considered that many times before. Take Anton, for example. He could make light bulbs and tools. And even robots!

But if someone else had taken his class, they would make cars or maybe would create phones with an apple on the covers. Against that backdrop Anton didn't look like quite such an idiot…

Okay. Who else did I want to put in my group?

It was simple enough to find Zorn. But I had not been expecting this kind of behavior from him. I caught him hiding behind the corner of a building and staring at something deep in the settlement.

It took a while of me circling over the dead idiot's head to realize that he was watching his granddaughter. In secret.

She won't accept me.

This thought was constantly coming up in his dead head, and he couldn't get away from no matter how hard he tried. I could help him with that. Give him confidence, force Masha to take her grandfather as he was, even if she was afraid. But I wouldn't. You had to decide these things on your own, without any interference from outside. But I could push him in the right direction.

"You worried?" I appeared behind him. "I would be worried too…" That wasn't true, of course. I hadn't had any close relatives even before the apocalypse, so it was actually really hard to understand him.

He simply glanced at me for a second then continued watching, not saying a word. We stood there like that for a few minutes, unable to find the right words.

"Listen, you don't even smell like dead flesh," I said, trying to calm my friend down in some way. But judging from how he looked at me, I hadn't really succeeded. "Gosha over there reeks like camel shit, so I wouldn't recommend sniffing him at all. He's a real zombie. But you, you're barely different from a human." I shrugged. Done. I did everything I could.

"That's because Gosha really is camel shit," croaked Zorn, turning back towards the ersatz children's park. "That's obvious both from the smell and his level of intellect…"

Who made that children's park anyway? I clearly remembered it not being there. And now there were slides, swings, and even a sandbox.

And a zombie acting like a pony! And just where had all these kids come from? They couldn't have all been born here, right?

"No argument there..." I scratched my head. "But anyway. Why don't you talk to her? She really wants to see her grandpa. When I got her out of that settlement she was constantly buzzing in my ear asking when she would see her grandpa, when, when, when..."

"She will see him. She will find out I am a zombie. I'm a deadie! You understand?" And for the first time in a long time there was emotion in his voice. Last time he had shown that was when I had given him his memories back. "And so I see that she is in danger. And I am doing everything to hold that off."

Ugh. So much expression. Even without that his hoarse voice had taken on a growling tone, and his eyes blazed yellow in the darkness. I was afraid to imagine what would happen to his enemies if they decided to come here.

"Chickenshit." And ended it there. "Fine, whatever. Accept this invitation..."

Group: Kaspophiles
Kasp — Ghost
Kamanta — Master of Shadows
Zorn — Overlord of the Dead
21:42:18 until a new test...

He had even got a class. He was totally becoming a person. Soon you'll see him breathing, and then even going to the toilet like everyone else.

Hmm... Could you do your business right into

your inventory? I would have to try that. I would be really convenient...

And his class was in no way gray. The most epic one possible. Not that I had had any doubt of that. The guy was seriously strong and I had never met anyone like him before. So it was really strange that it wasn't gold.

"Kaspophiles? Really?" groaned the Overlord of the Dead. "Even from you I wasn't expecting such flights of fancy..."

Oh, what? It's a normal name!

I wasn't about to get involved in the business between the zombie and the little girl, so I dematerialized and flew as high as I could. It was more than before. The people weren't sitting around idly and had already started building living quarters. A few buildings were already done, and judging by the new ones under construction, the rooms in them would be microscopic. But also with heating, plumbing, and all the other luxuries that we were used to.

I just had two more to get.

Obviously the bull would be worth taking, but god knows where he got off to, and I had no mind to chase him down. When he reappeared, I would invite him.

So who would the last one be? I recalled that before I headed back to Japan some chubby dude had approached me. He was the proud owner of a rare healing class which guaranteed us full medical insurance if we took him with us.

We didn't take him than. But whatever, he

would still heal us for free.

Did we need him in our group? I wasn't so sure of that. There was no point in healing me at least, not even cancer could get to Grugg, Zorn had no need of that healing, and Kamanta wouldn't fall anyway. If anything she could take a potion, no worries.

So pass on the chubster. But that still left the question of where he had gotten his class. I only knew one rare Healer personally, and he lived in the city. An hour of flying away from the settlement. Although there were others like him scattered around the world, but still, something was telling me...

Okay, whatever. I would see what Brownie was thinking. It wasn't hard to find him, since he spent most of his time around the stele. Or writing something in his notebook, but his table was right nearby.

Oh, everything is so fu—

One hundred percent agree with you! I read his thoughts for less than a second and I already got all of it. I got it, I accept it. Not touching it.

I wasn't even going to appear. The poor guy had his head in his hands and was working on some numbers. It looked like we didn't have enough building materials and nothing to buy them with. I had used up all our crystals.

Although you couldn't say they were expensive. There were a ton of camps in the cities that were just busy getting concrete. Some of the were dumping it, offering a ton of that material for just two gray crystals. Of course, deals like that only lasted a couple of seconds and you had to work hard to be that lucky. But just ten minutes of trying and I figured out how grab up all sorts of resources at the lowest possible prices here and there.

Soon our storehouse was filled with five hundred tons of stone, iron, sand, and other construction junk. I could afford it. And now the settlement would really change. It might be just five hundred tons of drops in the sea, with the System taking at least half, but that would definitely be enough for a good start.

And we got more experience in the treasury! Almost all the stuff made by Anton was bought immediately. A couple of things were still there, for some reason, but probably I just messed up their pricing.

I wasn't going to tell Brownie that the problem with the resources had been solved. Let him finish writing his notes first, calculate it all up, and then be pleasantly surprised. And realize that he had just wasted hours of his life.

So who would be the fifth? Hmm...

Group: Kaspophiles

Kasp — Ghost

Kamanta — Master of Shadows

Zorn — Overlord of the Dead

Kaman — Master of Daggers

21:28:54 until a new test...

The elf was young and had picked something that fit him. I didn't know he was good with daggers. But as far as I could recall from reading his thought, the blue-skinned boy had always dreamed of close-combat fighting. But he had been forced to use a bow, in respect of some sort of traditions and habits over there.

He immediately accepted the invitation as soon as I sent it. His class was blue, and designed exclusively around wielding two short swords. I would have to see exactly what a warrior like that was capable of.

We had gotten that class in the fight with the Japanese. If memory served, it was Grugg who had beaten the guy who was furiously brandishing two little swords, jumping and gleaming with bright flashes. But a powerful fist had simply knocked him down to the ground, and a hoof had done the rest.

Oh right, about him. I could wait for the horned guy until I was blue in the face, so it made sense to just send him an invitation to the group right away.

Group: Kaspophiles
Kasp — Ghost
Kamanta — Master of Shadows
Zorn — Overlord of the Dead
Kaman — Master of Daggers
Grugg — Ruler of Flame
21:28:54 until a new test...

"RAAAAH!"

A painfully familiar roar of fury could be heard in the distance, and next second a pillar of flame slammed into the firmament. Everything around was lit up by a bright flash, but that wasn't the end of anything.

People, shocked, rushing out of their homes, could see a swirling whirlwind of fire lighting up the horizon off in the distance, constantly moving towards them.

The soldiers immediately got their weapons and armor out of their inventories, ready to throw all that on, and the bear appeared out of the town hall.

But I just stood there and shook my head. That stupid horned bastard. There was nothing else I could call the dumbass…

CHAPTER 21

"SO WHAT?" THE BULL GOT UP from the burned ground and plopped onto his ass.

So... You couldn't argue against that. But I would try.

"It's that you don't need a magical class at all! It would have been better to leave it for someone more... Someone smarter! What do you need something magical for? The Japanese had a ton of useful ones that would fit you better!" I kept chewing out the horned bastard, but he just stared right through me.

"So what?"

"F*ck it!" I just wanted to fly away. Was this really a bull? Maybe that's how donkeys looked on his world? "Fine, I give up." I turned around and headed back towards the settlement. Impossible to explain...

The ungulate was now a Ruler of Flame. No,

that sounded awful. But also cool, somewhat. But goddammit, he had passed out the first time he used his ability. And what had Grugg made a pillar of fire hundreds of feet high for?

He saw a zombie! A single deadie wandering through the forest. The poor son-of-a-bitch had just gotten lost, separated from his horde, and wandered off in some direction, not meaning to cause anyone any problems.

And some angry stranger had turned him into a pile of ashes. Plus the forest had suffered, to a radius of about 100 feet.

But still, it was better than if someone who was not from our settlement got the gold class. We would teach Grugg, level up his Conduits and Repository, and then see if we could make something sensible out of him.

19:56:34 until a new test...

No sense in sitting around and waiting for the System to give us something interesting. Everything in the settlement could run smoothly without me so there was only one unresolved issue left. So I could confidently head for the city to check if my hunch about the death of the old healer was right, visit the pack of dogs, and maybe track down the golems and chimeras. Those assholes were definitely hiding somewhere not too far away, and if I followed their creations, I would be able to discover where their vile lair was.

Vanishing into thin air and moving under the dome, I floated in the air and called up the interface. It took an extraordinary amount of will to overcome my stinginess. I couldn't avoid having to spend dozens of skill points to achieve my goals. And saving them up had turned out to be difficult and complicated.

But you had to spend money to make money. So let's do this.

Appropriation (epic) (30)

Description: Active skill. Allows you to sneak into another person's inventory and move System items and rewards from there into your own. The choice is random. Costs 10-100 mana, depending on the value of the item. Chance of success, 34% to 79%, depending on the value of the item. Recharges in 31 seconds. Area of use, 3 feet.

In case of failure your target will notice you, and for 31 seconds they will see your location in spite of any protection or distance.

Additional Effect. Chance. After a success you may try to appropriate one more item immediately, and the chance of success increases by 10%, but no more than three times in a row.

Additional Effect. Choice. Offers you a choice from three possible options.

Excellent. A list of three possible additional effects appeared before my eyes.

Corpse Looting

Quick Recharge

Skill Appropriation

I have nothing to say. In fact, I wanted to say less than nothing. Ever.

But...

My only goal in leveling this skill up was to get

the ability to loot corpses. That would be an amazing ability that would let me get rich in no time. Getting more than just one pointless crystal and a set of worn-out clothes from every person killed. Just everything that they had collecting in their short post-apocalyptic life.

But Skill Appropriation. System, my dear... Let the devil take you for giving me names like this right now in what you're allowing me to appropriate. Over and over. And for putting such a difficult choice in front of me.

But I knew what she meant, actually. Once I got the skill up to level 40, I would be able to steal stat points, skill points, and ability points. Which I had completely forgotten about even before I ended up in fricking Japan.

But we got a good laugh out of it. We would have to do it again some time.

Appropriation (epic) (30)

Description: Active skill. Allows you to sneak into another person's inventory and move System items and rewards from there into your own. The choice is random. Costs 10-100 mana, depending on the value of the item. Chance of success, 34% to 79%, depending on the value of the item. Recharges in 31 seconds. Area of use, 3 feet.

In case of failure your target will notice you, and for 31 seconds they will see your location in spite of any protection or distance.

Additional Effect. Chance. After a success you may try to appropriate one more item immediately, and the chance of success increases by 10%, but no more than three times in a row.

Additional Effect. Choice. Offers you a choice from three possible options.

Additional Effect. Corpse Looting. Enables you to use the skill on corpses. The crystal must not have been removed from the body, and the corpse must still be warm. In the case of failure, the item will disappear.

The description was confusing and convoluted, but still everything was clear. The corpse should be fresh and warm. What if I warmed it up? Would that work, System?

I think everything has already been worked out. But I could keep bodies in my inventory, in any case. Their temperature wouldn't change in there at all, even after a year. I think that's what the System had in mind. Not an hour after death, so I could immediately put all dead bodies into my two-ton backpack.

Attention, I have a question. Could I use Skill Appropriation on the dead? No matter how crazy and necrophiliac it sounded, the question was still vital!

The Emperor fulfilled all the System's demands. He was definitely still warm, so it should work on him.

The only thing that bothered me was the bit about items disappearing if the appropriation failed. But still better than nothing.

I ended up sitting on the roof of the town hall and started defiling the corpse under the shocked gaze of passersby. No, he just lay back and thought of England while I, extending my Aura of Vampirism to the fullest, set about snatching item after item out of the Emperor's inventory.

A gray potato, some kind of spear, a green iron...

Two hours. You had about two hours after death to fully loot your fallen enemy's inventory.

The figure was an estimate, but I thought that was about right.

The job took me a lot longer. Up until dawn I spent my mana, put the corpse back into my inventory, and waited for it to fill back up. And I still couldn't get all of it out.

But I did get a lot of valuable stuff. His Imperial Majesty wouldn't have kept that gray potato. All his items started at uncommon or higher. That led to a bunch of failures, causing me to waste time and mana for nothing.

But the bastard had kept crystals, a purple potato, a few irons, and items that had already been opened.

There was even a gold potato, but just one, and that one disappeared when I failed to appropriate it. But I did manage to get out enough blue and purple ones for the ten skill points I had spent to pay for themselves in spades.

Most of the things I simply dropped into the town hall. There was also rare plate armor, a whole set, and light armor for war mages. All sorts of weapons and some magic stones. Including two things for teleporting to a stele.

I was only interested in the abilities. I knew

that he had already studied the most valuable ones, but not all of them had gone into slots. I didn't have any martial ones, for instance. And this guy had two rare abilities for shooting a bow. It would be a shame not to use them.

Konnor's Bow Shooting (rare)

Description: Teaches the ability to shoot a bow in the style of Connor.

What Konnor? Another scroll with a stupid-ass name. Urn was definitely some crappy people, so I would give that one to someone else. Cole, or maybe Igor. Whoever it wouldn't be wasted on, at least.

But before studying the ability I tossed all the potatoes I stolen into my mouth. No reason to leave them lying around. The Emperor had, and what good had it done him. Now they were all mine.

Plus a pure gold crystal, which could save either my life or that of many other inhabitants of the settlement in a pinch. You could buff up anything you wanted with it, and the last time I used that purple energy focus I had gotten great results.

Energy focus... Was that the soul, by any chance?

I looked at the crystals I had pulled out of people once more. For comparison I also looked the normal ones that I had gotten from zombies.

The difference was striking. The zombie crystals were muddy and all the same. No, in the rays of the rising sun they both gleamed and sparkled, but the human ones were still different somehow.

There was a little fire tumbling about the solid walls. It was like it was trying to break out, looking for an escape. But no such luck.

Definitely a soul. Trapped in a goddamn crystal for all eternity by the System. Or until someone used it to buff their abilities.

I would have to check that. A new resource opened up new possibilities.

But first I would have to check the interface and see how much better I was after eating something like fifty blue potatoes and fifteen purple ones.

Name: *Kasp*

Level: *32*

Class: Ghost

Stats:

Body (48): Strength (18), Dexterity (14), Constitution (16)

Mind (62): Intelligence (22), Reaction (23), Perception (18)

Spirit (95): Repository (33), Conduits (61)

Available Stat Points: 3

Skills:

Active: Appropriation (epic) (30), Aura of Fear (rare) (1), Aura of Ice (epic) (10)

Passive: Energy Vampire (rare) (30)

Additional: Dematerialization (Class Skill)

Available Skill Points: 6

Abilities:

Martial:

Craft: Concentration of Energy (10)

Available Ability Points: 38
Inventory 4320 lbs.

Not bad at all. I could put all the stat points into Conduits without a second thought. Without them I would be basically armless and legless and died long ago.

The blue scroll sent me far far away. I had gotten down from the sloping roof in advance, landing in the green grass, ready to watch a group of people entirely new to me.

The Konnors were monkey-like beings. Their world looked like a thick, dense forest with a vast collection of living things that were both harmless and extremely dangerous. They moved exclusively by using branches, jumping from one tree to another. Their cities were located up there too.

Down below was just hell. Any time of the day or night creatures down below were eating each other, trying the gain the upper hand and eat everything around, and the fight for survival never flagged for even a moment.

The ability was just right for me. It was good that I picked Konnor, since aiming carefully and hitting a target a quarter-mile away from me was not what I needed at all. I could just fly up and shoot it into their skull from 30 feet away.

Here the monkeys usually shot on the fly. They let go of the branch and before landing on the next one managed to get off at least one round. Sometimes two or even three.

The main thing about their ability was the possibility of aiming and being ready on the fly, as well as very quickly pulling arrows out of their quivers.

The vision ended too soon. I was left with the desire to see what would happen next. I was taken out of the teaching right when a monkey kicked off of a branch, began aiming at some winged lizard creature, and then gone... Right at the most interesting part.

I spent those ten ability points without a sliver of regret. That would definitely come in handy, especially when you consider that shooting midflight was more comfortable for me than anything else. Just shut off my dematerialization and shoot to my heart's content.

04:21:15 until a new test...

How long was I out? About six hours?

But it was a really nice six hours. I was a monkey, jumping from branch to branch, constantly shooting my bow at all sorts of creatures. It would be interesting to visit that world for real. And it might even happen, since we did have an unlimited portal and who knew how far it could put me in the future?

The materials that I had recently bought in the new and improved auction had been put to good use. During the time that I was a monkey archer, a ton of buildings had gone up around me. And the ones that already existed had changed too. The workshop had gotten a second floor, becoming much larger and wider. Work was going on apace over there now, since we had all sorts of craftsmen at our disposal now.

Even though not everyone had gotten a class yet, I had personally told at least ten people to wait for something more useful. But somehow a hundred people had made their choice and since then we have had apprentices, potion makers, smiths, and other useful people.

And the fact that all the craftsmen had decided to be under one roof was quite good. Why? Everyone could work together, at the very least. A smith couldn't make tech armor alone, for that he would have to get help from Anton at least. And in turn, Gnominumbus couldn't just sit around crafting just for himself so he could hang his microchips on plate armor later.

And that's how it was everywhere. Leatherworkers, potion makers, metalworkers... Just to name a few. Especially since the Emperor had retained a lot of useful crafting abilities. I immediately gave the scrolls to my people, but I wasn't about to get involved in the distribution process. The bosses on the ground knew much better where what should go.

Now, in this new world full of fear and death, I could always watch three things. How my subordinates were working, how my treasury passively filled up, and of course, how a whole goddamn mountain of rare and epic rewards that I had gotten from the Emperor's corpse were taking up space in my inventory.

However, there were still question about that third thing. What was all that stuff doing in my inventory?

Even though I did take most of it out, I had decided to open up the interesting things myself. Later. And I think that later had come.

Brabbid Egg (rare)

Description: To activate you must sit on the egg for 12 hours. After activation a baby brabbid will hatch from it. The sex is chosen at random, to breed them get at least two individuals of different sexes.

Damn, I only had one egg. But I still had five more irons, so let's hope we get lucky.

Brabbid... Was that something like a rabbit? Or was I mistaken? System, help me out here! Put a picture on the egg at least!

But no. A heater, a powerful flashlight, a self-driving wheelbarrow, an axe that could chop down even an ancient oak in a single hit... Oh, a seed! That would go to Gosha so he could experiment.

And that's all. There was nothing interesting in the green ones either. All sorts of tools, field equipment, some pots, tents, and other junk. A couple of simpler seeds, a fruit tree sapling, and a few lamps. I sent all that trash straight to the town hall, and now it was Brownie's problem.

There were still a few hours left until the test started. So, not wasting any time, I headed for the city.

I dropped in on all my vassals to see what they were doing. Mostly they were reducing the zombie population, of course. Gorodoftsevgrad was still making traps and manufacturing cages, sending the majority of them to be sold.

Everything was still the same with the girls.

Half of them were hunting constantly, while the rest of them stayed at home and took care of daily life. Not all of them, of course. Some of them were just too lazy.

"What you all prettying yourself up for? Better come help me in the kitchen, goddammit!" The girl who was doing all the cooking was annoyed in spite of herself. Cooking for twenty friends really was not that easy. Plus, the food had been purchased, as far as I could tell. Were they tired of eating potatoes?

"Oh, I will come help! Just five minutes, that's all!" squeaked back the cute-looking blonde, continuing to paint her face. Really, what was she doing that for?

"What for? What's the point? We don't even have any men here!" said the cook with sadness in her voice. She was also fairly good-looking, with a very nice shape.

"What if he comes flying back right now and takes me away with him?" tittered the blonde, staring into space and daydreaming.

Ah. I'll take you, for sure. First learn how to kill zombies, or cook, at the very least. Then we'll see.

I wasn't going to appear. I was just checking in, making sure everything was in order. There were fewer zombies outside, but the increased difficulty had brought new problems.

They had become fewer in number. But the quality of the composition changed every hour, it seemed. New, even more tricky mutants had appeared. The big guys had started to split into un-killable and completely unkillable ones. The leap-ers into quick ones and holy f*ck that's quick ones. Same with all the rest.

Some winged monsters had gotten bigger and with new abilities. So, for example, I saw and bom-bardier with my own eyes. He had some balls hanging off his stomach which he could detach if necessary, sending them down the heads of his en-emies. They exploded into a ton of shards, damag-ing their target in a radius of about 100 feet.

THWACK!

Nah, screw that. My slungshot easily took care of things like that, so I would be left in peace.

I watched how the bombardier fell from a height of 150 feet up and landed on the ground, then exploded into little pieces because of his bombs and then I kept going.

Okay then, how was the old Healer doing?

I appeared in his room and saw a less than pleasant scene. Someone had cut them all down. Every one. And judging from the devastation in the room, there had been a lot of enemies here.

Some splinters, pieces of stone, oil smeared over the walls and ceiling...

Dammit!

I hadn't noticed at first. In the corner of the farthest room, right by a pile of corpses, there was a golem frozen still like a statue. The lights in his eyes just barely flashed in the darkness of the en-closed area, so I only noticed the mad genius's cre-ation by chance.

I knew who had killed everyone here. And what the golem was protecting the pile of bodies for. He wanted to give them to his brother for his unnatural experiments.

There was an argument to be made for staying her until the reinforcements came. Or even to track them back to their base. I couldn't hope to be that lucky. But I could wait…

Your group has been offered an Underground test.

Difficulty: Medium.

Are you ready to start the test? Yes/No

I had totally forgotten. Well, fine, the golem wasn't going anywhere. But it did make sense to move it to the next room, just in case.

CHAPTER 22

THE UNDERGROUND... So many happy memories from this place...

This was my first group test! Too bad that the individual ones had finished right when I got into my first group. Although it would have been interesting to test our strength on someone like us. But that was before. Now I knew perfectly well who in this world was the fiercest and trickiest destroyer of all Emperors.

This time the space was a little different. It was a lot more like an underground. That time we had shown up in a room that was clearly worked by hand, with smooth walls, a floor face with large stones, and columns supporting the ceiling. Plus there had been quite a lot space, we could spread out comfortably and even walk around.

It wasn't like that here. Narrow cave passages with rocks sticking down, covered in moss glowing with blue light.

It was even on the ceiling. It was impossibly damp, and in addition to that the sound of droplets could be heard coming from all over, and somewhere deep under the ground a raging underground river was roaring.

Gradually our eyes got used to the semi-darkness, and now I could see everything here, down to the finest details. Plain as day. Probably that was due to my Shadow Set. Which I was itching to give to Kamanta. The tight leather things would... Let's say they would fit her like a glove.

No, I also liked them, but I was really wanting something more fit for a Ghost. That would improve my Conduits and my ghostly abilities. But the auction was still empty and had no intention of giving me the pleasure of some interesting unique items.

"Hu-h-huh!" I was pulled away from my thoughts by the sounds of exertion. The bull was tense, a flame was burning in his eyes, and he was trying his damnedest to move the massive stone that blocked the way into the cave.

I decided to simply watch his exertions. He used his magic a couple of times, then decided to do it the old-fashioned way, running straight into wall with forehead.

There you go. A completely different thing. He calmed down.

There was no point trying to explain to the ram, who had somehow pretended to be a bull, that we just had to wait. A half hour, if memory served.

The rest of my group seemed more attentive, and so they, like me, simply watched what our unrestrained friend was doing.

"He's not going to kill himself kill that?" Kamanta seemed to care the most. She turned into a cloud and quickly moved over to the gigantic body laid out on the floor. "Oh! He's hot!"

"If he hasn't cooled down, it means he's alive." Kaman raised a finger. He had just been testing out his new daggers, seemingly unphased, and could not resist the opportunity to be a smart ass.

"hkKh..." coughed Zorn politely. "Cool ones also sometimes twitch, you know."

Nobody was going to argue with his hoarse voice. But it didn't matter. It was just too bad I hadn't taken Gosha with me. It would be a bit more fun with him, if not more effective. Plus he would have taken part in the argument about the necessary body temperature for normal bodily functioning.

While that was going on, I walked over to the green stone and placed my hand on it. A message from the System we were already familiar with informed us that the test would start soon, and I set about studying the enemies we would meet along the way.

Hmm... For the life of me I couldn't remember what the difficulty was last time. But something like easy or around there. Now it would definitely be a little harder, since we would meet much fresher corpses along the way.

The first and most widespread opponent was the normal zombie. Of course, he was made half from a rat and half from a person. Strange creatures inhabited this place, but that made sense. Normal, self-respecting creatures wouldn't be found living in burrows.

And these really were burrows. Although last time we had to wander through wide stone tunnels, this time it was like our group was in an anthill. A very big one. And judging from the map, all paths sooner or later led downwards. And all the paths upward had been sealed off tight by our friend, the System. She didn't want us breaking out into the world and wreaking havoc there.

The map would only help us to be able to kill absolutely everything here. There were very many branching paths, trapdoors, and side rooms, but they all almost unerringly led to the lower room where the boss would be waiting for us. Passing through two other rooms, where there were two more no less dangerous monsters. Although I would prefer to say that they were valuable.

All the local monster were like rats. But very big ones, about six feet, sometimes even nine feet tall. Some walked on two legs and used pickaxes, but there were four-legged ones too. Designed for powerful bites and extremely high survival ability.

We would also meet big guys covered in bone armor. So far so normal. But they only lived in the wide passages, access to the smaller burrows being blocked for them, it seemed.

But those beasts weren't too scary for normal

Systemniks. In the lower reaches we would start running into ghosts too. Not classes like mine, but still not fun. Semi-transparent, impervious to physical attacks, but they themselves could attack people just fine and tear their souls out.

But they also had a weak point. They were supposed to be afraid of fire, especially magical fire. And this time we had a large horned lighter with us. We would just have to feed Grugg something spicy, turn his ass toward the cave, and simply wait for him to go off. And then everything evil inside would be destroyed in mere moments.

In addition to those given above, there were a whole lot more. Archers, invisies, mages, and other junk. I didn't think they would give us much trouble, probably just the opposite, and I was glad for the variety. The question was just if they were zombies. They looked like living creatures in the pictures of the bestiary. Ugly as hell, but living.

It was possible that the System had endeadened the poor guys on purpose so we wouldn't be struck by pangs of conscience for coming here and killing innocent rats. Especially since this was just a test. Nothing was real here. But every day it seemed more and more that eventually everything would become real. Some kinds of portals would show up or something like that, who know what the System would do or what lengths she was willing to go to...

As usual, the System had no intention of showing the bosses in the Underground bestiary. But that was even more interesting. Nobody knew what we would be facing in just a few minutes.

Right, I didn't intend to grind here like I did last time. We would all go together, without any careful reconnaissance. Especially since the rats could easily sense me, and if I were alone all kinds of bad things could happen. And I wanted to avoid that.

"GRAAAAH!"

This stubborn ram! The bull had regained consciousness and was charging at the stone that blocked the only exit out of the waiting room once again. But I could understand him. It was pretty cramped in here, and fairly uncomfortable for the five of us. Especially since we were all trying to sit as far apart from each other as possible.

Some had started sharpening potatoes. Zorn was just staring off into space, lost deep in his own serious thoughts. Grugg, proud owner of a concentrated vacuum in his brainpan, kept right on attacking the stone, and by doing so brought some light into this insanely boring waiting.

00:01 remaining until the test starts…
00:00.
Warning! Avoid dead ends! There may be traps in them!

Oh! Thank you. Now we would have to check there, since nobody was just going to be placing traps. I was sure that one of the dead ends would definitely have a valuable and interesting reward in it.

I couldn't hold back, rubbing my hands in anticipation. And also checked the map one more time, marking it for myself and trying to keep as many branches like that in my mind as I could. Almost all of them led upward and those dead-ends were not worked by hand, but rather were blocks set by the System. Like the rock that covered the entrance to the Underground.

"Oww…" The bull had come to after yet another spell of unconsciousness and stared at the entrance, no longer blocked by the rock. "So, did I get it?"

"Yes, Grugg, don't you worry…" Kamanta rubbed his furry back, and the horned one started breathing somewhat easier. "You good?"

"Yeah, I… I wasn't worried, what's with you?" The guy was suddenly embarrassed. I believe that if it weren't for his fur, we would be seeing a blushing bull. And so, just two puffs of smoke came from his nostrils and he turned right around.

"Alright!" I clapped my hands, drawing their attention. "You ready?"

After waiting for an affirmative nod from each member of my team, I outlined our plan. And the main part consisted of just three words. Kill them all. That's what the System was expecting from us anyway.

But there were some details. For example, while we were waiting, I thoroughly studied the group menu. Yes, there was one now with the new System update, a pretty good one. In it anyone could see the state of all the other members of the team, seeing who had how much health and mana remaining at any given time, and most importantly, it was possible to highlight their locations!

That meant my guys could see me even when I was in my incorporeal form. Zorn already could, since he had never taken his mark off, but I was more worried about the bull. He was now a hothead and could unintentionally burn me to ashes in mere seconds. Especially if I wasn't expecting it.

We had to spend about twenty minutes explaining how and why he needed to use the ally highlight. At first he just didn't want to, then when we got to the negotiation stage, he didn't understand how to do it.

And once again Kamanta helped me. She had some sort of special influence over all male living things, so she could win the horned beast over in just a few minutes.

No, woman. Your tricks won't work on me. But she did have a beautiful smile, no argument there... And she had a hell of a bod... Okay, stop!

"Grugg and Zorn, you go first. The rest come after you. And I'll be flying high." I concluded my speech, and within a second Grugg had disappeared into the darkness of the tunnel entrance. "Uhh... Well, let's follow him, why not..."

Absolutely no light there. If the walls in the starting room had been covered in well-lit moss, then further down here we came across it only in some places, and then only in small clumps.

But that was no problem. But me and the elves could see just fine in the dark. Zorn could sense both living things and things like himself. And

Grugg lit the tips of his horns on fire. Which was really pretty comfortable, that he could be his own flashlight.

I had asked him in advance to not use his new abilities unless it was a case of certain death. He didn't have strong control over them, so he could hurt both himself and all the other members of the group. Not to mention that the bull's mana reserves were so meager that even those small fires lighting the way for us were using it up.

And I certainly wasn't about to tell him that I could give him as much of that mana as he needed back from my own reserves. Otherwise I wouldn't be able to stop him.

We came across our first opponents not fifty feet from the entrance to the Underground. Two large rat-like monsters were making some bothersome sound, reminding you first of a rustling sound and then a cracking sound, and then they rushed to attack the two fires glowing in the pitch darkness.

"Rrrahh!" As soon as the first rat ran up to Grugg his fires went out. That was because the bull had bent down his head and slammed his horns through the beast's stomach, lifting it over himself.

The next one got a solid blow from his hammer right on the head. Straight down, no tricks, but extremely effective. You could hear cracking and the zombie rat-person simply went out, splayed across the floor.

But the one stuck on his horns wasn't just going to give up. The monster tried with all his might to get his clawed paws on the bull's soft-looking skin, but he did minimal damage. Scratches, nothing more.

But the bull couldn't reach the bastard either. Stuck tight on his horns, his enemy still kept wriggling every which way, not letting him get a good hit in with the hammer. And Grugg couldn't get him off either.

For a while we just stood there watching how the furious bull was running around the tunnel. Sometimes he shook his head or ran into the walls, but he could not get the load off of himself. And eventually he just stopped, his eyes glowed with flame, and within a second there was a whole bonfire burning over his head.

Only now did the ugly beast scream, filling the endless caverns with his awful voice. But that didn't go on for long, since the flames got even stronger, and the bastard turned to smoldering ash within seconds.

"Weakling..." The heavy silence was broken by Zorn's creaking voice. "So big, but useless."

He moved forward, passing the frozen bull and headed deeper into the caves.

The first thing I did was look how much mana Grugg had used to reduce the rat to ash. More than half... Yeah, we really needed to level him up. And we needed to not forget to check where he was pointing his stat points. I wasn't going to share my potatoes, but what he got for his levels should be more than enough.

"Okay. That was awesome. You beat them in a cool way." Kaman clapped the horned beast on his shoulder. Oh what, had he and his sister decided to tame my bull together? Hey! He's mine!

But actually, it was a good idea. Not about taming the bull, but that this test could be used for teambuilding. Everyone would go one at a time, show off their abilities and then we would take out the bosses as a unified group. To me that seemed great. Later, when we ran into serious danger, we wouldn't have to guess who could do what. Everything would be clear in advance.

Well, I did know a little about Zorn, but I still wanted to see. Especially since, as far as I could recall, he had lost his main weapon. So now he would be tearing rats apart with his bare hands.

But before we went on, I stopped. For a clearer picture I even dematerialized and flew around the first enemy we killed a few times.

And yeah, it was a rat. Short, mangy, brown fur, long front teeth. The skull was crushed in, but that was due to the hammer. He had applied it with vigor, and the brains had flown all over, even splashing on the ceiling.

However, I would say that this was no zombie. Or it had turned very recently. The body still had some primitive kind of clothing on it. Something between a cape and a dress. And next to where we had found our first opponents there were two pickaxes. Were they digging up something before their deaths? Maybe even some kind of ore?

A vein of Blood Iron.

There you go. The System even told me that you could dig up something useful here. It would a shame not to take advantage of it.

The pickaxe was also a System item, and it had not great durability stats. I had to use a rare repair kit so it wouldn't be too bad using a tool like this.

I didn't get any ore with the first hit. Or the second…

"What's wrong with you? Everyone's waiting for you, jeez…" On the twentieth hit I was distracted by low mooing.

"If you're so smart, do it yourself." I threw the pickaxe to Grugg and showed him the place he should hit. "You know that the first up is also the first down?"

Grunting somewhat in spite of himself, the bull picked the tool up off the dirty floor and sauntered to the vein of Blood Iron.

CRACK!

Oh, you prick.

Chunks of rock, faintly glittering red, fell over the floor, and the pickaxe turned to dust. One f*cking hit…

Fine, at least I'm good-looking.

"Your axe is a piece of shit." The bull waved his paw and went off to join the group. You could hear the sounds of a fight from here and he was anxious to join in.

Blood Iron (uncom.)

Description: An uncommon material. May be used to make weapons, armor, and other items.

Huh… The description could be a bit better,

that's for sure. But thanks anyway.

In any case, the System wasn't going to add any kind of nonsense, so I took all the pieces that had fallen out of the vein. They would definitely come in handy. The question was, for what? But I would figure that out at home.

It was interesting to see that the highlight on the vein had disappeared. It seemed that Grugg had knocked out everything valuable in one hit, and there was no point in digging there further.

There was one thing that was annoying. By the time I reached our group Zorn had already defeated his enemies. I didn't get to see the process, but the results were clear enough. The bodies, torn to pieces, all but hung from the ceiling. And with a pair of hands clinging on to the moss, now the scene pleased the eye like some sort of photograph or work of modern art.

I had grabbed two red crystals from the first enemies, and now I could add three more to the budget. Doing that I would slowly and quietly build a whole fortune. Especially since I still had some scraps left over from the last time. We had to stock up. The question was just, what for... Everything was still ahead of me.

The next person to show off their skills was Kaman. I can say right away that the elf had really been waiting for when he would finally get to fight. He had been given identical swords, after I spent some crystals to get them. Sure, they were only green quality. He could enough for something better himself. I mean, I really didn't even know how useful this dark-skinned boy would even be.

THWUNK!

And I had underestimated him. No, fighting him in the past had made me sweat. I was surprised by both his skills and his bravery. Now he gotten what might not be the coolest class, but one that was quite respectable. And if we recalled the previous owner of the class, who had been more powerless than dangerous, then my respect for the elf was starting to grow.

You shouldn't forget that almost more depends on the owner of the class than on its rarity. Just like now. Within literally a couple of seconds Kaman, flying past a lone ratperson, turned the poor bastard into finely minced meat.

His daggers flashed with a rhythmic crimson light, as if burning red-hot, and sliced the dead flesh with a barely audible hiss, as if through butter.

Plus that speed was more a skill than an ability. So now the grace with which the unlucky zombie had been dispatched was actually an inherent racial ability that our blue-skinned friends had.

"Not too bad." I nodded. It was clear that Kaman was waiting for my approval, so I wasn't going to make him suffer for nothing. Honestly, it was good. And that was at a low level, later he would get even better, absolutely.

Okay, who was left? Kamanta... This would be the most interesting. I was waiting with bated breath for her to show off her abilities.

"Oh-ho-ho!" The kind brother chuckled wickedly as soon as we got out of the narrow passage, ending up in a wide and spacious corridor. "Your turn, sis!"

"Maybe... I should?" The bull frown, counting up all the enemies heaped up not too far away. "I'll do it fast. And the girl can show us next time..."

He was about to step forward, but I stopped. This time there were a lot of enemies, and the majority of them were mutants. Big guys, six-armed leapers, skinny tricky shooters, hiding behind large boulders, waiting for the right moment to hit their target. And even a dead rat mage, dressed in some kind of dirty loose-fitting robe and armed with a gnarled wooden wand. He was standing within a circle of guards, so getting to him wouldn't be easy.

"So? You got this?" I stared at the girl. She studied her coming opponents carefully for a while, and then lit up the darkness of the caverns with her radiant smile.

"There's not a lot of them... I won't even get to enjoy it." She winked at me, turned into a cloud, then blended into the darkness of the caverns and headed for her opponents.

Well, this would interesting at least.

CHAPTER 23

"KIAAAI!"

The mage, under the protection of his body-guards, only gave out a short, sharp shout. Then the cloud materialized behind him and the next moment the rat's head was rolling on the floor. Thankfully she flew in silence, otherwise the sound would have been terrible.

No, these rats were definitely not zombies. Even though they bled profusely, even when they had superficial wounds, their intelligence was definitely not like that of zombies. Much higher.

But now. As soon as Kamanta blended back into the shadows, the rats started lighting their torches and candles. And in light like that the girl couldn't move so freely from one rat to another.

While the rats were busy lighting everything, the elf girl managed to cut down two more ugly bastards. I didn't even see her weapon. It was like her hands had turned into concentrated darkness, turning into a deadly weapon in an instant.

Ah, I want that too! Where are my Psy-Claws?

All I could hope for was success in the next System update. It seemed like it ought to be a celebratory one. We would be able to level up to level 50, and there, you'll see, we'll really be having new possibilities.

While I was standing around, lost in thought, Kamanta, skillfully avoiding all spots of light, attacked first one and then another one of those freaks. And she wasn't just attacking at close range. Sometimes the cloud of darkness that formed in the girl's hands become solid and flew towards her opponent in the form of a jet-black spike.

Or a figure might separate out of a black hole in the wall, immediately attacking the nearest enemy, landing multiple swift blows into their back in just a few seconds.

Basically, the rats didn't have time to get bored. The darkness of the elf girl moved at a great speed, so all the beasts' attacks missed their target. And that noticeably annoyed them, since every second that passed they attacked more wildly and with greater fury.

Interesting...

"Catch!" I shouted, throwing my bow into the darkness. I was curious to see how the girl would handle a weapon that was no not just her people's weapon, but her class one too.

A hand appeared out of the darkness of the

cavern, deftly catching the weapon in midair, and the next second a black arrow pierced the first beast. Right in the eye! The tip went through the other side, and the mutant immediately sank down to the stones. He was a goner.

The elf girl literally needed just a few seconds to land arrows in the heads of her enemies from all angles. I even had to throw her some of my reserve arrows since the mana in the bow ran out almost immediately. But the girl handily caught every arrow in midflight, sending them right off into her enemies, leaving no chance for anyone to survive.

"That was…"

"Fast." Zorn finished my thought for me. "Well done, young lady."

What a surprising test. Everyone was praising each other, and nobody was swearing at anybody. Something wasn't right here. Surely it can't be like this!

Ah, we had forgotten to bring Gosha, that's right. That's him, the root of all evil and strife.

"Is this really for me?" Her endless, wide eyes stared right into my soul as soon as I took a single step. The girl, appearing out the darkness, was carefully cradling the Bow of Shadow, almost as though she was rocking it to sleep, like it was the most valuable thing in the whole world to her.

What a tricky devil.

"No." I shook my head. "I will give it to you someday, but only if you behave yourself." No reason to give away property you earned through backbreaking labor. And you won't break me down with that stare. "But you can finish the Underground with it, sure…" That would be more effective. She could hide and shoot from completely unexpected positions. The enemy definitely wouldn't be able to dodge it.

"Well, I can be bad too, if necessary…" said the beautiful girl quietly, giving me a mischievous smile and turning into a cloud of darkness.

"What are you staring at, you demons?" I shouted at Grugg and Kaman who were throwing angry glances at me. "Get, go, fight!" I waved my hand at the passage where some rats had piled up and vanished into thin air. They were still staring at me. I would jam this slungshot where the sun don't shine and make them push it out. With their own strength, too, I wouldn't even pull on the chain.

We moved forward quickly. No unnecessary stops or foreplay, just Grugg and Zorn throwing the unlucky rat people aside and then we finished them off, passing by like a fatal second wave.

And me, I went last, diligently putting every single crystal into my inventory. Especially since I was the only one who could do it in a relative clean way. Even though there were a few times that the Bull knocked his opponent so hard that their red crystal dropped on the stone floor all on its own, most of the beasts were still killed by the elves. And their methods were a lot more humane.

"Stop!" I commanded, noticing the first dead end we had come across. And it would be pretty hard to miss, since right over the fork in the road there was a tablet with some incomprehensible writing and a very understandable picture. Plus it had been written in red ink, which meant it could be nothing else but a danger warning. "I will go alone from here."

Brute force was definitely not needed here. Grugg's hammer, Zorn's power, or even Kaman's skills as the Master of Daggers couldn't help against traps. I could have taken the girl with me, since she could fairly easily dodge any attacks, even the most unexpected ones. And she was familiar with dematerialization, we had learned. Physical attacks certainly couldn't defeat a cloud of darkness. It might be for only a few moments, but she could dip her toes into my incorporeal world.

But there was no point. It would be easier for me to avoid all the System's tricks myself. And to get the reward all by myself, if there was one at the end of the path, of course.

The dead-end tunnel itself was fairly wide. I would even say it was like a highway, since pretty much the main road which led somewhere into the very heart of the rat hill passed right through here. And now I was facing the prospect of going up. The angle was pretty steep too, 30 degrees at least.

Plus, it was only here that I could notice any traces of a long-forgotten fallen civilization. The ground was strewn with large stones and the walls were relatively smooth. And only the ceiling, with stalagmites or stalactites hanging down from it, hinted that some ancient person had been too lazy to work it with their hands all the way up.

Nobody even asked to go with me. That was a little annoying, since I had expected to have to force them to leave me all by my lonesome. They would rush into battle, worrying about my welfare and showing at least some concern for my health.

But no. The guys, as soon as I gave the command to relax, really just started to relax right away. They plopped onto large boulders, plucking off the shining moss to sit as comfortably as possible, and set about discussing their recent battles with fairly powerful monsters.

"I think you have to break their skulls," announced the bull, leaning backwards with a look of importance. "Their bones are weak, and breaking them is easy. You remember that... Oh, what is it... The big fellow. Dumb one."

"We remember. He's called Grugg." Zorn nodded. "How could we forget him?"

"Hey! What the f*ck, you!" The bull lowered his head, pointing his horns at the zombie and stamped his foot on the floor instinctively. You could open a factory for making gravel like that for a while.

"Calm down!" exclaimed Kamanta, barely holding back a smile. "Say what you like, but killing them from a distance is easier than anything else."

"Decapitation." Kaman shook his head, disagreeing with his sister. "Quick, accurate, and without too much noise."

I wasn't going to listen to any more. This argument could last all of eternity, and even then they still wouldn't get to the truth. Clearly everyone knew that the best method for fighting with your enemies was a slungshot. I couldn't think of anything as effective, no matter what anyone said.

The first trap was a simple tripwire. Nothing special, just tripped you, and then a stick covered in rusty metal spikes hit in the back from out of the wall.

If you could see well in the dark then noticing traps like that was pretty easy. And especially if you had a light.

At one point the sticks had been hidden with a cloth. The large strips of flags that had once, long ago, decorated the high arches of this cavern hinted at that.

And right, the ceilings were no less than 15 feet high, in some places reaching as much as 30. Very likely that the city had been built right over some deep and expansive caves. The first rat people had come here first, then something went wrong and they decided to dig out more burrows, gradually widening their living area until it was a megalopolis.

But there was no reason for me to dig into the history of a people I didn't know. Then I might spend a whole week here, and a golem was waiting for me at home to lead me back to his master. My goal was to get a reward, no more, no less.

So headed forward right away, gradually getting higher and higher.

Holes, mines, some decomposing nets and

other tools for sneaky annihilation. Every step I encounter all that stuff and it didn't bother me at all. Some bricks on the ground looked very strange to me. Especially when you consider that most of the floor consisted of stones no smaller than five square meters.

Oh! What's this?

A semi-transparent thread had appeared in the air in front of me. It hung in the air like a spiderweb, completely covering the passageway forward. It stretched from one wall to the other and floated almost unseen through the air as if it were in weightlessness.

Thank you skill. I could see and clearly differentiate energy in the surrounding space. Not only in my ghost form, but also while I was a human, so if I ran across something like that I would probably manage to pick it out.

But this chunk of energy here was hidden deep in the wall, and no matter how hard I tried to get at it, something stopped from doing it. This tricky System, no doubt. And this was a normal tripwire, actually made in a non-corporeal form.

All I could do was applaud and go around the piece of crap as far away as I could. And also to admit that it was better for me to move around in my ghost form. Anybody else would definitely have got caught on that wire.

But the rats turned out to be more well-thought than I expected. Some more of those spiderwebs were waiting for me under the ceiling, and squeezing past them without hitting even one would be impossible. This trap would work no matter what.

What if I ran through them as fast as I could? Only one way to find out.

Although, no, there were two.

Using my ability, I began searching through the floor, walls, and ceiling for concentrated energy hidden within them. In places the threads stretched right to the chunks, but it turned out that this network of traps was a lot more extensive than I thought at first.

And the network extended downward, by which I mean back where I had come from! That meant if I activated a trap, the hit would come from behind. And if I ran through this tricky spiderweb, then everything behind me would be destroyed.

Hmm, I had long ago noticed that all the traps that came across were intended for people going up. Those spikes were supposed to fly into your chest, not your back, like all the rest.

So that meant all these were created to protect against someone inside? So it made sense to try flying through this whole mess of traps, not stopping until you reach the very end.

Pfah, let's go.

CHK!

I got a good running start, and without worrying about mana rushed up through the tunnel. I heard a clicking sound, then the pitch-black darkness of the tunnel was broken by a bright light from numerous flashes. The explosions threw centuries' worth of dust into the air, sweeping the solid walls down into shards and filling the passageway with a raging flame. But, as I expected, all of that happened far behind me.

I was tired of the Underground. I had to go faster. So, not wasting my speed, I rushed toward the dead end, activating trap after trap.

Loud? Yes. Risky? Absolutely. Effective? You bet!

Within a minute I ran headfirst into a pile of stones that completely blocked me from going farther.

Hm...

There wasn't a damn thing here. Just rocks, that's all. I had expected to find at least a vein with extremely rare metals here. Or a treasure chest. Gold, rewards, crystals and other System treasures.

But no. Just stones which had long ago fallen from the ceiling, completely blocking the main entrance to the underground city.

Was that it? A pile of stones? So who knew what was buried under it?

No, it couldn't be that easy. In the name of curiosity I kicked the first stone, causing a small landslide. You couldn't destroy a single stone in the System underground. And you think it's so easy to clear out a caved-in tunnel? The rocks won't give up that easily. Knowing the System, she wouldn't have even considered leaving any flaws in place.

I spent about twenty minutes throwing back rocks, pieces of masonry, and even rotten chunks of wood, until my curiosity was finally rewarded.

First there appeared a barely noticeable flickering in the dark, and I immediately redoubled my efforts. As it turned out, I had managed to catch sight of a gold metal, untarnished by time among the stones. A cuirass, to be precise.

Then I dug out all the other pieces from the middle ages, along with a very expensive-looking suit of armor, with the bones of an unknown creature still inside.

But why was it unknown? A rat is a rat in Africa too. They were just two-legged, and judging by the clothes, fully intelligent.

In theory this discovery was useless. The armor itself, along with a massive golden scepter, were not System items. Just chunks of precious metal, nothing more. But under the cuirass there was a semi-transparent blue crystal just jangling around. A rat soul... This would certainly be interesting. Especially once I figured out the trick to using these souls...

If need be, I could use it to buff my abilities, no problem there... Plus the System had gifted me a unique sphere. It was inside of a small bag embroidered with gold, and catch my eye only by chance.

It looked like going through the traps had all been worth it. The worse all this System stuff was for you now, the better it would be later. No matter how dumb that sounded.

"RA-A-A!" The bull's roar could be heard from hundreds of feet away. I had to hurry because they might need my help over there. Right before I flew out of the tunnel I got out my slungshot, extending it to the maximum, ready for a heated battle.

"Let's go! Let's go!"

Seriously? Who did I pick for my team? They seemed like decent people... Sure, in the previous group there had been some people who hadn't taken part in even a single battle, but what was this?

"Zorn, them I get, but why you?" The deadie was standing off to the side, but he was watching the action with undisguised curiosity.

"Twenty-eight... Grugg, two more! Or are you all talk?" he croaked at the bull without paying me any attention.

"I am not all talk!" roared the horned beast, and then took a green potato out of his inventory, opening it up right away. "Beef again!" he howled. "Why?"

It turned out that while I wasn't around, Grugg and Zorn had argued about whether the horned guy could eat the contents of thirty green potatoes all at once. The clever zombie knew that some-times beef steaks would drop from them and thought that the bull would certainly not eat his own kinsmen. But far from it, since our horned friend was no stranger to cannibalism. But thirty meals at one time... Just judging from his face you could tell it was too much, even for him.

"What did you bet?" Having accepted that the experiment would end soon anyway, I asked Zorn the question.

"For a wish." The deadie waved his hand. "Don't worry, I won't mess with him. But I had to settle him down, he was going crazy..."

And the elves were happy. At least some kind of entertainment. They were shouting out words of encouragement just to make it more fun to watch the suffering of their friend.

"No! I can't do it!" The bull forced down the fatty steak and opened up the last potato. But from that one, almost as if on purpose, food poured out like from a cornucopia. First one meal, then another, and even a compote. That was the moment when he gave up, realizing that even just one more spoonful and the contents of his stomach would be coming right back up. "You win, you dead piece of shit... Make your wish."

"No, not yet." Zorn's face broke into a smile. "I will make it at the most unexpected moment!" After saying that he let out something like a wicked laugh, which made all of us a little bit uncomfortable.

"Now I will give you a new competition!" I clapped my hands to get everyone's attention. "Whoever kills the most rats will get... Will get a slap in the face! Okay, let's go."

After saying that I disappeared into thin air and headed into the tunnel. After a few seconds my companions got back to normal, chattering happily, and followed behind me.

Now the worked quickly and brutally, not wanting to stay too long in the damp, dark underground. Just like before Zorn and the bull went first, then the rest of us. We were headed down the main corridor, getting closer to the first boss room.

Sometimes small offshoots came off the main corridor where we constantly met whole hordes of beasts. The elf siblings took to clearing them out. There were very few enemies hiding there, so the guys didn't have any problems.

And I, simply flying in the back, grabbed crystal and tried to find something valuable. One way or another I had to get everything from here that wasn't bolted to the ground. We had to maximize our profit.

But even if a plan like that could be extremely effective, I still could control what was happening in front. And what was happening there was Grugg and that was terrifying and sad at the same time.

"Stop!" I heard the hoarse dead voice croak out. "Stop, you idiot!"

But Zorn's words fell on deaf ears. It turned out we had already reached the first boss room, and the horned idiot had decided to attack right away, without waiting for the rest of us. And so, taking his hammer in his hand and raising it over his head, he rushed forward ready to land a decisive blow onto the enemy's skull.

"Unlessssssss..."

BOOOM!

END OF BOOK FOUR

Want to be the first to know about our latest LitRPG, sci fi and fantasy titles from your favorite authors?

Subscribe to our **New Releases** newsletter:
http://eepurl.com/b7niIL

Nanomachines
A Progression Fantasy Adventure Series
by Nikolai Novikov

The Afflicted
A LitRPG Apocalypse Adventure Series
by Konstantin Zubov

The Dark Summoner
A Portal Progression Fantasy Series
by Andrei Tkachev

The Last Paladin
An Action & Adventure Progression Fantasy Series
by Roman Savarovsky

The Other Side
A Progression Fantasy Adventure Series
by Rodion Korablev

Me and My Demons
A Portal Progression Adventure Fantasy Series
by Oleg Sapphire & Alexey Kovtunov

The Blood Code
A Historical Progression Fantasy Adventure Series
by Michael Borz

The Banned
A LitRPG Adventure Series
by Michael Atamanov

How I Built a Magic Empire
A Portal Progression Fantasy Series
by Konstantin Zubov

The Order of Architects
A Portal Progression Fantasy Series
by Oleg Sapphire & Yuri Vinokuroff

The Selected
A LitRPG Action Adventure Series
by Vasily Mahanenko & Yuri Vinokuroff

The Hunter's Code
A Portal Progression Fantasy Series
by Oleg Sapphire & Yuri Vinokuroff

The One Who Changes the Future
A Dystopian Portal Progression Fantasy Series
by Boris Romanovsky

An Ideal World for a Sociopath
A LitRPG Apocalypse Adventure Series
by Oleg Sapphire

The Healer's Way
A Portal Progression Fantasy Series
by Oleg Sapphire & Alexey Kovtunov

The Last Portal Jumper
A LitRPG Progression Fantasy Series
by Konstantin Zubov

The Dark Healer
A Historical Progression Fantasy Series
by Alex Toxic & Nadya Lee

Lord of The System
A LitRPG Progression Fantasy Series
by Alex Toxic & Furious Miki

A Shelter in Spacetime
A LitRPG Apocalypse Series
by Dmitry Dornichev

The Coming of God of Death
A Portal Progression Fantasy Series
by Dmitry Dornichev

The Village
A LitRPG Progression Fantasy Series
by Dmitry Dornichev & Alexey Kovtunov

Condemned (Lord Valevsky: Last of the Line)
A Progression Fantasy LitRPG Series
by Vasily Mahanenko

Living Ice
A Portal Progression Fantasy Series
by Dmitry Sheleg

The Goldenblood Heir
A Portal Progression Fantasy Series
by Boris Romanovsky

Law of the Jungle
A Wuxia Progression Fantasy Adventure Series
by Vasily Mahanenko

Crossroads of Oblivion
A Portal Progression Fantasy Adventure Series
by Dem Mikhailov

More books and series are coming out soon!

In order to have new books of the series translated faster, we need your help and support! Please consider leaving a review or spread the word by recommending *Ghost in the System* to your friends and posting the link on social media. The more people buy the book, the sooner we'll be able to make new translations available.

Thank you!

Till next time!

www.ingramcontent.com/pod-product-compliance
Lightning Source LLC
LaVergne TN
LVHW020724200726
843506LV00009B/616